Praise for *A Kettle of Vultures*

"I love this book!!! Sabrina Lamb puts you in the center of the action with her descriptive writing style. As a former record industry publicist, it was like re-living the record business through these pages. The personal struggles of Iris—the consummate professional who has to keep it all together to save her own image—are on display here proving life is NOT glitz all of the time. If you have any family at all down South, Iris' family is a mirror image of yours...forcing you to face your upbringing in spite of what you have become."

—LaJoyce Brookshire, Author
Ask The Good Doctor, *The Last Listening Party of Notorious B.I.G.*,
Faith Under Fire: Betrayed By A Thing Called Love,
Web of Deception, and *Soul Food*

"A funny book about race, love and Cuban coffee—among many other things."

—AJ Jacobs, Author *The Year of Living Biblically* and
My Life as an Experiment

"Witty and deliciously humorous, Sabrina Lamb interweaves a bona-fide satirical piece of literary fiction with *A Kettle of Vultures* that's sure to be a classic for generations to come."

—Terrance Dean, author of the *Essence* best-seller,
Hiding In Hip Hop

"Sabrina Lamb's a rock star, as she confidently takes chick-lit to a whole other level with her superb writing style. Her latest novel is fittingly clever, funny and charming."

—Abby Finer, Television Executive Producer/Author

"Sabrina has always been...one step ahead! Catch up to her, if you can! She and her writing is a winner, in every sense of the word!"

—Bob Sumner, Creator/Producer of Laff Mobb,
Executive Producer of HBO's *Def Comedy Jam*

"The multi-talented Sabrina Lamb has put her comic talent to excellent use in this barbed first novel. *A Kettle of Vultures* is a pungent, fast-paced tale that follows the escapades of protagonist Iris Chapman as she journeys from Atlanta to her Florida hometown and on to New York City seeking to come to terms with herself and her family. With stinging satire, Ms. Lamb unveils a host of eccentric characters that include a grandmother whose down-home observations often echo a Moms Mabley routine, and a jackleg preacher reminiscent of Reverend Ike. Filled with ironic insights and wicked caricatures, this is a tightly written lampoon, a feel-good story that will leave you laughing. Finally, it's great entertainment with a keen, satirical edge."

– Mel Watkins, professor at Colgate University and author of *On the Real Side: A History of African American Comedy* and *Stepin Fetchit: The Life and Times of Lincoln Perry*

Zane Presents

A KETTLE of VULTURES

...LEFT BEAK MARKS ON MY FOREHEAD

Dear Reader:

Follow the journey of Iris Chapman who takes readers on a course from Opa Locka, Florida to Atlanta to New York in this adventurous tale featuring a cast of eccentric characters.

In her debut novel, *Kettle of Vultures*, Sabrina Lamb showcases her humorist side through the main character and her family, which includes her cantankerous grandmother, Ms. Chickie; her snobby mother, Lee Artist; and her evasive father. When she heads home to the Miami suburb for her brother Victor's wedding, she is unaware that a low-flying kettle of vultures is above the plane. Upon arrival, she is reminded that her family is its own brand of vultures.

Many of you can relate to a woman whose family and the men in her life attempt to mold her into their own idea of perfection. However, she rebels against their ideals; she is pleased with her current state.

In addition to dealing with her non-traditional family, she owns an image consulting firm and experiences challenging encounters with such clients as an NBA draft pick, a comedienne and a recording artist.

Sabrina Lamb is a New York City-based media personality, a familiar voice with a background as radio show host and magazine columnist. She has also appeared on numerous television specials and has interviewed cultural and political figures. While she has addressed serious topics, she has shown the flip side with her comedic skills as she does with her new novel.

Thank you for supporting Sabrina Lamb's efforts and thank you for supporting one of the dozens of authors published under my imprint, Strebor Books. I try my best to bring you cutting-edge works of literature that will keep your attention and make you think long after you turn the last page.

Thanks for the support of the Strebor authors. To find me on the web, please go to www.eroticanoir.com or join my online social network, www.planetzane.org.

Peace and Many Blessings,

Zane

Zane
Publisher
Strebor Books International
www.simonandschuster.com/streborbooks

ZANE PRESENTS

A KETTLE *of* VULTURES

...LEFT BEAK MARKS ON MY FOREHEAD

SABRINA LAMB

STREBOR BOOKS
NEW YORK LONDON TORONTO SYDNEY

Strebor Books
P.O. Box 6505
Largo, MD 20792
http://www.streborbooks.com

This book is a work of fiction. Names, characters, places and incidents are products of the author's imagination or are used fictitiously. Any resemblance to actual events or locales or persons, living or dead, is entirely coincidental.

ISBN 978-1-59309-335-8
LCCN 2010934201

First Strebor Books trade paperback edition October 2010

Cover design: www.mariondesigns.com
Cover photograph: © Keith Saunders/Marion Designs

10 9 8 7 6 5 4 3 2 1

Manufactured in the United States of America

To my literary agent, Sara Camilli,
for her unwavering loyalty, support, wisdom and friendship

To my brothers, Paul and Jason,
for their love and friendship, and tolerance of their hovering big sister

To Zane and Charmaine
for their hard work, dedication and for embracing and sharing my writer's voice

OPA LOCKA

[1]

Hauling off and whacking your grandmother is downright wrong, felonious, and can be regretful; but my left hand twitched another opinion in response to her whining interrogation, forty-five seconds into my homecoming.

I wonder what it's like to do felony prison time. The wrinkle-faced lifers would crane to get a glimpse of the new hard-ass as I swaggered, bopping along the corridor of the musty cellblock in handcuffs and returning the glares with my mock intimidating stare. "What you in for, light-skin?" they would ask, as I drag on a nauseating high tar cigarette. Hacking under the smoke, I would sneer, "Not dat iz any of yo biznesses, but dat old lady had it comin'…and if you hussies don't want what she got, you'll get off me, unless you know where I can get real dick." And there it was. My jailhouse reputation would be sealed. I would be dubbed "dat batty bitch." Anyone who thought they were tough by calling career criminals "hussies" had to be batty.

I had already been assaulted today, first by the ninety-eight-degree heat and hundred percent humidity. And mosquitoes waited at the baggage terminal, holding placards with my name on them. By the time I entered the taxi, sweat was oozing down my pant legs. It felt as though a cow's tongue was lying on my face.

So I was in no mood for "Why you got to go around looking like Bob Marley fa?" Ms. Chickie ordered or asked, I forgot which, as I stretched my neck back out the front doorway to see if the pimpled-faced, Middle Eastern cab driver could facilitate a rescue and return me to the airport. Though it was a sun-splashed, cloudless noon, it would have been prudent to instruct him to wait until I waved a white handkerchief, indicating it was safe to leave me with my eccentric family. Instead he was off chasing another fare, dreaming of less humidity and an upcoming Noori concert.

The wrinkles in my forehead mirrored the wrestling match my thoughts were experiencing, wondering how this high-cheekboned, olive-skinned octogenarian, wearing her beloved pink pearls, knee-high stockings, and nothing else under a flowered housedress, simultaneously blasting three Miami gospel radio stations and a television blathering *The Wendy Williams Show*, could have somehow found disdain for, or had intermingled with, Bob Marley.

I didn't have to be here. More attractive options were available, like undergoing a colonoscopy, listening to Indian sitar music, or perhaps remaining in Atlanta to join Tammy in returning, like breeding salmon, to Cisco's—the headquarters of Atlanta's decadent, elitist ritualistic nightlife—to spawn conflict, or attract love, however fleeting.

But destiny has placed me here.

In Opa Locka, Florida. A suburb of Cuba. And about two and a half blocks away from the sun. Located in the northwest section of Miami, the name of this middle-class, African-American enclave was derived from the Seminole Indian word *opa-tisha-wocka-locka*. Ms. Chickie was notorious for amusing herself by telling white developers who relentlessly knocked on her door begging to purchase the house, that it meant "I'm snatching your land."

In Opa Locka, polite social interaction, foreign in many cities, still remains. Everyone waves when they pass your house, whether they know you or not. Though my little friends and I preferred giving passersby our middle finger when they waved, no one seemed to mind. My family has resided here for fifty years, segregated from but yet a part of Miami, successfully staving off rising crime. But to Ms. Chickie's despair, citizens of Opa Locka have not been able to escape the encroachment of a city dominated by Cuban culture and gentrification. She complained often, "Everybody speaks Spanish! If the English language is good enough for Jesus Christ, it's good enough for the Cubans!" Carmen Esperanza Beiro, my best friend from high school, cackled when I would tell her about Ms. Chickie's irreverence, over a late-night plate of chicken *empanadas* and *medianoche* at her family's restaurant.

Change in Opa Locka occurs in tiny ebbs; perhaps the family on the corner has added a patio or paved their driveway. Or somebody's sister joined the military or had a sex change. Or as my taxi turned the corner passing the pastel-colored homes, onto my block, there was Ms. Janette, still hunched over with her ass up in the air, like a Red Kangaroo, picking up non-existent debris, under the guise of beautifying the neighborhood. In reality, her ass was poised in the air, so that she could catch an out-of-control penis from one of the sanitation workers who happened by on their truck at the same time each day. Ms. Janette graciously batted her fake eyelashes at their catcalls, and would constantly invite them in for breakfast. "Big men, like yew, must be hungry for some cheese and eggs, pancakes, sausage and grits…come on in and let me, Ms. Janette, feed your bellies."

Ms. Chickie instructed Lee Artist to never let my father outside in the yard, without being chaperoned when Ms. Janette was performing her morning bend haunch. "That's how she stole Sally's drunkard husband. And he hasn't been back home since."

Whenever our family was preparing to travel somewhere together, perhaps to a christening or a family friend's barbecue grill, Ms. Janette would holler from across the street, "Yew hew! And how is Mr. Chapman on this fine morning?"

Tightening her jaws, Lee Artist would tell my father, "If your eyeballs even look like they want to move in that direction, you can forget about ever getting a blow job again for the rest of your life."

When news of my arrival swept the neighborhood, it ranked right up there with the news that my brother, Victor Chapman, had renounced his vow to bachelor life. I've flown home to dutifully participate in the marital rites, which will somehow add either a period or a semi-colon on his new life, depending upon Victor's level of commitment, which often wavered like leaves in a hurricane. Figuring out what it all means—resolution—isn't a necessity. What is more pressing is the uneasy feeling I have about the percolating havoc that may lay ahead.

However, being a moment-to-moment optimist, I wiped puddles of perspiration from my forehead, hung my burgundy suit bag in the vestibule closet, and attempted to restart the conversation.

"Ms. Chickie, how are you?"

As my lips brushed against her cheek, her arms flew around me like an octopus hugging the belly of a seaward tugboat. Under threat of a cracked rib, I squeaked out an appeal to breathe freely again. Ignored, I resorted to pimp-slapping her on the back, as if burping a Sumo wrestler. Though I feigned suffocation, Ms. Chickie's legendary hugs were comforting, expected, and signaled that my visit home was now official.

"You gained weight, huh? Spread out like a Sunday buffet. I knows ya hungry. Ever since you were a little baby, you'd eat the wood off of the side of a barn."

Ah, the interrogation continues. A blinding prosecutor's spotlight flooded my face as I sought refuge in Ms. Chickie's hazel blind eye.

It didn't work.

"I didn't know what you wanted, you eat so funny. Back yonder in the kitchen, I cooked ya grilled chitlins, oxtails, collard greens with the chitlins or collard greens with ham...because I knows you likes to eat healthy."

"Um, Grandmother, remember that I'm a vegetarian?"

"Youse still in that Bin Laden cult....and Iris, you didn't have anything better to wear than that?"

My creaseless Gap khakis and limp white shirt developed an inferiority complex.

Not knowing what to respond to, I gained strength, and retorted, "Nope. I stole these off shipwrecked Chinese immigrants down at the Port of Miami!"

"If it was up to me, I'd send all them Chinamen back. Back to Korea where they belong!" she replied, pouring two glasses of fresh lemonade. It was not my responsibility to correct Ms. Chickie. I left that insurmountable task to a higher power.

"You ain't got no sex appeal," Ms. Chickie shared. "And whatever boy you messin' wit don't know what he doin'. I can tell by the way you walk."

Her fascination with my sex life occupied much of her time, and she would often mail celebrity sex videotapes to make sure that I was updated on the latest sexual techniques. "*Dear Granddaughter, I could tell how that girl moved on* Dancing With the Stars *that she didn't know what she was doing. Watch this here video. This is what not to do. I repeat. This is what not to do. God Bless, Chickie.*"

After my flight to freedom at graduate school, Ms. Chickie had moved in with my parents at the insistence of her daughter—my social butterfly mother—and to the dread of my hermetic father.

It wasn't that she was a cause for concern due to infirmity, indigence, or *non compos mentis*. She was lucid, strong, and as cunning as a crocodile avoiding the shoe rack at Jimmy Choo's, but Ms. Chickie was fond of injecting miscommunications or outright lies into already fragile relationships, just to see what hell erupted. She feared that the world that she once knew is disappearing faster than green grass running through a goose. And the older she gets, the more adept she becomes at emotionally disrupting the lives at 321 Napier Avenue, and using everyone as a pawn in her mischievous chess game.

The relationship between Ms. Chickie and Lee Artist, my mother, is a curious one; a combination of master and disciple, puppeteer and marionette, and as emotionally distant as Michael Strahan's two front teeth. Ms. Chickie had encouraged her daughter to do what she, herself, had been prohibited from accomplishing—to create a new American dynasty.

Early in life, Lee Artist set about studying the Kennedy clan, utilizing Jacqueline Bouvier Kennedy as a template and ignoring Negro royalty such as the King family, who were in her backyard, because she believed that all of that marching was undignified and that Reverend Dr. Martin Luther King, Jr. dreamt too much. Lee Artist craved a life of adventure propelled by the traditions of the royalty she and Ms. Chickie would cast, but she was stymied by her own conjured superstitions, believing the Kennedy curse was created by Rose Kennedy.

"Rose Kennedy must have preserved pickles during her monthly menses. That's why she gave birth to all of them boys," Lee Artist would often say.

So theirs was an unusual bond, devoid of the familiar mother-daughter mutterings and affection, but melded in a fierce determination to forge a Chapman dynasty. In my mind, historical figures lived in dynasties and for thousands of years were never served Spam and oxtails. Later, as my father became increasingly sullen, seeking comfort under the hood of his Oldsmobile and blues collection, Lee Artist would trail behind him muttering the late John F. Kennedy to characterize her relationship with her mother after watching (again) a tribute to Rose Kennedy on the Biography Channel: "Geography has made us neighbors. History has made us friends. Economics has made us partners, and necessity has made us allies."

When the sound of keys jingled in the lock, Ms. Chickie yanked my neck in a death grip, forcing my face proximate to her strawberry-pink lips and sour milk breath, and with urgency, loudly whispered with tinged mustard breath, "They took my money! The thieving bastards—" Then she shoved me away at such a throttle, my brain rattled inside my cranium.

While I attempted to realign my vertebrae, Ms. Chickie completely transformed, donning the halo of an angel posing for Michelangelo in the Sistine Chapel. By that time, Lee Artist entered carrying a myriad of boutique shopping bags and Cocoa, her Tasmanian Devil Pekingese. When Lee Artist saw me, she peeled off her white gloves, and assailed me with staccato Dorothy Dandridge air kisses while Cocoa growled around my feet.

Hostile furry flatulent bitch.

When I was in elementary school, my mother had gone to wherever you go to adopt a satanic beast and brought Cocoa home announcing, "Iris, look, you have a precious puppy." However, Cocoa made it clear from the beginning that she hated my guts. When my parents were around, she would yap and wag her tail, curling up in their laps. But each morning, while my parents argued behind their closed bedroom door, I would attempt to get a bowl of Cheerios from the kitchen, but the little heifer would snarl, blocking the entrance and chase me so that I jumped on top of the granite kitchen counter. The only way I could enter the kitchen would be to distract Cocoa by turning on the vacuum cleaner.

"Iris, what has gotten into you, girl? Cocoa ain't thankin' about you! Turn that thing off! It's way too early to be tidy. The Kennedys would never vacuum this early," my mother would bark, standing with her hand on her hip in the middle of the dining room. Respecting my mother as her pack leader, Cocoa suddenly bounced about, wagging her tail, gaining a pat on the head from my mother. "See, Cocoa is just as sweet as she wants to be," Lee Artist would observe, before returning to the bedroom to argue with my father.

Lee Artist thought that it was perfectly normal behavior that I was sitting on the kitchen counter with my knees drawn around my chest as if I was setting up for an Olympic high dive.

Ms. Chickie pulled a piece of grilled chitlin from the pocket of her housedress and fed it to the eager Cocoa. Lee Artist exclaimed, "Mama, I have repeatedly asked you not to feed Cocoa the same food that we eat!" Ms. Chickie ignored her daughter and ambled down the hallway to her bedroom singing to a gospel radio commercial for gas relief: "Precious Lord, take my hand, lead me on, help me stand; I am tired, I am weak, I am worn. Thru the storm, thru the night, lead me on to the light. Take my hand, precious Lord, lead me home."

"Oh my goodness, look at you! Were you in an accident?" Lee Artist asked incredulously, her eyeballs bouncing like fruit on a casino slot machine.

Ms. Chickie shook her head as she gingerly eased down the hallway. "Lord knows, I told her. I told her, praise Jesus."

"And what *happened* to your hair?"

"Nothing *happened* to my hair! I just don't relax it anymore."

Lee Artist stared at my natural locks, inspecting, as if she was seeing pig vomit for the first time. "Well, Iris," she began, plopping into a plush, pale yellow Ethan Allen armchair, opening her tissue-wrapped packages, "Birds have made a nest on top of your head. Now you'll never attract good fortune. Call Helena; I'll treat you to a full touch-up—er—makeover. My dear, you'll never be like First Lady Michelle Obama with napp—I mean, kin—"

"Let me help you, Mother; it's natural. They are twists," I informed her. There was no point in correcting her again; telling her that I had no interest in being First Lady—hadn't since junior high school. And that being First Lady was Lee Artist's fantasy, not mine.

"You never see First Lady Michelle Obama running around the White House with nappy hair. Just think how that would impact foreign policy, and I betcha the President wouldn't get reelected because of it." Ignoring my clarification, Lee Artist examined the extra button packet attached to her cream and gold Norma Kamali silk tunic. "Iris, I've told you a thousand times, image is everything." Then suddenly aware of competing voices, Lee Artist yelped, "Why are all these goddamned radios on?" as she flitted, like a bee pollinating a sunflower, to the radio, console stereo, kitchen clock radio, and television, silencing promises of deliverance, hell, and damnation and the promotion of a multi-level marketing spiritual cleansing opportunity.

"I was listenin' ta dat!" Ms. Chickie croaked in a muffled tone from behind her slightly ajar bedroom door, where she watched *The Young and the Restless*—better known as her "stories."

Lee Artist's fair, translucent complexion still held those infamous high cheekbones and the mole below her right nostril. When she was a young girl, her light skin, high cheekbones, and long hair were coveted, and even more so in college, where she was highly recruited to pledge membership in the Alpha Kappa Alpha sorority. In Opa Locka, she was the closest thing to a movie star that anyone knew. In a world that idolized anything resembling Caucasian features, Lee Artist was considered royalty, especially by Ms. Chickie, who had a high regard for white people. Lee Artist still had the figure of a centerfold and moved with an air of superiority that did not always match her surroundings or the economic struggle she and my father endured early in their lives. Ms. Chickie recalled, "We were so poor that we couldn't jump over a nickel to save a dime." Though the army promised worldwide travel, they omitted the part about low wages, cramped overseas apartments, and the German natives' stares at Negroes, a sight that was, at that time, rare.

Lee Artist's idiosyncrasies were groomed under the tutelage of Ms. Chickie. She was taught that because of her looks, she was guaranteed to have the right friends, go to the right college, marry the right man, and damn it, be happy about it. So when lanky Willie Chapman threw his fourth touchdown to clinch the win for Florida A&M University's Rattlers in the Southern Bowl, she knew that this restrained, incompatible, pedantic seeker of ancient truths would complete her formula for the *right* life.

The fence made a whining sound, annoyed it had been awakened from its afternoon slumber. Through the pale green window treatments, I spied my father entering the front yard. A big smile erupted across my face, making it appear as though I had a hanger in my mouth. I waited, poised, for Willie to enter. As the door opened, the relentless heat barged in, gaining temporary advantage over the central air-conditioning.

"Keep that door closed, Willie!" Lee Artist hurled.

"He must be 'touched' in the head," Ms. Chickie interjected from her bedroom.

"She could make a preacher cuss! How am I supposed to get in the house without opening the door? I tell you one thing— well, wouldja lookahere…" His dark brown eyes compressed into slits, awakening the spider lines on his forehead. "Iris! Hey, little girl! Come give your daddy a hug!"

"Hey, Daddy! Howya doin'?"

"...so hungry my belly thanks my throat done been cut out, pretty little girl," he answered, smiling.

❖ ❖ ❖

Willie Louis Chapman left Quincy, Florida, and lied about his age to get hired to build connecting highways to the Everglades. After which he entered the Army, serving in Korea and Vietnam, receiving the Purple Heart medal. Through the GI bill, he received a degree in religious studies, determined to enter the seminary, until he accepted that traditional religions did not satisfy his questions about man's relationship to God. Or explain why a light-skinned, city gal would want to be his wife. At least, that is what she told him, over and over, until he had dissolved into a puddle of defeat. Standing at a sturdy six foot four, with hardened, stern features, Willie married Lee Artist and spent the next twenty-five years gritting his teeth as he slept to mask his resentment and his ambivalence toward the woman whom everyone thought he should have. Now a recently retired accountant, Willie indulged himself in his responsibilities as treasurer for the Order of the Opa Locka Free Masons, believing essentially:

"You are to act as becomes a moral and wise man; particularly, not to let your family, friends, and neighbors know your concerns, and wisely consult your own honor."

Being held in his comforting, lean arms resurrected memories of riding his shoulders and picking mangoes in our backyard, fishing at Port of Miami, and of him catching me making out with random boys and not telling my mother.

Lee Artist's demand that I not leave our front porch on Saturday evening played right up my teenage alley. Using the front porch as our stroll, my older cousin Nikki wore extra-short hot pants and halter tops and greased our brown legs. Then in the evenings, while the adults were engrossed in a lively game of Pinocle, we posed in our chairs, angling our bodies, to seduce passing boys to stop and visit with us on the porch. Timing when I knew my favorite would pass by, Nikki and I would pretend that it was a spontaneous occurrence; that Dwight and T.J. were now on our darkened front porch, and after my parents had gone to bed, that their tongues had somehow accidently plunged down our throats. Our makeout sessions never made it anywhere other than the front porch or included the inconvenience of knowing Dwight's and T.J.'s last names.

"I'm glad you could make it down, dahlin'," Willie said, giving me an extra squeeze.

"No problemo. Just wish I could stay longer," I lied, remembering the laundry list of projects waiting for attention back in Atlanta. "...kinda surprised that Victor is getting married, Daddy. Aren't you?"

"Well, you never know when it's your time," he replied, as if he was referring to a sudden tragic death, over his shoulder as I followed him down the hallway, past the dusty mummified replica of Ms. Chickie's husband, Woodrow, which I thought was an unusual knickknack, since my grandfather wasn't dead.

Never knowing Woodrow, Ms. Chickie told me when I had asked the whereabouts of my grandfather, and why I had never met him, nor saw any photos, "Woodrow done drove his truck up North delivering oranges. He'll be back when he good and ready. Never ask a man who is set on leaving, when he coming back. The only thing that'll do is keep him gone longer."

To an eight-year-old, that seemed like a plausible, folksy explanation for his long absence. After all, truckers were known to make long hauls for weeks, sometimes months, at a time, delivering their goods and screwing bus stop prostitutes across America. And since I had horny boys and the beach on my mind, I couldn't be bothered with investigating a possible missing grandfather.

Tall and precocious for my age, but in the eleventh grade, I was hired one summer as a nursing assistant at the South Florida Evaluation and Treatment Center and assigned to the pyromania ward. Located along the bustling Twenty-Seventh Avenue, which connected Carol City with Pembroke Pines, to the casual observer, you would assume that the South Florida Evaluation and Treatment Center was a junior college campus. Instead the expansive foliage and green lawns with white, small cottages hid patients that were segregated according to their psychiatric *solution* as the brunette, unibrow New Hire Trainer explained, during my orientation.

"Words such as 'crackpot' and 'looney' are not permissible in our rehabilitation. We categorize our 'guests' according to their solutions; not their alleged problems." While she droned to our slack-jawed group of new nursing assistants during our tour, I wondered what the *solution* was for the *guest*, who had just sprinted past us around the security guard booth, and over the wooden fence, which bordered the property, into morning rush-hour traffic. At the same time, a chubby, square-faced man flattened his body against the roadway, and dangled his arm through the metal slats down into the sewer drain.

"Grab my hand!"

"Oh for the love of God, Henry! Satan is not down there," she screeched, stomping her foot.

Nursing Assistant. Fancy title for what I was doing, emptying bed pans, cleaning lice out of hair, flipping bedsore-prone patients, while dodging the groping excrement-tinged fingers of hallucinating staff members. Nothing like what they did on television hospital dramas. There were no late-night calls for me to perform an emergency lobotomy or yelling, "Clear!" and saving the life of a child with the heart resuscitator. Well, there was that one makeout session with that handsome boy, who I assumed was an medical intern. "I'm dating a doctor," I looked forward to bragging to my friends.

Turned out, he had stolen a doctor's lab coat and disappeared from the sex offenders' cottage.

It became apparent that each patient on the pyromania ward had a unique relationship with fire. "Would you be so kind, Ms. Chapman, to let my dick set fire to your pussy? It would really make my day...really it would," drawled Bernice, the buck-toothed, gray-haired patient matriarch of the ward, who would then cackle like the wicked witch of the south. When I would insist that she did not have the equipment necessary to set my pussy on fire, she would ponder the merit of my statement, as if appearing before a Congressional hearing, then respond, "Well, I do declare, you are one negative bitch, now ain't cha?" Bernice was confined twenty years ago, when she had a nervous breakdown watching the film *Backdraft*. She was arrested after burning the films of Kurt Russell in the straight-to-video aisle of a Blockbuster store in Coconut Grove. From then on, she linked setting fires to vaginas with Kurt Russell. *I completely understood the connection.*

I found the guests quite liberating. Secretly, I dreamed of greeting my supervisor, "Good Mornin'! You redneck, bald-headed sonabitch," just like Bernice did, without any consequences. *What a wonderful world it would be*, I often thought, to utter something inspiring like that before continuing on with my day.

❖ ❖ ❖

One of my duties was to engage the *guests*, to entertain them, and prevent them from drifting into their internal worlds. Keep them focused on their solutions. One afternoon, after returning from lunch, I approached and then sat across from a silver-haired gentleman, whom the staff nicknamed Blues. He had a long narrow face with silver hair, and silver gray eyes, who looked like a blues singer. "Would you like to play a game of checkers, Blues?" I asked. Since Blues spent most days sitting in the corner chair, facing the wall, I was happy to see him facing the ward.

"Why, yes, I would, dahlin'. Yes, I would indeed. Hopefully, the fire department will come on time today." I placed the checkerboard in the middle of the wooden table, and arranged the chips, as Blues stared out of the window, mumbling, "Whatn't nobody messin' with that sonabitch; all he had to do was make her a dancer, though she can't dance a lick, can't dance a lick; nobody cared 'bout her more than me. I could drive a Studebaker, but she still thought he was a better man than me—"

"Who you talkin' about, sir?"

"Da datgum Studebaker, dammit!" Blues insisted, slamming the palm of his hand on the table in front of me. "Da mango man that owned that Studebaker come round my house but didn't brang the fire department wit 'em." Blues leaned back in his chair, making his first move, diagonally, without even glancing at the checkerboard.

"Did the man forget to call the fire department?" I asked, now making my move, and realizing I cared about his answer.

"Chickie! Call the fire department! Chickie! Call the fire department! It's burnin' down! Call the fire department!" he suddenly screamed, abruptly rising, overturning the checkerboard and the wooden table. Nurses, whom had been engrossed in reading the *National Enquirer* behind their tiled work station, rushed over to restrain him. "Did Blues take hiz medication this afternoon?" asked one plump Jamaican nurse.

"Him say, he no like de medication. Him say, it make he sad," said the other plump Haitian nurse.

"Chickie, call the fire department. Call the fire department," Blues continued screaming.

"Mr. Chapman is crazy like a fox. He only act that way 'cause he tinks we gwanna make him see dis Ms. Chickie."

"Dat's right. He figure he better off stayin' right here."

"Mr. Chapman?! His name is Chapman?!"

"Yes it is, same as yours, dear. Wouldn't it be a big tickle if that kuh-razy old man was related to you? Hmmm, dear? I'd definitely get a tickle outta that," the plump Jamaican insinuated, her jowls under her chin, quivering with the thought of an impending embarrassment.

"What's his first name?" I asked, hoping to put her accusation to rest.

"He name Woodrow 'Blues' Chapman."

No one in my family ever thought to mention it, as it would have been sacrilege to expose what had been secretly and neatly, tucked away.

"Daddy, you sound like we're going to a funeral," I said, chuckling. Willie didn't crack a smile, rubbing his oil-stained hands with soap in the bathroom sink. His furrowed eyebrows remembered the state of his own marriage.

"Have you met Avril?" I asked while Willie patted his face with a white cotton face towel. He considered my question, making kissing noises against his teeth, trying to remove a sliver of conch fritter lodged between his back molar.

"She seems nice enough. But I don't have to live with her. Your brother does. That's all that matters."

"Her family. What they like?"

"Never met none of 'em. She planned a fancy engagement dinner down at the Marriott, but Victor wouldn't have none of it. Which don't make no never mind to me, 'cause if they're gonna be family, we'll meet 'em soon enough."

"Knowing my brother, it is a miracle that he invited us. How'd that happen?" I asked, sitting on the edge of the cool, porcelain bathtub next to a large cup of Ms. Chickie's teeth.

"She threatened to place an announcement in the Sunday *Miami Herald* if he didn't." "She" and "Huh" were how Willie always referred to my mother.

Victor developed a penchant for secrecy shortly after adolescence, even locking his bedroom door when he began junior high school. When I tried that tactic, I was admonished. The distinction, as Lee Artist explained after conferring with Ms. Chickie, was that "men, the carriers of the family name, need their privacy; while women need protection."

Hence, Victor never introduced his friends, fraternity brothers, or girlfriends to the family. But we knew he was popular by the amount of phone calls he received every night and the thong panties that were strewn beneath his bedroom window. Either that or he operated a home lingerie shopping service. However, that too stopped when his private telephone was installed, but the orphaned panties remained. Meanwhile, my private telephone calls were received at Carmen's house, where her parents didn't care how often *el Negroes* phoned.

Ms. Chickie shuffled out of her bedroom and stood in the bathroom doorway. "Y'all come on outta there. I got bitness to tend to."

Willie stuffed the face towel between the crystal clear rail and pink tile, mumbling, "Dammit, I can't find peace in my own goddamn bathroom. It's the one damn place that don't smell like *Robitussin*!"

My charming older brother, Victor, had, since his engagement to Avril, a recent Haitian immigrant whom he'd met during Atlanta's Freaknik, campaigned for, then later lost a City Council seat to a Cuban attorney. The attorney had inserted Victor's alternative religious leanings into the campaign, incurring public rancor. Miami-Dade County, being the Jewish/Baptist Bible Belt capital of the East Coast, strangled on its Bible verses when Victor's affiliation with Yahweh bin Yahweh was leaked. No matter how much he renounced his ties to Yahweh, the voting public rejected him, and the other half didn't care and didn't vote. A fringe element of Yahweh believers became annoyed when Victor denounced them and sent him a threatening email:

"This is for him whose family is not present in the Sacred Mosque, and be careful of your duty to Yahweh, and know that Yahweh is severe in requiting evil."

Although Victor was guilty of many misdemeanors during his formative years, which my mother chose to ignore, he still remained in good standing with the family. But all of that was threatened now that Avril was about to become a permanent fixture. Ms. Chickie did not find her Creole accent in the least bit fascinating. Avril, by her very existence, had violated many of the tenets in Lee Artist and Ms. Chickie's Book of Judgment: She was short; thus stunting the gene pool of future heirs. She didn't speak English. She had a gap in her teeth, which to them was a characteristic of liars.

In their view, Avril's only redeeming quality was that she was a homeowner, which was uppity enough for Ms. Chickie.

Willie said, turning to face me, "You really look good, little girl."

"Thanks, Daddy." I beamed, sticking my tongue out in the direction of Ms. Chickie and Lee Artist.

And as if sensing an opportunity to contradict him, Lee Artist called, "Iris, unpack; let me see what you're wearing to the wedding. We must look our best."

Before I formed a sigh, Daddy hugged me again. "Go on and get ready." Silently, I wished that at that moment he and I could become warriors, standing up against injustice and any attempts to re-create me in someone else's image. But without a willing compatriot, I felt powerless to rise up on my own.

"Lawd, Lee Artist, look what your daughter done brought," Ms. Chickie squawked, from deep inside my suit bag.

"Granddaughter, what the hell are you wearing? What happened to those purple golf cleats I gave you for your birthday? Why didn't you bring those with ya?"

"Well, I don't golf, and—"

"Oh gal, you ain't got no sense of style. I got those purple golf cleats from the white lady, I used to clean for, over on Miami Beach. The white lady loved those purple golf cleats, that it was so hard for her to part with 'em. Both her and her husband always be wearing golf cleats."

"Maybe that was because they lived on a golf course?"

"Well, what happened to that white dress with the attached lavender bow and...and all the ruffles and with the...with the sash and the two beautiful bows in the back? What happened to that?"

"Um, that was a bit too young."

"Well, the white lady liked it."

Ms. Chickie liked anything the white lady whose house she used to clean on Miami Beach preferred. For the life of her, my grandmother could not understand why I didn't like the same things white people liked. For the first two years after I left home, my dorm room was decorated in Early White Lady furnishings donated by Ms. Chickie.

"Well, what happened to the green Members Only jacket that the white lady gave you?"

"Too boxy."

"Well, the white lady liked it. Hmph, heifer!"

My earliest memories were of being inspected and prodded, like a cocker spaniel at a dog show. Victor used to tell me that Lee Artist had been ecstatic shortly after my birth. When she saw that her only daughter had blue eyes, announcements and telegrams were dispatched, causing relatives to sprint to Opa Locka to see the prized blue-eyed child and to puff their chests out, strutting like roosters around my crib. But as I grew out of infancy, my prized blue eyes changed to dark blue, then brown. Lee Artist was crushed, then embarrassed. Ms. Chickie accused her of dropping me on my head. Pediatricians from Miami Beach to Coral Gables assured her that there was no cure, that this was a natural evolution. My cataclysmic beginning gave birth to the prodding in an attempt to somehow resurrect those prized blue eyes.

But now I was tall, with a coffee-brown complexion (quickly blamed on my father's side); shoulder-length hair that had been processed for years before I had, last summer, let its natural consistency grow out; high buttocks; firm thighs; small bread-basket stomach; and pert breasts. *Not bad. I think.*

My early predilection for tomboy activities had put my beauty-pageant stage mother on course with a nervous breakdown. Like her mother, Lee Artist force-fed me the notion that my power was in the shape of my body and the styling of my clothes. To cement those messages, when I was seven she dressed me in low-cut dresses and spike-heeled boots, with enough foundation to open a makeup counter. Rebelling, I used every opportunity to sabotage the message by accidentally-on-purpose soiling a yellow chiffon dress, scuffing white ballet shoes, or suddenly becoming ill the morning of the Little Miss Opa Locka talent competition.

As I matured, the curvature of my ash-free Vaseline-shined legs attracted attention from men of all ages, and sometimes disdain from women. The power of my body was apparent each time I hiked up a skirt, or sat at a premeditated angle. While I battled the expectations of Atlanta's bourgeoisie lifestyle, still the voices of Ms. Chickie and Lee Artist whispered, "You need to be fixed." I have often tried to quiet my tomboy, devil-may-care voice. "Hmph, but not hard enough," according to Lee Artist.

[2]
Delray Beach

In Daddy's air-conditioned-less Oldsmobile, squeezed in the backseat between cousin Lenore and her teenage son, Poot, I soon realized my efforts to iron creases in my lavender pantsuit had been for naught. Daddy didn't believe in air-conditioning. Thought it prematurely ruined a car's engine. Willie had also intentionally removed the air-conditioning months ago in an attempt to discourage anyone—such as Lee Artist and Ms. Chickie—from wanting to ride in *his* car. After all, this was his private bastion. However, on this day, my mother insisted that it was more royal to arrive together as a "dynasty," in the only family vehicle that could accommodate the egos of the Chapmans. As he locked the front door of our house, I heard Willie grumble, "Dammit, damn, dammit."

Sitting between two cousins known for their humongous thighs, I knew what it felt like to be a piece of grilled steak on a shish kabob skewer. In the front seat were Lee Artist, Ms. Chickie, and the mumbling Willie, who drove, blasting B.B. King's "The Thrill Is Gone" on the cassette player.

"Seem like you would know some other song," Lee Artist scolded, cooling herself with an autographed Diahann Carroll limited-edition fan.

Poot and Lenore were never allowed inside our house, because they were dairy kleptomaniacs. If you had a stick of butter lying around, one of them was sure to swipe it. According to Willie's calculations, the two grifters had contaminated pounds of butter, ice cream, milk, cheese and sour cream over the three years, mostly by licking. The night before a holiday or family gathering, my father would stock up on the ingredients he needed to bake his recipes of pies, cakes, and macaroni and cheese. Family and friends would gather in the living room watching *Roots* and the Lou Rawls United Negro College Fund Telethon. And just when Kunta was going to renounce his slave name, Lenore and Poot would slip into the kitchen to lick and sniff anything connected to the curd of a cow.

After one Lent celebration, Willie caught Lenore and Poot, sticking their tongues in the organic milk that my father coveted. "Goddamn it! Are you two calcium deficient? I leave the room for one goddamn second and you're in here wit your nasty tongues in my organic milk! And don't be sittin' there looking like all that lactose done bother you none. Looking like bull-frogs, which your eyes bulging out your heads! Y'all ain't in no danger of having osteoporosis. But I know one goddamn thing, you better stay the hell out of my house! Just nasty! I wouldn't trust ya in a shithouse with a muzzle!"

In spite of Willie's tirade, Ms. Chickie still had Poot to perform her errands, but from the yard. My grandmother would hand him her errand list through her bedroom window, while Lenore waited at the fence, hoping for a calcium fix. Later, when Willie protested about Poot and Lenore riding in the car with us to Victor's wedding, Ms. Chickie told Lee Artist, "That man you married may be madder than a mule chewing on bumblebees, but dey is family and dey is goin' and that's all there is to it."

We rode in combustible silence, as Ms. Chickie fumed over the idiocy of being without an air conditioner. Lee Artist didn't mind at all. As children, Lee Artist sheltered Victor and me from drafts. Other mothers protected their child from weird strangers, gagging on string beans or running in the street and getting hit by a wayward ice cream truck. But Lee Artist had only one fear and that was that Victor and I would catch pneumonia from anyone breathing on us or from a sudden breeze.

"Roll up the car windows," my mother would order Willie on an eighty-degree temperature Opa Locka day. "Make sure the wind is not blowing on the children. And cover their little noses with a wet towel so they won't suffocate. You can roll your eyes if you want to, but I'm only doing this for their benefit."

Benefit. Lee Artist is consumed with benefiting humanity. Not the charity of saving the snotty-nosed orphan with flies buzzing around them in the church pew next to you. Instead, my mother believes her calling is reminding you that whatever she does for or to you, usually of the uncomfortable variety, is only for your own benefit. Like the time she visited my elementary school and announced to my class, "Please ignore little Iris when she lets out poop bombs. It's not intentional. She just does it for attention. Must get from her father's side of the family."

"Well, it was only for your own benefit, Iris," she later explained, when I requested legal representation for immediate emancipation and political asylum, preferring to serve out my adolescent years on the red sofa in the principal's office. "Forewarning your classmates was to put their little minds at ease; otherwise, they would've thought that the sound of your air biscuits were bullets shooting up the classroom. You didn't want your little friends diving for cover every time you decided to let her rip, did you? I only did it for your benefit."

"Don't worry, Daddy, you'll get your car back soon," I whispered as I stood with him to purchase gas at the 7-Eleven off Twenty-Seventh Avenue before we headed north, draped by an orange-red sunset, toward the heart of Delray Beach's Little Haiti.

One summer, Carmen and I had traveled to Delray Beach to party, and arrived thinking there was a celebration in honor of Toussaint L'ouverture. Then reality set in—the anarchy of these streets was not a carnival, but a drug supermarket. Skeletal, bug-eyed humanoid creatures had splayed themselves against my car, pleading for another dose, hit, drag, puff, or snort. *Everyone with twists or dreadlocks does not smoke weed.*

Since all I had was an aspirin, I floored it, dumping the unlucky ones who had not read their horoscopes off the hood onto the sidewalk, and U-turned it for Interstate 95 South back to Opa Locka. Now, due in large part to Haitian immigrants, the city had undergone a renewal, reducing the likelihood of anyone asking if I was there to procure anything.

"Seem like he could have found a gal in Miami. And who gets married at night, anyway? Like some old country bumpkin," Ms. Chickie mulled while penciling on a new pair of eyebrows in a tiny mirror. Often her statements would belie her own agricultural past and that of her parents. She wanted to distance herself from whatever pained her and others of her generation.

"When we gonna get there?" asked Poot for the fifth time in the last hour, sensing my father was lost. We traveled along St. Laurent Boulevard, bustling with girls in sundresses tottering on platform sandals, loitering reggae-blasting boys, Judaica Treasures, and Haitian shipping services. *Reliable Taxi* drove alongside us near the bustling intersection.

"We done circled the statue of Gloria Estefan ten times, Willie!" Ms. Chickie yelled. "You need to get a GPS aviation system like the one Victor Newman has on the *Young and the Restless* in this clap trap!"

"I'll be damned if I let some machine tell me which way I oughta go. When did man follow a machine? One day, that same ESP thang, or whatever you call it, it's gonna tell somebody to drive right off a bridge. And I guess y'all go right over there with 'em...Tell huh to get that driver's attention," my father said, to no one in particular, staring straight ahead. In the same manner, she called him "Chappie" during the rare occasions they actually did speak.

"I know how to ask for directions, Chappie," Lee Artist snapped before batting her eyelashes at the driver. "Sir? Directions, please?"

The Haitian driver, pinching a cigarette between his lips, leaned out of the window, gracing Lee Artist with an easy yellow smile. "Where you wanna go?" he said with a rich Creole accent.

"Tell huh to tell the man the address," Willie responded, irritated that his role as Head Explorer was being usurped. Lee Artist rummaged through her patent leather handbag until she found a small sheet of paper underneath a pile of tissue.

"Three-twenty-seven Toussaint Boulevard, Delray Beach, Florida," she informed the driver, as if he would have assumed she meant Alaska.

The taxi driver's yellow smile vanished instantly as he slowly leaned back inside his car. "What you want to go dere for?" he asked suspiciously.

"Immigration, dammit," Ms. Chickie answered wryly, to which I cut my eyes at her impishness.

"Three-twenty-seven Toussaint Boulevard!? Three-twenty-seven Toussaint Boulevard!?" he shrieked in stunned recognition. "It's the devil! They're dancing with demons!" he shrieked, twisting himself across his front seat to jerk open the glove compartment. Drivers behind furiously honked their horns, as the traffic light signaled to proceed. Leaning back outside his window, and shaking his pamphlets in the air, the driver shouted to the heavens, "Strike dem down, fadda," and hurled "Message of Love from God" pamphlets in our window:

CHRIST JESUS RESPONDED: I AM HIM. MARK 14:62.

The cab driver rolled up his window, changed gears and screeched his tires to speed away, leaving us in a cloud of black carburetor smoke. One of his bumper stickers flew away proclaiming in English and French:

JOHN 3:16
FOR GOD SO LOVED THE WORLD, THAT HE GAVE HIS ONLY BEGOTTEN SON, THAT WHOEVER BELIEVES IN HIM SHALL NOT PERISH, BUT HAVE ETERNAL LIFE.
Pour un dieu a ainsi aimé le monde, Quil a donné son seulement fils, Celui qui croit en lui ne mourra oas, Ayez éternelle lavie.

We froze, resembling Montserrat volcanic ash, as we stared at the cab driver speeding past Pineapple Grove, a bustling pedestrian mall, until he was swallowed up in stagnant rush-hour traffic.

"People here are mighty unfriendly," Lee Artist piped in.

"Sho is," Ms. Chickie agreed.

What stunning events of historic proportions. Ms. Chickie and Lee Artist agreed on something, I surmised as a skinny, black cat sauntered past our car into the intersection.

"Which direction did that cat come from, Chappie?" Lee Artist asked.

"Tell huh I don't know."

"He came from the left," advised Poot.

"No, he didn't," said Lenore.

"Well, since none of y'all know, Chappie, I want you to turn this car around, this very minute!" There was no sense in arguing with Lee Artist when it came to her black cats or any other superstition. "It's not superstition. If you want to argue with evil, you go right ahead and let a stray black cat cross away from you. But I won't be with you, when it does. The Rayburn family were on their way up to Myrtle Beach and they let a black cat cross away from them. And the smart alecs kept driving and nobody has heard from them since. They haven't even been to church."

Finally arriving after sundown, the frenetic drums emanating from inside dissuaded us that this was the location of the wedding of Lee Artist's First Son. From the music's intensity, you would have thought that white farmers had decided to return the land in Zimbabwe and Nation of Islam Minister Louis Farrakhan was leading the celebration. Lee Artist re-checked the address: 327 Toussaint Boulevard, Delray Beach, Florida.

The Chapman dynasty sat in the Oldsmobile craning our necks for a full six minutes before a silent vote resulted in me unfolding my legs from the backseat and tiptoeing to the narrow door of the brown, dimly lit, ramshackled building. My tender knocking was ignored by the pulsating drums. I glanced back at the Oldsmobile, with the engine still idling, saw the slack-jawed expressions of my family, sloshing in their own perspiration, and then opened the door and stared into the expansive, candle-lit interior. When I stepped inside, my sweat glands fully exploded in response to the funky air, steamy with musk oil.

Victor, dressed in a summer-white, floor-length caftan, was chatting with a handsome, muscular woman with long auburn dreadlocks spiraling from under a white gele wrapped around her oval-shaped head. About two hundred people, dressed in colorful formal and casual floor-length robes, were crammed into padded, metal fold-up chairs. A white sofa was positioned in front of a wooden altar piled high with multi-colored cakes, fruit and various bottles of liquor. On both sides of the altar were caged reptiles, whom either slept or flickered their tongues. Sweaty, middle-aged black women sang in French Creole, smiling and swaying in front of the appreciative throng. Sweaty muscular youths wearing FREE TIGER WOODS and FREE OJ T-shirts pounded on their sacred conga drums, throwing their heads back, and swirling their long dreadlocks like octopus tentacles. Before I could gather myself to haul ass out of there, Victor and the handsome woman glided over to greet me.

"Mgbeke! My treasured sister. You have arrived!" Mgbeke was the name Victor bestowed upon me, despite my protestations, when he was going through his Yoruba phase.

"I told you not to call me that Victor—er, um—Prophet Yechetzwyah," I responded through clenched teeth. Prophet Yechetzwyah was from his Yahweh phase. *Mgbeke* means "a child born on corn-shucking day," an honor I could do without.

"Have you traveled this distance unchaperoned?" Victor asked. My eyes rolled back in my head until the whites showed, appearing as though I was performing an exorcism on myself. Victor, or whatever he was calling himself these days, spoke in high-falutin' Biblical tones, as if he had handed Moses the Ten Commandments himself. This was hard to take from a brother who wet his bed until he was twelve, becoming defensive when I called him "Tinkle."

"What's going on here?" I answered, my eyes darting around the room. "I thought you were getting married."

"Ah, the seeker begins her journey. My treasured sister, meet Montreuil. Montreuil is the Mambo for the ceremony." Noting from his tone, this Montreuil must have been in charge of something, but did I need to put my image consulting business on hold to learn how to do the mambo? Nevertheless, I extended my arm to shake hands with her.

"Nice to meet you. I'm Iris." Perhaps it was the firm manner in which she held my hand that made me notice the intensity of her gaze. In point of fact, Montreuil was not going to release my now-wilted hand until she was ready. "You don't remember me, do you?" she said in dramatic alto tones, peeling back a wry smile. In the recesses of my mind, the North Miami Dade High School yearbook flipped open and spiraled through pages of promises, best wishes, faculty/administration, horny janitors, sports teams, organizations, then paused on the Young Soldiers for the Moral Majority (*which were neither*). Front and center was the four-term president, Edwina Arnold, with press-and-curl bangs, cat-eye glasses, and a penchant for declaring anything contrary to her moral platitudes to be the lynchpin that crumbles the universe as we know it. Edwina had now, obviously, made a horizontal or vertical evolution (undetermined as of yet) to—*voila*—Montreuil!

"Edwina! Small world."

"Small world indeed," she responded, nobly bowing her head.

"Tink—, Vict—, Proph—," I said to Victor.

"Come, my beautiful sister. Excuse us, Montreuil?"

Montreuil again bowed nobly, which I remembered was what she did to suck up to teachers in high school.

"Oh that Edwina, such class, such grace, what carriage," teachers would coo. And here I was attending charm school and dance class and all she had to do was bow nobly and smell like cherry incense.

Victor guided me by the elbow like I was a toy sailboat, into a small, damp office containing two caged, outraged chickens. "Victor, everyone's out in the car. What the hell is going on?"

Victor smiled patronizingly, nodding patiently. "My sister, I am indeed holding my commitment ceremony on this enchanting evening that Damballah has blessed us with—"

"Who?" I quizzed. "Wait a minute. Don't answer that. The last time I asked 'who,' I got the genealogical history of Netjer!"

"Ah, you were always so impatient, my young, impetuous sibling," Victor responded, weaving his fingers together.

"Okay, that's it! I'm gone!" I barked, turning on my heels to leave this coffin, um, office. Victor followed, yanking on my elbow, which I jerked from his reach and moved with long knock-kneed strides toward the front door. Before I reached the doorknob, Victor ran in front of me, blocking my exit.

"Iris." Wonder of wonders. He remembered my name. "Iris, allow me to explain."

"Sure, just drop the verbosity. I was the one who convinced you that nose-picking was unattractive; remember, Tinkle?"

"Shhh! Lower your voice, ya feel me?" Victor pleaded. Now that's the Victor I knew, the one who ended every statement needing to verify if the world *felt* him.

A group of smiling celebrants dressed in bright orange and white garments entered the office, greeted and hugged Victor, then joined the assemblage. I pointed to my Movado watch to signal that his time was rapidly expiring.

"Iris," he began slowly. "Tonight I will pledge loyalty, service, and sexual fidelity to Erzulie, the spirit goddess of love. Avril, my fianceé and I will live separately. I will be free to live my life as I wish, though two nights a week I must sleep alone and wait for the spirit of Erzulie to visit. If I must work, I work. If I have things to do, I do them. But before midnight, I say my prayers to Erzulie. She is always in my heart and in my house. And this ceremony is my way of saying that I am at her disposal."

"Wait a minute. I thought you were marrying Avril," I said. Before he could answer, Victor was whisked away by Montreuil, who nobly nodded toward me before they disappeared behind a beaded, multi-colored, cheap motel-styled curtain.

By the time Victor returned, whisking me outside, I had erased any illusions that a carrier pigeon would swoop me away from this hell. I had also departed from the notion that this was going to be an ordinary night. Waiting in the sultry heat for my return, Ms. Chickie and the rest were fanning themselves so hard the Oldsmobile was levitating off the ground. During the requisite hugs, Victor's eyes met the glares of two menacing-looking black men lurking across the street, wearing white sheets and turbans by Yahweh. Rattled, Victor, glancing over his shoulder, ushered Lee Artist and Ms. Chickie toward the warehouse door. "Don't step on any sidewalk cracks! Ten years bad luck," Lee Artist advised. Lovingly gazing into Victor's anointed eyeballs, the pair stroked his forearm, but turned chartreuse when they crossed the building's threshold. Seeing chickens strolling around didn't ease their horror. Willie remained outside, cursing out Poot, whom he suspected of stealing a case of egg nog from the trunk of the car.

Victor sat the bewildered Lee Artist and annoyed Ms. Chickie in the front row who peppered the ushers with requests for a program, corsages and champagne, which they deemed was their right as mother and grandmother of the groom. As the sweaty, middle-aged black women ended their songs, the congregants continued with improvised moans and chants. Victor whispered into the ears of a group of petite Haitian men, pointing out the menacing white-sheet wearers, who had entered the warehouse. Their eyes bulged out of their heads and searched Victor's lying eyes for confirmation. Victor nodded, crossing his heart. Then, like a colony of bees, the Haitian men gathered baseball bats, chairs, and hammers and chased the now fleeing white-sheet wearers out the door, shrieking:

"Oh mon dieu! Oh mon dieu! Il est le Klan! Mate el Klan! (Oh my God! Oh my God! It's the Klan! Kill the Klan!)"

Back inside, dancers wearing kerchiefs knotted around their heads and gigantic hoop earrings, chanted, "*Sina, sina, sina dogoue.*" They clapped and tapped their feet ritualistically. "*Nou pou ale vwe sine dogoue* (We are going to see God of the universe)."

A wiry, dark-brown woman next to me suddenly jerked upright, spinning wildly, arms and legs flailing, with her eyes rolling as if she had also heard one of Victor's diatribes. Two men rushed to her side, supporting her in their arms. Her yellow kerchief slipped off her head causing her shiny, straightened hair, arranged in a French bun, to unwind. Her body became rigid, muscles taut, as she stomped the ground with her bare feet, whipping her head from side to side, eyes stretched wide, sweeping the room with her fierce gaze. And all of this was during Montreuil's welcome remarks. I decided to inch over to a chair near the front door in case a swift, early departure was in order. After all, I had a lot to live for.

Victor and Avril entered separately, as Montreuil held her arms spread wide like Rio de Janiero's Christ the Redeemer statue. Avril's eyes focused solemnly on Montreuil. The more hypnotic the drumbeat became, the further I slid down in my chair, completely wrinkling my clothes. A green-eyed young girl seated across from me, clad in a white golf shirt and navy blue capris, asked, "*Est-ce que tu veux tomber en-trance?* (Do you want to fall into a trance?)" Not waiting for my answer, the girl-woman fell to the floor, thrashing. Someone handed me an ice-cold beer, but it was intercepted from behind by a trembling Lee Artist who prayed aloud, "Michelle would never be caught dead in this situation." Women wearing white kerchiefs rushed to the young woman's side, holding down her arms. By the time, the young girl stood erect, she was in the throes of spiritual possession.

Montreuil announced, "Erzulie, the goddess of love, will join Jobu, Victor's new alias, with Avril. I notice others have come to embrace their union as well." The congregants moaned and chanted incoherently their approval. Montreuil clapped her hands like a lightning strike, transforming those close to me. A young girl was inhabited by a vamp, who sashayed over to a table, anointing herself with perfumes. Then a large, square-headed man flailed his arms and fell into a chair, shaking, then rose with lust-filled eyes to flirt with me.

A flirtatious, rhythmical circle formed around Victor and Avril. Each person placed *clairin*, a white, raw sugarcane rum; Barbancourt rum; a bottle of strawberry fruit punch; or perfume vials on the altar. After the offerings were made, everyone danced to their seats.

Montreuil gestured for Victor and Avril to stand. "For eternity, we unite the eternal spirit Erzulie with Jobu and Avril." Montreuil placed a gold coiled-snake ring on the middle fingers of Victor's and Avril's left hands. The frenetic drumbeats signaled the end of the ceremony and the beginning of the feast of delicacies, from a local Indian takeout restaurant.

A sweaty, thin black woman wailed a Creole hymn:

"*Kouman ouye la. Mwen bien. Nap kebe.*" ("How are you? I am well. We are here.") "Ke ke ke ke ke ke ke ke ke," she chanted frantically in an eerie staccato rhythm. Her eyes rolled back in her head, and sweat appeared on her upper lip. "Ke ke ke ke," she sang bawdily, lifting up the hem of her dress, gyrating lasciviously.

Ms. Chickie, exposing her pink gums, exercising her prerogative to embarrass the Chapman clan, danced with the drummer wearing the FREE O.J. tee shirt, while Willie and Montreuil had an apparently titillating conversation near the altar. My father hadn't smiled that way in decades.

As a sliver of sunlight signaled the morning dawn, Victor and Avril found Lee Artist and me massaging our feet, with our high heels dangling from the Oldsmobile hood ornament. "We wondered what happened to you two," Victor said.

"Victor, how could you?" scolded Lee Artist.

"How could I what, Duchess?" Victor asked, using "Duchess" when he wanted to rapidly retreat to her good side.

"How could you have a wedding here? In this sordid place? I will be the laughingstock of Opa Locka. My sorors will never understand. 'No wedding announcement in the *Miami Herald*, Lee Artist?' they will ask over and over. And thank heavens, this travesty wasn't in the newspaper...I can see it now; a dozen roosters dropped feces in honor of the newlyweds—"

Victor released Avril's hand and drew Lee Artist close to him, patting her on the back. "You look stunning, Duchess," Victor said to Lee Artist, at which she blushed and pressed a rather large rabbit's foot into his palm. Expecting money, instead of a tear-stained good luck charm, Victor frowned.

"And what is up with 'Jobu,' Victor? You change your name more than most people change their underwear!" I asked, knowing that whatever he said, my mind could not wrap around his explanations, his insights, or his spaceship that will retrieve black folks next year. I introduced myself to Avril, who only smiled and ignored my extended hand.

"Ah, she doesn't speak English, only Creole," said Victor, squeezing Avril's hand gently.

"*Mwen anvi vonmi.* (You make me sick)," Avril managed.

"What she say? What she say?" I said to Henry Kissinger, er, um, Victor.

"Um, I'm not sure. I haven't gotten that far in the translation book yet."

Montreuil strolled over to bid farewell, urging us to cleanse our spirits by entering into a spiritual marriage with Erzulie as well. I flatly refused. I have a hard enough time keeping track of my boyfriend, Achilles, in this world; forget about one in the spirit world.

While Willie shoved a "Voodou For Dummies" brochure into his monogrammed shirt pocket and waved forlornly to Montreuil, until she was surrounded by a group of admirers, Lee Artist flung herself into the Oldsmobile in a huff, ordering that we leave instantly.

"I've had the embarrassment of a lifetime. And I will never live this down! The laughter has already begun." Poot and Lenore, who had fallen asleep in the backseat, awoke, wiping the dried white saliva from their chins. Once we had returned to Opa Locka, I went online to the name generator website to destroy your child's life and learned that *Jobu* meant "one who is born to create storms."

My mother now blames Avril for the brown-wrapped package consisting of a new ceremonial dress, a necklace of blue and white snake vertebrae, a pair of white roosters, Florida water, barley water, strawberry soda, sugar cookies, eggs, herbs, powders, and photographs of St. Patrick, the Virgin Mary and the Rolling Stones, anonymously delivered during her Alpha Kappa Alpha Boulé board meeting. Victor, with his customary hurt look and virtuous disclaimer, denies and defends his wife. Avril neither confirms nor denies, these allegations as far as we can tell, as none of us understand Creole.

[3]
TIL DEATH DO US PART

Little did I know that a looming flock of low-flying vultures had convened by the time the proposals for new clients were prepared and retrieved by FedEx. Tammy had phoned again, this time hinting for details on Victor's wedding.

"Tammy, give it up," I said, transferring the cordless telephone to the other ear as I prepared scrambled tofu and a toasted bagel.

"What?" she asked innocently.

"What, my ass. Why would you care about someone who dogged you as much as my brother did?"

"No, no, no, no, no, I was just making conversation," Tammy lied.

It defined logic why Tammy believed she needed to repeat her "no's" more than once, as if I was too retarded to comprehend the first no, no, no. Her verbal language tics were akin to those people who believe that people who can't speak English, will only understand if you scream loudly.

"Sure, sure. Sounds like your heart was making tracks to get back with him. Victor is my brother and I love him, but he attracts women with low self-esteem from around the globe. Loving the drama, the chaos, the tangled web of infidelity. And Victor is the only one who emerges from his bullshit unscathed."

After the discomfort I experienced being tossed between two people who used more subterfuge and intrigue than an Ingmar Bergman film, I now forbade any of my friends to date Victor as I no longer want to play psychologist or referee.

❖ ❖ ❖

Victor had chatted up the then born-again Tammy during his visit with me in Atlanta, meeting her during my firm's launch of a client's product. On her failed search to find a saved, Christian man, Tammy had decided to construct her own. And since Victor was capable of being all things to all women, in Tammy's eyes, he was the blessing she had been praying for.

"No, no, no, no, no, Iris," Tammy explained, after I told her about my brother's predatory history. "Amen, you just don't understand that the power of prayer can change all things, including a man. It takes a good, Christian woman to make a good Christian man. Amen."

Tammy had only been a full-time Christian for about six months; during which she renounced all forms of fornication, intemperance and pilates. As though she needed to constantly remind herself of her full-time status, Tammy began and ended her sentences with "amen" or "blessed and highly favored." Since I had been raised with Victor, I was used to observing those near to me undergo seasonal changes, with weight, religion, and political viewpoints.

Next thing I knew, Victor had moved to Atlanta and in with Tammy, and began cheating with women in Tammy's church like a sexual evangelist. Victor was on a mission to anoint as many women as possible, in case his rendezvous with Tammy didn't pan out.

Tammy and I became fast friends after meeting at a Women in Business Empowerment seminar. Like myself, she sought information on how to make her then needlepoint business, more marketable. Using a 5" x 8" design over dyed floss, dyed perle, rayon thread, silk thread, and metallic thread in various colors, one had to follow hard-to-understand, small-print instructions, and later be surprised by the design created.

Securing her first business contract on a ward of mostly black, amputee war veterans, Tammy encouraged them to use whatever extremity they had left to needlepoint. However, after a concerted effort, the veterans were incensed when the surprise design was not an image of Lena Horne, as they had been promised, but had an incredible likeness to Tammy, whom Ms. Chickie often said, "Dat gal is so ugly, she'd make a freight train take a dirt road!" Despite Tammy's physical presentation, she had a heart of gold, though she needed to frequently shave the whiskers on her chin.

When Tammy needed a job to pay off debts from her failed needlepoint business, I also needed someone to help operate Image Control, which was steadily attracting new clients, requiring more of my time. Tammy began as an assistant, then rose to a junior associate, as she demonstrated a knack for public relations, maintaining her own client list with her small-town charm.

Tammy's heartbroken sniveling pierced the middle of many of my nights, whining questions to which she already knew the answers, while Achilles lay in the bed, next to me.

Still, Tammy continued to deal with him. Victor must have a gold dick because otherwise I can't understand what she saw in him. He was ten years older than her, separated from his first wife, had a potbelly and bad credit. He would look perfect on a Stylistics album cover. Plus, the old fucker moved in with Tammy 'cause he couldn't afford a decent apartment. The last one was so small that when he walked through the front door, he tripped over the back fence.

Victor's fate with Tammy was sealed during one of his *sudden* business trips to the Washington, D.C. headquarters of his company, for which he was a sales account executive. In an effort to have one of those "do you still love me" conversations, Tammy phoned his company's headquarters and was told the facility was closed for renovations. As I was in the middle of issuing another ultimatum to Achilles for a commitment, I barked to Tammy when she phoned to complain, "Tammy, just dump his ass!"

"No, no, no, no, no, no, no, Iris. I believe in the power of prayer. Amen!"

"I thought you had given up fornication, Tammy?"

"No, no, no, no, no, no, no, Iris. Amen, the Lord is still working on me. And working on you, too, Amen!"

Working on her indeed. Shortly before laying eyes on Victor, Tammy was swooning for someone who called himself a reggae singer. It was the leather guitar strap hanging around his thin neck and gold front tooth, which captivated Tammy. The singer explained with a lilting accent that the actual guitar was stolen from the tour bus. He also claimed that his father was a member of the 1988 Jamaican Olympic bobsled team. Unfortunately, he continued, his father was subsequently crushed outside of Ocho Rios, under a watermelon pushcart. Incredible what bullshit some people choose to lie about. And what other people choose to believe.

Tammy believed all of his proclamations of love, country and a dire need for a green card. Since her legal affairs were all tied up with another green card situation, the singer accepted her desperate offer of a roof over his unemployed head.

"Tammy, why don't you just open up your house as a bed and breakfast for wayward fools? That way, you can cut through all of the crap!"

"No, no, no, no, no, no, no, Iris. We're just going through a rough patch right now. Amen."

Rough patch, my ass.

"…all I know is that I'm not comin' to your house anymore… can't get the smell of his reefer smoke outta my clothes!"

Soon after, Tammy arrived home to find her jewelry stolen. Together, she and I donned black-colored clothes, and visited every Jamaican nightclub and eatery in Atlanta, including the One Love Rastafari association planning meeting, only to learn that reggae boy had evaporated into a puff of smoke.

When Tammy wasn't working on her men issues, she was involved in every multi-level marketing scheme known to the capitalistic free world. Her Toyota Rav4 was filled with each new business fixation. Multi-level marketing products and brochures were scattered throughout her home. Why she would try to recruit me, reading from her MLM training manual, as if I didn't know what she was doing, was always puzzling:

"Hey Iris!! I wanna set up a meeting with you to discuss my new business venture and pick your brain about some ideas and concepts. This is an urgent opportunity! We can help people and earn a six-figure monthly income! I would love to have our meeting about my business ASAP. What works best for you, mornings, afternoon or evenings? Call me!"

When I would return her telephone call about an unrelated matter, I asked, "Well, Tammy, what is it?"

"I can't discuss it over the telephone. But if anybody needs to do this, it's you! With all of the people you know."

"Is there any selling involved?"

"This business sells itself. It's a fantastic opportunity."

"More fantastic than AshAway, TightSkin, WholesaleIncense, ShoesForSale, Cheap Travel, Prepaid Bail and Dream Body?"

❖ ❖ ❖

As planned, Tammy picked up Victor from Atlanta's Hartsfield-Jackson International Airport, meeting him outside of Delta airlines' baggage claim. Smiling broadly, Tammy hid her knowledge of his transgression into evil. Victor galloped toward Tammy's care like an illegal alien over an Arizonian border fence.

"How was the flight?" Tammy asked nonchalantly, a fire slowly building in her belly.

"Oh, it was fine. The usual," he answered, looking out of his window.

"How was D.C.? Get to see anything?" Tammy continued.

"Nope," Victor muttered. "Just went to the training meetings at headquarters and went back to the hotel."

Anticipating his arrival, Tammy prepared his favorite dinner—barbecued spare ribs, wild rice, and black-eyed peas—then screwed him so hard he got heart palpitations. When he fell asleep, scratching his belly, Tammy rifled through his pant pockets and wallet. There in his wallet was the proof she needed: a credit card receipt for $425.61 from a bed and breakfast in Savannah, Georgia.

Tammy stared at a muted television as Victor snored in the bedroom, the one she had let him sleep in rent-free for the past eight months. Her right eyeball twitched as she remembered starching and ironing his shirts, crisply hanging in her closet. Victor snored louder. She saw a mirage of hundred-dollar bills that she had lent him, "just until he got paid."

Suddenly, Tammy marched into the utility room where, on the top shelf, she found Elmer's quick-drying glue; then tiptoed back to hear Victor snoring deeper and deeper into hibernation. Victor didn't feel Tammy apply the glue between his fungus-ridden toes. Victor smacked his lips as Tammy then glued his penis, making sure it stuck to his hairy thigh. After sticking it to him, Tammy quietly stuffed his clothes into Winn-Dixie plastic shopping bags and watched the glue dry, like a toddler, watching ants build a colony.

When the sun rose, Victor didn't, until he stumbled, around noon, to the bathroom, raised the lid on the toilet seat, and realized he had to pee sideways. While he screamed, "What the fuck!?" Tammy read aloud Judges 15:7: "Samson said to them, 'Since you act like this, I will surely take revenge on you, but after that I will quit.'"

Like other men who charmed Christian women into believing that they enjoyed Bible study classes, Victor lied, cajoled, and begged forgiveness. When that plan failed, he snatched Tammy's Bible, because he didn't own one, and flipped to Romans 12:19, reading: "Never take your own revenge, beloved, but leave room for the wrath of God, for it is written, 'Vengeance is mine, I will repay.'"

Before he could slam the door that he didn't own, Tammy went to the book of Revelations, which is where she should have been reading from all along, and barked: "From the relevations of Tammy: Get the fuck out, 'cause this bitch is blessed and highly favored."

Victor returned home to Opa Locka, to pee again in Willie and Lee Artist's toilet, and plot to find the next woman with low self-esteem he could move in with.

And then along came Avril.

"Iris, get dressed. I need you to run me and Walter up to the church," Ms. Chickie said, not waiting for an answer as she trumpeted puffs of gaseous odors while waddling back to her bedroom.

"Achilles," I said to the telephone receiver.

"Uh-huh."

"I gotta—"

"I know. I heard her."

"We'll be together tomorrow. Promise."

"Iris, all I hear from you are promises."

"Look—"

"Before you went down there, you gave me an ultimatum. But how do I know that if I commit, you'll be there?"

"'If'?"

"Iris, I'm ready to go," Ms. Chickie snapped. She was dressed in a Talbots embroidered crepe floral dress with a pink straw hat, purse and shoes. As she stepped onto the front porch, she left the screen door open so the humidity could duel with the central air conditioning. Ms. Chickie had returned to her cantankerous self after the white sugarcane rum had filtered through her bloodstream.

"Achilles, I'll talk—hello?" I said to a dead telephone connection.

We traveled through the winding roads of Bunche Park to Twenty-Seventh Avenue in the late-model Acura I had rented to prevent a recurrence of the suffocation I experienced in my father's car. We waited for a house-moving trailer to pass before turning on 183rd Street, whizzing by fast-food restaurants, large-size retail stores, discount shoe outlets for large feet, and wig shops for big heads.

"You goin' too fast," Ms. Chickie warned.

"Sorry," I said, easing my right foot off the pedal slightly.

Silence.

"You gonna marry that boy? What's his name?" Ms. Chickie asked, turning toward me.

"Who?" I stupidly asked.

"Don't be asking me 'who.' The one you be breathin' heavy on the phone with. Every time he on the phone, you go—"

"Okay! Okay. Are you eavesdropping on my conversations, Ms. Chickie?" I asked, trying to distract her off the subject.

"My momma didn't raise no fools. Answer my question."

Laughingly, I answered, "Achilles."

"What kind of name is that for a Negro?"

"Names aren't reserved for Negroes only, Grandmother!"

"Well, he may be working some roots on you. Been calling every night since you got here."

Whenever I was away from Atlanta, Achilles wanted to substitute his physical needs with phone sex, even though I was uncomfortable huffing and puffing into a telephone receiver when the object of my affection was in another state.

"What you got on?" Achilles would begin, during a late-night telephone call.

"Pink cut-out panties, lover man," Ms. Chickie interjected, barging into my bedroom, to verify that the bedroom windows were locked. Framed by the light of a muted, flickering television, I sat in a cushioned chair in the corner, wearing Lee Artist's borrowed plaid housecoat.

"Nothing," I would giggle coyly, after Ms. Chickie exited, advising, "Don't be leaving no slobber on my telephone. Other folks in this house got to use it, ya know. Mess around and give everybody ptomaine poisoning."

"Did you rub the kama sutra oil between your thighs?"

"Uh-hmmmmmm."

"Iris, you sound fantastic."

"You miss me?"

"You know I do."

"What do you miss?" I asked with a plastered grin, muting the television and sliding onto the bed.

"Your chocolate thighs around my waist. Your liquid moans. The sound of your heart beating."

"Uh-huh."

"Let me hear you," Achilles said, arousing himself to a full salute.

Doing my best Donna "Love to Love You Baby" Summer imitation: "Uhhhhhhhh! Uhhhhhhhh! Uhhhhhhhhh!"

"Yeah, baby. I want you to feel me."

Ordering a red blazer from the Internet on my Apple iPad, I continued groaning into the telephone: "Uhhhhhhhhh! Uhhhh-hhhhh! Uhhhh-hhhhhhh!" Until Ms. Chickie barged back in demanding: "What the hell is all that dadgum noise? You got asthma?"

"Don't act like I'm some crazy, old woman," Ms. Chickie said, spitting her snuff juice out the window. "Is you in love with him?"

"Ms. Chickie, okay." I surrendered.

Silence.

I waited for a school bus to unload a group of parochial school children.

"Sometimes I think, yes. Sometimes I think, no," I explained.

"Well, time ain't waiting on you, ya know."

"Huh."

"A girl got a little bit of time to use herself to get herself a man. Shoot, by the time I was your age I was on my third husband and others I had to run off." Clapping her knees together, Ms. Chickie continued, "You keep on acting like time waits on you, and you'll get so old, dust will fall out when you walk."

"Ms. Chickie, I don't want a third husband. Just one. One will do."

"Don't go wasting your life on that business of yours. It's good to do for yourself and what not, but I don't want you to look up one day and you're all by yourself. Ms. Chickie ain't gonna be here forever, you know. Whatchu need to do is to buy some porn. My favorite is *Pirates*." The biggest-budget porn film in history.

"Ms. Chickie."

"Yes, baby."

"I love you."

"I love you, too."

I drove into the parking lot of Mt. Herman Tabernacle and Judgments of the Blessed and Highly Favored. The expansive parking lot was empty except for a 2011 Lexus and a black Roadrunner.

"You remember Lottie Taylor," Ms. Chickie mumbled.

I turned off the engine. "No, can't say that I—"

"Oh, you remember Lottie Taylor."

"Not really."

"Lottie used to come to the house every first Sunday to give me my payout when I hit the number. And she used to let you count the money. You don't remember that?"

"Can't say that I do—"

"You don't remember when I cussed her out, when I told her to play 362...'cause I dreamed I saw three Tyler Perry movies, he was wearing six different dresses and—"

Then I understood that the sooner I did remember, the sooner we could move on with this conversation. "Oh yeah, I remember Lottie," I lied, as the temperature rose in the car.

"I knew you did."

"How is she?"

"Dead."

Ms. Chickie is a walking obituary announcement for the dead in Opa Locka. If you're dying or dead, my grandmother believes it's her duty to inform the community, whether or not you are related to the dearly departed or infirmed.

"You know Hazel Dupree finally croaked."

"Oh my goodness. She just celebrated her ninety-ninth birthday, didn't she?"

"Yeah, she's gone up yonder to be with the Lord."

"How did it happen?"

"Whatchu mean, how did it happen? How did it happen? What, you thank she was tryin' to break Evil Knievel's record by jumpin' over fourteen Greyhound buses and suddenly broke her hip? Or she got the bad end of a fight with an arthritic alligator out in the Everglades? Or she got elbowed in the Roller Derby championships? Punctured her lung? How you thank a ninety-nine-year-old, chain-smokin' diabetic with a arthritic double-jointed hip die? She croaked, dammit! I tell ya, granddaughter. You can ask some dumb-ass questions sometimes."

I followed Ms. Chickie's tiny, erect frame through the red carpeted corridor lit with gold-embossed lamps and inside the church rectory. The paneled walls held portraits of the church founders, including Ms. Chickie and her deceased sisters, Essie, Jesse and Erma.

Without knocking, Ms. Chickie pushed opened the door marked PRIVATE OFFICE, interrupting an intimate conversation between

Irene, the coal-complexioned, ruby-red-lipped, lonely church secretary, and the flamboyant, slick-haired, pencil-mustached, piano-toothed man, who called himself a prophet.

Upon seeing us, Irene hid her eyes as Prophet smoothed his lapels and flashed his piano-tooth smile, bellowing in a nervous voice, "Sister Ingram? This *is* a surprise. And your beautiful granddaughter! How are you both today?" Luckily for Irene, the telephone sprung to life as she was about to erase her epidermis in a fervent effort to hide the passion mark on her neck.

Prophet puckered his lips up to Ms. Chickie, which her glare froze in mid-pucker. Not to be deterred, he grasped my hand, using his index finger to circle my palm.

"I need a word with you, Foster," Ms. Chickie said, with a pointed familiarity, continuing into Prophet's interior office, which was decorated with oil paintings of Caucasian renderings of Jesus Christ.

"Of course. I'm always available to Mt. Herman's founders. Shall we?" he said, as I followed them, with Prophet closing the heavy oak door with brass doorknobs behind us. Ms. Chickie smiled, which is rare and never a good thing.

"The usher board was superb this past Sunday, Ms. Ingram. Absolutely superb, praise Jesus, amen. I am continually amazed at the outpouring, amen, my ministry receives as a result of my cable show, thank you, God. And if it were not for the usher board, amen, there would have been no way on God's green earth, praise His name, that we could have enrolled those new members. Forty-five at last count, thank you, glory. Forty-five new angels of Zion! Praise Jesus."

"You killed Lottie Taylor," Ms. Chickie said, her left temple suddenly pulsating. Prophet attempted to sit up in his executive chair but accidentally struck the recline button, which flattened him to a horizontal position. My eyebrows narrowed as I sat in the red leather upholstered chair, tightening my grasp to prevent a guffaw from erupting.

"Now, now, Sister Ingram. It was one year ago today that Lottie met her Maker by mistaking rat poison for Sweet n' Low. The Lawd came to me the night before, told me her low-sugar diet was going to do her in. By the time I called to warn her, it was too late. Now I can imagine you're still upset—"

"You killed her, just as sure as I'm sitting here," Ms. Chickie said, shaking her fist.

"Ms. Chickie—," I began.

"Be still, child. This is grown folks' business," Ms. Chickie said, cutting her eyes so sharp I got razor burns. She didn't see me roll my eyes as I crossed my legs, wondering what was my purpose here, when I would rather be in Calle Oche hanging out with Carmen.

"When you removed me as president of the usher board, that really hurt me. It really did. Hurt me like a root canal with no novocaine. But I swore that I'd git you for that. You would be handled," Ms. Chickie threatened, pointing her finger toward the nervous prophet.

Prophet chuckled as he twisted his wedding ring up and down his hairy finger, trying to conceal his nervousness.

"Lottie could not handle running the numbers, the members, especially your battle-ax wife, and she could not handle you. Poor thang ate herself to death and ate my winning ticket."

Prophet reached for his Bible and asked, "Are you in need of prayer, Sister Ingram?"

"I am in need of my goddamn money!" she said, slamming her fist on Prophet's desk. The good prophet abruptly stood up, clearly offended. "Now, Sister Ingram, as your prophet, and as a man possessing a doctorate in divinity from Internet Distance Learning University, praise God, I won't take these groundless accusations—"

"Walter wants you to siddown," Ms. Chickie ordered. Both the offended prophet and I looked to each other, trying to understand who Walter was. Ms. Chickie nodded toward a steel gray .45-caliber handgun that she held pointed in the precise direction of the prophet's vas deferens, threatening to dismantle the tubes that carry sperm from his testicles. The now humble prophet slowly eased into his chair. "W-What can I—" he whimpered. Ms. Chickie threw a thin, green plaid accounting ledger on the desk in front of the devious, whimpering prophet.

"Open it," Ms. Chickie suggested with a smile. Prophet mopped away tears that fell steadily onto the ledger pages, smoothing a pile of receipts paper-clipped to the back cover. "Sister Ingram, why must we resort—"

Ms. Chickie rose, silencing his suggestion; handed me her purse, saying, "Hold my pocketbook, child," and moved to stand behind Prophet, still holding Walter.

"Ms. Chickie, whatever he did, why not report him to the Bishop? 'Cause murdering him is just gonna be plain messy," I suggested, envisioning a grand jury indictment naming me as an accomplice.

Since Lottie had no family to speak of, it was left up to Ms. Chickie to settle her estate, which consisted of an abundance of liniment and S&H stamps. The usher board had been in chaos due to the members' agonizing over the removal of Ms. Chickie, the appointment of an interim president, and the board members' scattered loyalties. The older members supported Ms. Chickie and openly campaigned against Prophet, wearing black armbands and purposely disrupting church service by stomping into the rectory during his sermons. The newer, single, female members were loyal to Prophet, who rewarded them with repeated overnight prayer vigils and lingering conversations in his private office, out of earshot of his flat-chested, devoted wife.

Ms. Chickie and her devotees had observed that immediately after her removal as president, Prophet became more affluent, sporting diamond pinky rings, taking trips to Europe, and trading in his scratched-up Toyota for a Citation Sovereign aircraft stowed at the Opa Locka Executive Airport in its own private hangar. Prophet's trademark sermons had previously centered on preparation for the next life. Now he stressed prosperity in this life, demanding an increase in tithing and contributions to a *building* fund, for which, not one brick had been laid. Initially, many in the congregation were encouraged, jumping on the prosperity gravy train, tithing money that they did not have, resulting in many of them losing their homes.

My father, Willie, stopped mumbling long enough, and audited, then confirmed for Ms. Chickie what she already knew, that the prophet had withdrawn millions of dollars without the board of directors' approval. The good prophet obviously believed that it was within his right to drain the church's coffers to ensure prosperity for himself in this lifetime.

The muffled sound of the telephone ringing in the outer office provided the tense backdrop for the sweat beads percolating on the prophet's forehead.

"See all of the money you took?" Ms. Chickie said, guiding her wrinkled index finger down column after column, her other hand relaxing Walter so that it—he—the barrel of the gun wavered in my direction. "I worked my hands to the bare bone to build a nice place so peoples could come to worship His Holy Name. Now all of it is gone. And it got so I was hitting the number every week. And now all of that is gone, too."

The prophet kept his eyes closed, hoping his life would not end today without him ever riding in the fifty-foot sailboat he had just purchased.

"Me and my sisters built this church when you were just fore-play, punk!" Ms. Chickie threatened, jerking open the prophet's eyes at the suggestion. "Sister Ingram, where there is forgiveness of these things, there is no longer any offering of sin," the prophet whined into the palms of his hands.

"Hmph, you weren't saying that when you were touring Buckingham Palace, huh?" I instigated, to which Ms. Chickie repeated her warning to keep out of grown folks' business.

"While we were praying for God to come into our lives, Satan was standing up in the pulpit," she continued. On the walls, the Caucasian portraits of Jesus Christ shook their heads in disgust as male voices rumbled nearby. "You know what they do in Saudi Arabia and Detroit when you steal?" Ms. Chickie asked, slowly raising Walter.

Suddenly, the oak door flew open, revealing agitated Miami-Dade police officers standing in the outer office with revolvers drawn. Irene, nursing a handkerchief, retreated through the sea of blue and white uniforms as the telephones continued to sound.

"Officers! Thank God," the prophet exclaimed, standing behind his desk. "This woman—"

"Hold it right there, Prophet," an officer with a reddish complexion said. Ms. Chickie leaned toward me, passing Walter behind her back and into her open Coach purse that I held.

"Excuse me—," Prophet said.

"Prophet, you are under arrest on three outstanding warrants for grand larceny, fraud, and embezzlement."

"But—," Prophet blubbered, as he was spun around, his hands knitted together and silver handcuffs tightened around his wrists, and shoved out of the sanctuary of the Lord.

"You have the right to remain silent…," the officer continued until they disappeared with the remaining officers following, the loud phalanx of walkie-talkies dimming.

Ms. Chickie and I followed the officers and a sobbing prophet out to the parking lot, where Irene waited, holding her packed belongings in a small box. "It was me who turned him in. He used alla the church money to buy fancy things. And when some of the members stopped tithing, he wanted my little money. I went to him for spiritual guidance on how I could get closer to God. Instead, he wanted me to worship him. If it is one thing I learned from you, Ms. Ingram, it's to put no man before God."

"And I learned something too, baby—" Ms. Chickie replied gently.

"What's that?" Irene answered.

"I shoulda never let Lottie outta my sight before I got my money—"

The usher board members, consisting of grandmothers with long-running bingo games, had formed a caravan around the parking lot. When Ms. Chickie exited the church, they hurried over, applauding and embracing her.

"Were you really going to shoot him, Ms. Chickie?" I asked, turning into our driveway as the clouds opened for an isolated rain shower while the sun still shone.

"He was dead long before he came to us, child. Long before, but yes, I would've split him right open. The hole would've been so big you could see all of the way down to purgatory. It woulda been the only Christian thang to do," Ms. Chickie answered, chewing on a fresh piece of tobacco.

[4]
CUBANO

"Whatchu going over there fa? Messin' 'round with dem Mexicans?" Ms. Chickie accused later that afternoon, replenishing her jaw with a pinch of snuff.

"I'm going to welcome Fidel Castro back to America," I answered sarcastically.

"Oh really?" She grinned. "That's nice. That's very, very nice."

Lee Artist, on her way to a Chamber of Commerce dinner dance, agreed with Ms. Chickie's original stance. "Iris, how can you spend time with those people? On your last night home. Most daughters would want to be with their family," she hollered out the car window, sprinkling salt over her shoulder as she drove off. Chapman family values. Good idea. But even good fish starts to stink after three days. And with Victor's wedding behind us and Prophet taking a permanent vacation from the pulpit, we were at three days and counting. Before I leave Opa Locka in the morning, I wanted to drive south, in search of warmer memories.

Within a passport's throw of the Atlantic Ocean, slightly west of Miami International Airport and north of South Beach, past foreclosed high-rises, beyond the car rental companies, is the nerve center of Miami's passionately political Cuban community, Calle Ocho, the business center of Little Havana, where very few can or need to speak English, or a broken version of the language, at best.

Calle Ocho, a vibrant section of Miami, always awakened my senses, as nothing is subtle here. The sights and sounds are designed to jolt you out of your cultural slumber. When I was a teenager, Lee Artist blamed the café cubano, a caffeine-laced jet fuel, for my bounce-off-the-wall energy. Here, heavy aromas abound, coupled with the smell of cigar smoke.

The emphatic conversations among the *abuelos* (grandfathers) playing checkers and dominoes against the backdrop of murals at Maximo Gomez Park were nonstop, particularly after another raft of Cuban refugees had washed ashore. I would listen in awe as my high school friend Carmen would recount the harrowing journeys of her family members aboard a five-foot raft for days, with too-close-for-comfort encounters with sharks, treacherous waves, and even more frightening, the United States Coast Guard. Her father, Alturo Beiro, was returned to Guantanamo Bay, Cuba, three times before he finally made it to the United States, reaching the shore during a shift change at the Key West Coast Guard station. Many of the Beiros' remaining relatives migrated to the United States during the Mariel boatlift, when Fidel Castro permitted any person who wanted to leave Cuba free access to depart from the port of Mariel. Today, Calle Oche continues to be the hotbed for all those against Castro and Atlantic ocean-rafting. The modest, pastel-colored frame homes previously owned by Jewish families are now occupied by former boatlift survivors, recent refugees, and those who can play baseball *berry, berry* well.

As I drove down 95 South toward Calle Oche at dusk, with a furious orange-red sky merging with the Western horizon, the memories of my childhood returned. Carmen's Uncle Eliades, who understood English, but refused to speak it, had assured me that Carmen would definitely be at the restaurant this evening.

Small gatherings of Cubano men turned to stare as I meandered down S.E. Eighth Street, while others were too consumed with arguments over whether they would return to Cuba once the U.S. embargo was lifted. In the background, Latin jazz maestro Eddie Palmieri played pulsating, urgent rhythms to heed. Spanish billboards promoting liquor, beauty enhancements, and politics framed the tree-lined street.

Beiro's Cuban Restaurant was just as I remembered, except for the new white siding that made the wooden structure glisten next to the drab storefronts that bordered the property.

The salsa of Arsenio Rodriguez's *La Vida Es un Sueño* greeted me as I entered. Beiro's always played vintage Cuban music, I thought, side-stepping rubber-necking patrons dressed in business attire. Mr. Beiro influenced my taste for Latin music; releases by Fania All-Stars, Compay Segundo, and Tito Puente littered my CD collection.

Arranged groupings of autographed photos from Venezuelan president Hugo Chavez were hung on the wall. A small candle burned in front of a painting of Panama's former president Manuel Noriega, and dusty memorabilia from the Beiro's Cuban childhood were scattered around the restaurant. Male patrons, nursing on unlit cigars, compared new stories from their Cuban newspaper, while a grandfather extolled the intellectual virtues of José Martí to his table of grandchildren. Posters of Cuban tourist attractions were on sale behind the bar. Where it had always been, in the main dining room was a large painting of Cienfuegos, where the Biero clan originated. The take-out service entrance had been updated with a dessert display with coconut flan and egg custard. Chrome barstools were positioned in front of an expresso machine, in an attempt to compete with the Starbucks franchise opening across the street.

❖ ❖ ❖

As I began to salivate at the coconut flan, I heard: "*¿Lo puedo ayudar yo, el fallo?* (May I help you, Miss?)" A white, thick-necked bouncer, wearing a rented two-sizes-too-small monkey jacket, regarded me with serious eyes. Craning my neck above the crowd, I searched for Carmen or Mr. Beiro as Thick-Neck obstructed my view. "I'm here to—"

"*Somos cerrados esta noche. El partido privado. Arrepentido.* (Sorry, we're closed. This is a private party.)"

"What? *¿Qué? Yo sólo entiendo un español pequeño.*(I speak very little Spanish.)"

"I said, we're closed. Private party."

"Why didn't you say it in English in the first place?"

"*Esto es Havana Pequeño. Esto no es la Ciudad de la Libertad,*" Thick-Neck responded. That part I understood. At the very least, I got the message his tone was sending. I had heard it before. Know your place. This is Little Havana. This ain't Liberty City—the el Negro part of town.

A Cuban waiter with a heavy tray of *lechon asado con platinitos maduros y congris* (roast pork with fried plantains and rice and beans) stared before passing through to a family headed by an elderly patriarch and his adult sons. There was no recognizable face amongst the waiters. What happened to Carlos, Ruben, and my favorite, Arnesto? Arnesto would give me a few dollars when I helped him set up the tables with fresh linen and silverware after school. And Carlos would scoop a large helping of diplomatic pudding.

Thick-Neck blocked my way when I attempted to go around him into the kitchen to find a Beiro, any Beiro. "Where are the—?"

"IIIrrris!"

There was Carmen, exiting through the swinging doors, dressed in a yellow sarong skirt covered by a black apron and a spaghetti-strapped blouse, and carrying a cocktail tray. She had lost weight, a lot of weight. She was skinny compared to her former corpulent figure. And she had dyed and straightened her previously dark brown hair to a striking platinum blonde, including her eyebrows and persistent sideburns.

Aside from the fact that she was Cuban and I, African-American, or black, as we called ourselves then, the insecurity about our looks initially bonded us. In elementary school, we were called the sweater girls, because during recess, we wore yellow, black, brown and red sweaters on our heads to emulate the flowing locks of our Caucasian classmates. Flailing our heads and imaginary sweater hair made us feel close to an idealized standard of beauty. Though other classmates were awe-struck when I placed at a local beauty pageant, Carmen really understood how denigrated I felt participating.

Ms. Chickie and Lee Artist were my self-appointed drill sergeants in preparation for the annual Opa Locka "Light Is Right" beauty pageant. "Smile, Iris, why you thank we paid all that money for your teeth? You should be proud your family could afford a proctologist," Ms. Chickie would remind me, as our living room became a mock runway. "And come to think of it, where did I put *my* teeth?"

"Iris, you might as well forget about buying your evening gown off of eBay. That kind of behavior is reserved for trailer park trash and hillbillies who don't have the sense God gave them to drive to Nordstrom," Lee Artist added, addressing pageant invitations to her sorority sisters. "And, you really need to tuck in your derriere. You don't see white girls walking around with their asses on their shoulders, do you?"

Careful to glide one foot, slightly crossing the other, wearing tan pumps and white girl nude stockings, I imagined the audience of obsessive parents, who only cheered for their own daughters, throwing an evil eye, at the would be frontrunners.

"Now Iris, when you cross in front of the judges, make sure you smile and look them in their foreheads. Never look white folks directly in the eye, because then they'll want to fight ya and take over your country, just like they did with the Alamo. So just look them in the forehead and they won't know no different," Ms. Chickie opined like she was a panelist on *Meet The Press*. Being the courageous man he was, my father, Willie would tiptoe through the living room, surrender his credit card to Lee Artist, and scurry out and under the hood of his beloved Oldsmobile. My father knew better than to intervene. Early in the process, Willie was attacked by Ms. Chickie and Lee Artist because he had the temerity to make a suggestion in his own house about his own daughter. Foolishly, losing touch with reality, Willie had suggested that perhaps a professional beauty pageant coordinator be hired. "What kind of absurd idea is that? What could a professional beauty pageant coordinator do that we can't? With us, our Iris will be surrounded by two people who can support her best. And who'll be there to support her when she falls flat on her face during the talent segment, 'cause the child can't sing her way out of a paper bag."

Mr. Beiro forced Carmen to participate every spring in Calle Ocho's debutante ball, even finagling her appearance in the

South Beach debutante variety by way of some under-the-table payoffs. By any means necessary, Mr. Beiro was going to ensure that Carmen received a large piece of the American pie. And since his wife, had passed away, Mr. Beiro was even more determined.

"CCCaaarmen!" I squealed, giving Thick-Neck a dirty look. Carmen gave me a long neck hug with her right arm while she balanced the other with a tray. "Go on over to the bar, I'll be right back," she said, flipping her hair, before sashaying over to serve a young, perky-looking couple. It was good seeing Carmen move with such confidence, fully aware of her feminine wiles. I'd last seen her three years ago when she and Ms. Chickie saw me off at the airport when I moved to Atlanta.

Carmen had not been accepted to any graduate school, which caused conflict with her father as he felt graduate school would put her in the right circles to meet a well-to-do husband, and to get her away from Jerome, her black boyfriend, who had been banished from Calle Oche after Mr. Biero caught him climbing through Carmen's wide open bedroom window. From the beat down Mr. Biero and his *los compatriotas* put on Jerome, he is probably still leaping fences, trying to escape.

Flipping her hair yet again, Carmen wiped her hands on her apron, returning to the bar. "Uncle Eliades told me a woman had called—*el Negra*—he said. And I thought and I thought, and I realized that you would be the only *el Negra* I knew," Carmen said, flipping her gold-streaked locks twenty times as she spoke. My jaw-flopped open. I was stunned that Uncle Eliades had identified me as el Negra.

Dumbstruck customers slowly strolled past, staring at Carmen, then me, then Carmen, then me, trying to rationalize the connection. This was familiar, too—whenever I was in a social setting with a white friend or white client, morons would try to wrap their brain around why on earth we would be together. "Is the black one the nanny? I wonder if she could watch little Benjie for us," their facial expressions would say. When I brought this to Carmen's attention, she responded, "They're not used to seeing people from outside the neighborhood."

Outside of the neighborhood.

Never feeling like I was an outsider as Carmen's friends, me included, would eat *coquitos* after school, warranting extra visits to the dentist. We would talk about boys over broken *tostadas*, dunking the pieces into the *café con leche*. And on Fridays, I would purposely miss the last bus that would connect with the last bus back to Opa Locka so I could stay at the Beiro home on the weekends.

Had the social contract changed that much in three years?

about 1 second ago via twitter for BlackBerry

"Outside people," I replayed in my head. When did I become an outside person? Carmen handed two gin and tonics to another waiter, telling him to serve two women engaged in a spirited conversation. "This is a fund-raiser for Manuel Pagalas. You heard about him, right?"

"Yeah, he's running for mayor of Miami. Running on the Tea Party ticket?"

"Of course. We all are. It's the only way to go, if you want your rights and take this country back."

My forehead wrinkled as I tried to process what I almost couldn't believe I was hearing.

"Carmen," I said, touching her forearm.

In response, Carmen's eyes blinked, attempting to process data she could not comprehend. I blinked this time, noticing that Carmen was wearing blue contact lenses. "This is obviously not a good time, maybe—," I said, reaching for my car keys.

"Oh, no, Iris, stay. Say hello to Papa. You know he hasn't been well."

"I'd heard. I'd like to see him."

"Ever since Mama died, he hasn't been himself, you know. So I'm running the restaurant now." Thick-Neck lurched over to get a patron's parking validated. After he moved away, Carmen said, "That's Tony. You remember him, right? From high school?"

My brain flipped through old yearbook photos of classmates until it paused on a skinny, angry kid who always got into fights with the black kids. My eyes widened. "Tony Hernandez?! That's Tony Hernandez?" I said, pointing.

"Uh-huh! He's been hanging around here since he got out of high school. You should go over and say hi."

"No thanks. I already did."

"Okay, *uno momento*. We'll go next door. Tony can take over," Carmen said, running her fingers through her hair as tipsy politicos took notice.

Reaching me on my BlackBerry, Ms. Chickie checked on my whereabouts. "Ms. Chickie, you know I am at Beiro's."

"Well, whatchu want me to do with these conch fritters I fried for you?"

"Grandmother, put them in the refrigerator. I'll have them for breakfast," I said.

Inside the Biero home, a hushed stillness filled the house. It would have been vulgar to speak loudly. In this house, one did not know which emotion to convey other than just to be. Be still. The remote sound of a Spanish language radio station whispered from deep inside the cavernous house.

In every corner there was a dusty, illuminated statue of the Virgin Mary and the Christ child in Mary's arms. On the dusty coffee table were yellowed photographs of babies and social events with blurry, inebriated people. On the dusty bookshelf adjacent to the front door were framed autographed photographs of Pat Buchanan and Glenn Beck. In another framed photograph was Mr. Biero holding a sign demanding the president to show his birth certificate. "Oh Lawd, it's worse than I thought," I mumbled, rubbing my weary eyes, creating patterns with my toe in the thick-pile brown carpet while Carmen checked on her father upstairs.

"What did you say?" Carmen said, skipping down the stairs like a tap dancer in a Broadway musical.

"Oh nothing," I responded, slightly startled. "Your father?" I asked, rising from my chair.

"He's sleeping," Carmen said uncomfortably, her previously confident hands trying to find a place to hide themselves. "*¿Café con leche?*"

"Sounds good. But what I want to know is how you're doing, gurrrl? What's up?" I said, trying to ignore the desolation that hung in the dusty living room, and to see if our friendship could be jumpstarted again. Carmen returned, carefully handing me a cup of *café con leche*, and a framed photograph was stuffed under her armpit.

Blowing the rising steam across the cup, I stared into the eyes of a blond, crew-cut, square-jawed marine, standing in an erect soldier's stance, wearing his blue dress alphas. The photograph was signed: *To Carmen, with love. Sergeant Scott Jones, USMC.*

Brushing my fingers against my temple, I said, "Can I get a little detail here?"

Carmen told me that she and Scott met while he and his marine buddies were on leave, hanging out on South Beach. It was lust at first sight, and they consummated the attraction in an overnight stay at the famed Fountainbleu Hotel, utilizing his fifty-percent-off military discount. Since then he had phoned her every day from Helmand Province, Afghanistan.

"It's serious. Scott asked to marry me," Carmen said with sour-puss eyes.

"This should be a cause for celebration, shouldn't it? What's the problem?"

Carmen looked to the ceiling for answers, then finally blurted, "He doesn't know I'm Cuban."

"Say what?" I retorted, suspending the cup of *cafe con leche* in mid-air.

"He doesn't know I'm Cuban," she had the nerve to repeat.

"What the hell—sorry," I said to the statue of the Virgin Mary. "What does he think you are?"

"Irish mix."

Blink.

A burst of lung-expelling wind. The Virgin Mary and the Christ child and I cracked up, as I spilled the *café con leche*. "Har-har-har-har-har!" My first guffaw blew at least an inch of dust off the living room. It was a shame with Mr. Beiro upstairs, perhaps on his deathbed, for me to be heehawing like this, but it couldn't be helped. When I could contain myself, I stared at her and tear-fully asked, "You're kidding, right?"

Slowly, she shook her head.

Rustling through my purse, retrieving a tissue, I asked, "How could he *not* know? Girl, the only Irish been in you was that surfer dude in Daytona Beach."

"He doesn't think I'm Cuban because of all the bad things he says about us, the blacks, Jews, everybody. I knew he was serious when he showed me a photo of his pickup truck. And the rifle rack, he said, was Alabama law."

"So you just sat there and let him demean you—your people. Didn't you punch him in the balls and give him a real Purple Heart?" Carmen again sadly shook her head. Her passive response was getting a little old, even in the twenty minutes I'd been with her. "Why didn't—"

"Iris, look at my life. I'm thirty-three years old, I'll be thirty-four in August, and I still live with Papa. All I have is this restaurant, and it isn't really mine. Nothing changed for me...nothing really changed until I dyed my hair blonde. Even the Palm Beach Republicans like me now."

My eyes narrowed, indicating I wanted to interrupt, but Carmen retained command of the floor.

"I'm not like you. All I have is a sick papa and a restaurant. But you, you're the one who left Opa Locka. You have your own life away from here. I never had that choice. In my family, it is against tradition for a girl to leave home without being married. I didn't even date until I became a blonde. Jerome sneaking in and out of my bedroom window was not dating, but with Scott, it's different now. He wants to take care of me. Take me with him all over the world. Europe, Asia—Birmingham, as soon as Papa gets well."

"Carmen, you don't have to become a blonde to—"

"You black women wanna be blonde too. Don't deny it."

Enraged, tears streaming down her face, Carmen abruptly rose, gesturing for me to follow her into the walk-in hall closet, which she opened to reveal neatly stacked boxes of Clairol No. 355 Born Blissfully Blonde hair lightener. "This is my ticket out of here, and nobody is gonna take it away from me," Carmen screamed, bending over, frenetically shaking her blonde hair.

❖ ❖ ❖

Carmen stood in the doorway of Beiro's Cuban Restaurant, tossing her blonde hair, the key to her newfound power, and holding the door open for her infirm father, who slowly followed her inside. Burning rubber, I sped from Beiro's parking lot, loosening my rusted carburetor on the speed bump. Flooring the gas pedal, I yelled, "*Adios*!"

Veering off 95 North to the Palmetto Expressway, I pressed redial on my BlackBerry. "Ms. Chickie, could you warm up those conch fritters? I'm on my way in."

And then, dialing. "Delta Airlines? Do you have an earlier flight to Atlanta? Yes, I'll take it."

"You sure you can't stay another day," Willie said, from underneath the hood of the Oldsmobile, the oil seeping underneath his nails, framing his cuticles. B.B. King's "The Thrill Is Gone" replayed for the eleventh time this morning. The air was thick with humidity, causing an almost desert haze, and silencing birds to reserve their chirping until after the sun went down.

"Sorry, Daddy, I've got a ton of work on my desk," I said, swatting a mosquito against the side of my neck.

"Well, seem like something got you tore up inside. I hate to see you go like that, Daughter." The term he used when distance would again separate us.

"I'll be alright. Just have a lot on my mind," I answered, my face resembling a Picasso painting.

"With the wedding and my Mason lodge meetings, I didn't spend as much time with you as I wanted." Our most intimate moments were while my father was in the bathroom or under the hood of his Oldsmobile.

"Come visit me in Atlanta," I suggested, knowing that a fatherly visit was a pipe dream. Willie never traveled anywhere outside of South Florida, using his Oldsmobile as an excuse. At least verbally, Willie never refused me, saying as he slammed shut the hood of the car, and climbing behind the wheel, pumping the gas pedal, then turning the key to the ignition."We'll see, Daughter. We'll see. First, I gotta make sure this old car is up to the trip first," he said over the rattling din. "Guess I gotta run over to Carol City and get some more engine oil."

I opened the passenger door, and climbed in next to Willie, who turned, and gently patted me on the shoulder. Gazing into his gentle eyes, he said, "Daughter, be happy." I nodded a reply. "And whatever you do, don't bring no sawed-off boy to my house, you heah me? That kind of pressure, I wouldn't be able to take. Seemed like all the little girls you growed up with, done got caught up with some short runt of fella...look like they were laid off from the circus. Don't look! Don't look over there...don't want 'em to thank we talking about 'em, but all of his daughters is shackin' with some runt....but that's what he git...never did pay me for my brake oil that I lent him...and that one gal that used to live on the corner? All her babies look like they haven't growed since they were five years old...Boy, Iris! I'm tellin' you the truth...seem like young people today just don't think thangs through...don't think how their actions will affect anybody but themselves...don't even thank about their families. I don't thank that I ask much of you...Did all I could for you. Raise you up to be a beautiful young lady. Made sure you got an education. I know there is a lotta pressure on girls today, 'cause it seemed like everywhere you look, there's some midget sniffin' around some innocent gal...they even organized themselves, don't want nobody to call 'em what they is...Little people? When I was a boy, they gave them a choice; either be happy about being called a midget or a leprechaun...but daughter, I wasn't then...nor will I now not call it as I see it...and the best I can do now, after knowing what I know is to protect what's mine...so all I ask of you is that you don't brang me no sawed-off runt, claimin' you gonna marry him. That's all your daddy asks."

Later, Ms. Chickie placed a plate of conch fritters with pasta salad on the table as my father and I entered the house, our taste buds salivating. "You're just in time. Both of you get washed up."

Like dutiful schoolchildren Willie and I followed her directive, returning to the kitchen table as Lee Artist swept into the house, joining us at the dining room table with fanfare.

"We sho' enjoyed you, child," Ms. Chickie said, chaperoning, but not eating the meal.

"Me, too," I answered, though my mind was reeling from the myriad of expectations Opa Locka had handed me.

"That boy that called here last night; he ain't black, is he?"

"Of course, he's black, he—"

"You know what I mean. He ain't dark blackety Africa black black, is he? 'Cause I be worryin' about you...around all dem crazy people...I see it all on the news...ain't nothin' up in Atlanta but vultures… a kettle of vultures," Ms. Chickie shared, shaking her head, using a rag to wipe grease off of the top of the stove. From Ms. Chickie's bedroom, a gospel radio station broadcasted "Precious Lord" again.

A cataclysmic split was occurring in the left lobe of my brain. Willie, Lee Artist, and Ms. Chickie appeared hazy, in slow motion, and spoke as if they had spiked my conch fritters with an ounce of Timothy Leary's personal stash of LSD.

"Yak-yak-yak-yak," Lee Artist said.

"Hmph-hmph-Huh-She-Huh, sawed off. Sawed-sawed," Willie countered.

"Child-child-child-child," Ms. Chickie argued as Lee Artist led me to the kitchen sink, massaging my scalp and parting my hair down the center, then from left to right, applying cool cream to the edges of my scalp, and then lowering my head underneath warm water. When I regained consciousness, Ms. Chickie and Lee Artist were standing around me grinning, which is never a good thing, and admiring my beauty.

"Child-child-child-child," Ms. Chickie said.

"Yak-yak-yak-yak-yak," Lee Artist countered, holding a small gold-rimmed mirror up to my face. I recognized this person as someone I had abandoned long ago, with straight, shiny hair styled in a sixties' upward flip. Ms. Chickie and Lee Artist continued to grin, admiring their handiwork.

Gathering my words, I asked, "So, will straight hair guarantee my happiness in this lifetime?"

"See how happy we are?" Chickie and Lee Artist answered in unison, with their arms threaded together.

Lee Artist pressed an acorn in the palm of my hand for good luck, confiding, "Now if it starts thundering and lightning while you're up in the air, throw this here acorn out your window." Weighed down by my suit bag, Always Straight moisturizer and three sweet potato pies, I settled into my leather, first-class seat and nibbled on conch fritters that Ms.

Chickie had wrapped in aluminum foil. The aroma had caused a German Shepherd in airport security to growl at my purse. When the plane reached altitude, I waved out of the window at my dear Opa Locka. Tears squirted from my eyes, until I fell asleep with my mouth draped open.

I knew from the start
I'd spend the best part,
The time of my life in—

ATLANTA

[5]
HOME AGAIN

"Don't answer it," Achilles whispered, as I attempted to reach for my BlackBerry on his oak night table. Since early dawn, it had vibrated that several messages were waiting on the Image Control office message machine. Whomever needed me at 7:15 a.m. was persistent, calling again only after a few minutes. Achilles draped his hairy, brown thigh with the black birthmark over my legs and kissed the nape of my neck, down my shoulders, and over my breasts.

"Don't answer it," he repeated. My arm went limp at the same time the ringing ended. Perhaps whoever was calling had someone seducing them, too. Achilles laid his six-foot-five body on mine, resting his head on my breasts with his eyes closed, humming the tune to "Lift Every Voice and Sing," the Negro national anthem. Warmed by our cocoon-like embrace, I folded my arms across his smooth, broad back as we snuggled under the black silk sheets on his king-sized bed. Caught up in a sense of nationalism, I joined him in the second verse, when his eyes peeled open. "Let me do this," he said, chuckling.

"Say what?"

"You obviously don't know the words and singing ain't one of your strong points, baby."

"I don't see anybody chasing you with a record deal."

"'Cause they don't know about me yet," Achilles said, rolling over with a smile.

"Oh, so you mean you're the next big discovery since Sisqo," I said, turning to face him, untangling my legs from the knot in the sheets.

"Uh-uh. More like a combination of Brian McKnight, a little Luther and throw in some KRS-One. It's gonna be wild, kickin' some revolutionary lyrics on top of an R&B beat."

"Yeah, okay, KRS." The alarm clock sounded although Achilles and I had been stirring for hours.

Returning to Atlanta the night before, I had first gone home to my three-bedroom gated condo near the Midtown/Buckhead border, to unpack, shower and change. My business, Image Control, had become successful enough that I placed a down payment, two years ago, so I could combine a home and work space.

Atlanta became the destination after college graduation. Unlike other students, who created a career roadmap to guide them to their next point in life, I chose Atlanta because it was the number one choice of *Ebony* magazine: "The Mecca For Young Blacks."

One week after college graduation, I was on an Amtrak train to the new Black mecca. "Some man is going to knock you up, you watch," said the crusty old Black man, who boarded the train in Orlando, and designated himself as a psychic for my life. "I give it a year and BAM, you gonna drop a truckload of kids for somebody. Wish it could be me, but I'm taken...hee-hee." In order to avoid his obsessive predictions of my fertility, I pretended that I was sleeping from Orlando to Tallahassee, during which I prayed that a serial killer would jump out of the overhead compartment and suffocate him with the plastic from a dry cleaning bag.

The Atlanta train station exuded the promise of pimp training, prostitution and drug trafficking, not a shining beacon for the aspiring middle class. The cab driver who dropped me off at a local bed and breakfast was kind to return later that evening to give me his personal tour of the shining star of the South—Lovely Atlanta.

In my first job out of college, I was the perfect example of incompetence. Flashing my degree in public administration, no one on the telephone operator third shift gave a damn about my bachelor of arts diploma. "Yeah, yeah, you sound just like me when I came here twenty years ago…all fresh and idealistic…Well, I got news for you, just answer the switchboard on the first ring, College Girl, and be happy with the job you got," said my supervisor while he polished his toenails, as he got high on cocaine in his back office.

For the life of me, I didn't understand the notion of corporate hierarchy. If your name was John Doe, then I would call you John. Unlike my co-workers who began to flutter with excitement, that John Doe was paying us a courtesy call, I couldn't have given a rat's ass that John was also the president of Universe. "Good," I would say. "Because I have issues that he needs to address."

It got to the point where hearing, "We decided to let you go and move in another direction," became commonplace between employers and me. While my college friends entered graduate school or began their careers in the corporate world, I was explaining to a professional baseball player that I had checked in at the Atlanta Marriott, why I wore two-toned eye shadow and why I wasn't going to let the team rub my vagina so that they could win the pennant the next day. What was most annoying were those employers who thought you needed a doctorate to work for them. "Let's see here. You only have a bachelor of arts? No additional graduate work? No law school?" Never in a million years would I think you needed a degree to mash grapes; otherwise, I would have prepared.

Parting of the employment ways became music to my ears until

I realized that I needed to employ myself, and if I needed to go in another direction, the other part of me was going, too.

Arriving at Achilles' Cascade area, athletically decorated, one-story brick house, complete with a basement recreation room, around midnight, the living room was strewn with every basketball trophy he had won since high school, plus framed photographs of every team he had been associated with both as a player, and now as a coach at Clark-Atlanta University. The narrow, beige wall next to his bookcase held his memorabilia from the year he played with the Los Angeles Clippers. Two basketballs, one deflated from Achilles kicking it after an Atlanta Hawks playoff loss, teetered underneath his gold-trimmed glass coffee table.

He was the first legitimately tall boyfriend I had ever had. Despite my father's frequent admonitions, the men I had dated were prone to rock back and forth on their heels in an effort to grow before my eyes. And frankly, in their presence I usually suffered from a curvature of the spine. The fact that I was here sharing overnights and swapping saliva with Achilles was a minor miracle, as I had not liked him initially.

Two summers ago, the Armstrong Room of the Auburn Avenue Research Library was filled to snobbish capacity with members of the influential Cascade Road Literary Group, gathered for their monthly reading series. An immense, shadowy mansion, if you wanted to know whom in Atlanta thought themselves to be important, you were welcome every first Sunday to tour the third-floor structure to see the many self-commissioned statues, paintings and busts of people, who wrapped themselves in self-importance, no native Atlantan had ever heard of.

As a favor to friend and New York City publicist Cleo Elliott, I had escorted author Ennis Raspberry, who had written an uncomplimentary, historical drone on Atlanta's black elite, of which these members considered themselves to be the epitome.

Black waiters dressed in starched, white smocks circled the high-ceilinged, formally appointed room with their right arms angled on their lower backs, their left hands balancing sparkling gold trays laden with marinated prawns with celery and sun-dried tomatoes or champagne in pristine, elegant glasses.

Cleo, who had missed her flight from New York, needed the impudent and controversial Raspberry, escorted or hog-tied, whichever strategy proved essential. Personally, I believed Cleo conjured up the missed flight excuse because she had run out of ways to protect Raspberry from being beaten about the head with his own book by his critics and by members of the media.

Picking him up in my black on-its-last-leg Honda from the Atlanta Hilton, the wire-framed-glasses-wearing Raspberry appeared harmless enough until, after a long silence, while riding alongside me in the front seat, he turned to me and asked deliberately, "So what did you think of the thesis I put forth in my book?"

"Um," was my first answer. Not only because I didn't know the answer, but because Ennis' breath was so stank that he could clear a chat room. For some reason, individuals suffering from halitosis always had the most conversation, aimed in close proximity to your nose. Not to be rude, I held my right nostril closed with one finger, and continued steering my car with my left hand. Still Ennis' question hung there along with his breath.

Noticing the brown, wood-paneled station wagon that sped

past us on 20 East, with sugar-addicted, rambunctious children leaping back and forth over their backseat, I wished they would have thrown me a life line and told me what the hell Ennis' book was about. Glancing again at the book cover, *Atlanta's Uncle Toms: The So-Called Black Elite*, which lay on the black dashboard, I swallowed and hazarded a bullshit answer.

"Undoubtedly, your premise is by and large representative of the view which many find—"

"You didn't read it, did you?" Ennis asked, adjusting his black suede beret on this eighty-degree summer evening.

"Mr. Raspberry, your reputation as an intellectual—"

"Did you?" he repeated, scolding.

"No." There, I said it. Now what was he going to do, cancel my subscription to *Black Enterprise*, prevent me from making peanut butter and jelly sandwiches for members of the New Black Panther Party or reconvene a meeting of the Negro Thought Police? Instead, he peered out the window, shaking his head, and no doubt concluding that the future of African people was doomed because another lost sister had not read his probably incoherent tome. Relieved that Ennis was now blistering the windshield with his waste dump breath, I released my right nostril and reached for a package of breath mints.

"These are really delicious. Would you like a few pieces?" I asked Ennis, as if I was the head waiter at the Park 75 restaurant in the Four Seasons hotel. Like most people, whom are intent on suffocating the world's population, by denying us uncontaminated oxygen, Ennis refused, waving my offer off with his left hand.

"...my sista, my life's thesis focuses only on the liberation of our people. And for that I will never compromise nor apologize."

Well, perhaps you should apologize for that stank breath, Huey Newton, I thought.

❖ ❖ ❖

Arriving at the library, uniformed valets swarmed my car to open our doors. Before I could set the emergency brake, Ennis was out of the car, and be-bopping toward the impressive carved marble entrance to the historical library. Tight security had been employed to examine the social status credentials of anyone entering the venue, just in case their human genomes were destroyed by the presence of "those people" whom might jeopardize members' ascendancy to their rightful place on the throne of the Negro World.

After being questioned about his unique attire and being denied his several attempts to enter, Ennis loudly demanded to speak with the "brotha" in charge: a Canadian library manager reading a biography of Rev. Martin Luther King, Jr. Ennis refused to have his complaint redressed by anyone other than someone of African descent. He pouted in the vestibule until I confirmed that he was indeed the author presenting that evening, and that I would vouch for his conduct.

Dressed in a black paratrooper jacket with pants stuffed into his shin-high black boots, and the black suede beret and dark sunglasses, Ennis resembled a backup dancer for Public Enemy. This uppity social set, that traced their families back six generations in Atlanta, did not know whether to clap or flee as Ennis approached the podium after my introduction. "You owe me big time, girl," I said to Cleo, still in New York, on my BlackBerry, in a hushed whisper, pacing outside in the palatial lobby.

"Achilles Henderson should be there any minute to rescue you. Ennis is a handful, isn't he?" Cleo responded with a giggle. "But his books sell. And Fox News just loves him."

"Oh, gee whiz, I wonder why? And how does he get people to

buy his books? At gunpoint? Look, I'll call you later," I responded, as a stout, silver-haired woman wearing a navy blue suit and large, white pearls tapped me on the shoulder. "Young woman, Sonia Herndon," she said, in a high-shrilled tone.

"Yes, ma'am. How may I help you?" I asked, slipping the BlackBerry in my purse.

"….and the last thing this country needs is a bunch of boot-lickin', grinnin', elitist Uncle Toms. Your kind of people has set us back a hundred years! And don't get me started on Barack Obama. I don't know whether or not to call him a brother, the inveterate collaborative raghead," lectured Ennis.

Members of the audience sucked their teeth, shaking their heads with disgust. With champagne glasses still in hand, half of the attendees gathered their belongings and made a beeline for the front door.

"Mrs. Herndon, this is appalling! You will hear from the board about this," an elderly gentleman, with an eye patch, wearing a gray suit complained, as he too exited the library.

Mrs. Herndon turned back to me, gesturing me to follow her to the rear of the Armstrong room, and ordered in a hushed voice, "Remove him at once."

"What shall I do? Run up and tackle him?" I replied regretfully when her hazel eyes turned to steel.

"My young woman, we have certain standards of decorum, which in ten minutes your Mr. Raspberry has managed to violate every last one of them. I don't know what forms of behaviors you accept back in the hood, but we will not tolerate ghetto insults and slurs on our beloved President Obama. Raghead? How immoral. Remove him or we shall telephone the authorities and have you both removed!"

"You donate money to what you call the lower class. But it has been out of guilt, not generosity, disdain, not compassion. And until Obama delivers a black agenda...," Ennis continued.

I was stunned to see there were only three people left: two cameramen from C-SPAN and a tall, handsome man who clapped enthusiastically like a hungry seal, as Ennis rallied his follower of one. Holding my right arm up, I waved at Ennis, trying to get his attention, which he noticed, then ignored. Ennis loved the television cameras, loved the fact that anyone was applauding what he was saying, even if it was just one person. He was enraptured with his own voice. I glanced back at the wrinkled brow of Mrs. Herndon, who pushed me, on the side of my lower back, toward Ennis.

Standing next to the brown-haired C-SPAN cameraman sitting in a director's chair, I asked, "How long are you scheduled to broadcast?"

"Eight more minutes," he answered, rubbing his beard growth and checking his Timex watch. "We're expecting a live feed from the Native American protest at the Department of Agriculture." Ennis' loyal fan whirled around in his chair, pressing his index finger to his lips, indicating he wanted us to be quiet.

When I returned to the lobby, Mrs. Herndon was surrounded by two worried-looking women who held their mouths agape as I approached. "Mrs. Herndon, C-SPAN has eight more minutes to fill."

"Eight excruciating more minutes of these insults," Mrs. Herndon whined. Checking my watch, I wandered back into the Armstrong Room, where Ennis was now opening the floor for questions. Didn't this imbecile see there was no audience? The hand of the tall, handsome man shot up. Ennis nodded toward him, urging him to stand. His fan of one rubbed his hands as if he was preparing to crack open a safe full of diamonds, before posing his question.

"In light of your comments tonight, why do you think the very people whom you address recoil from your wisdom?"

"Fear, my brother. Nothing but fear," Ennis answered. The C-SPAN director stood, holding an index card, indicating to Ennis he had one minute to wrap up. Ennis, however, was on his own time schedule, as he continued to drone on until the director twice gave him the cut sign, to which Ennis ignored.

Taking matters into my own hands, I borrowed a glass of water and a tray from a bored waiter, strode up the side aisle, and pretended to offer it to Ennis. As he leaned over to retrieve it, I whispered, "Ennis, you are no longer on the air. The cameras are off."

Ennis turned his gaze on the C-SPAN camera crew who were packing their equipment, and the lighting technician unscrewing the light bulbs. His chest caved, finally recognizing that an audience had evaporated. Ennis returned the glass of water to the tray and said abruptly, "Thank you, everyone, for attending. I will be signing copies of my book in the lobby. Get at me!" Following in tow, Ennis be-bopped away from the podium into the lobby, with his black briefcase in hand. Mrs. Herndon and the other women stared at him like a suspect in a police lineup, as he glided past them, nodding. "Greetings, my sistas!"

The other women and Mrs. Herndon clutched their pearls.

The follower of one caught up with Ennis, exclaiming, "Ennis, my brother. Excellent as always. Excellent." I made my apologies to the still-flustered Mrs. Herndon and prepared to escape when the follower turned to me, saying, "You must be Iris. Chapman? Cleo said you would be here."

"Yes. Yes, Iris is fine," I stammered. My feet were hurting and I really didn't want my name to be associated with Ennis. Like ushering a wild boar, it was going to be a hat trick to return him to his hotel, so that I could commence a late night of tub soaking at home.

"I'm Achilles Henderson. Helped Cleo to book the library."

Steam percolated out of my ears. "Mr. Henderson—"

"Achilles, my sister."

"Mr. Henderson"—to which Achilles revealed a glimmer of a smile—"you were supposed to have been here an hour ago so I could leave."

"I was here. Inside. Supporting the author. Not outside profiling on my BlackBerry or whatever gadget you have. Just another way for the man to track your movements. Big Brother is real, my sista." I had heard of this type of individual before. They operate under the radar of life. Almost like an alien from another planet. Undetected by Google, Yahoo or any other search engine, these types distrust all forms of detection, and are hyper-annoying about other people who choose to live in the twenty-first century. In my universe, if you aren't in a search engine, you just don't exist. If you haven't done anything worthy of detection, then you just haven't lived.

"First of all—," I began, my neck moving like a cobra.

Ennis moved from behind his table when he finally noticed that no one was requesting his autograph. "Ah, my brother Achilles, can't you go anywhere without stirring passions of a beautiful queen?"

Glaring at both Achilles and Ennis, I realized that somewhere a black mother had given birth to two idiots, and then dropped them from their bassinettes on their heads. And I was furious with her. Extending my hand to Ennis, I said, "Mr. Henderson will take over from here. Nice meeting you—"

"Was it really nice or is that what you image types are programmed to say?" Ennis interrupted and held my gaze with his kicking breath, knowing he had cornered me into silence. "Well then," he continued, "I'll take your silence as a reprieve and an opportunity to request your presence at dinner with Achilles and myself. After all, that would be the professional thing to do."

My head violently shook as if I was having an epileptic seizure.

Ignoring me, Ennis continued, "As you have probably surmised, Achilles can't be left alone without insulting a sister, so would you please save the sisters in this black mecca from a misguided brother."

Ennis, though self-involved, pompous, and confrontational had a way of stringing his words together. And it would have been improper to leave Cleo's client on a negative note, so I decided to have one hors d'oeuvre, stay for twenty minutes, make my apologies, and make my escape.

Ennis exuded a more mute persona at Justin's restaurant than he had at the book signing. With him sitting on the opposite side of the dinner table, gave room for me to breathe freely and to release the hold on my nostril when he spoke. Ennis explained that he needed to be incendiary if he wanted to get his point across through his numerous television appearances. "People want to be challenged by ideas. They want everything they ever knew to be turned upside down. And they know that when they read one of my books, or attend my lectures, that is what I will give them. I make great television. Pure and simple."

Achilles ordered a refill of pineapple juice and pored over every feature on my face. Without being equally as blatant, I too had examined Achilles, but in one glance. Coffee brown, with pouting lips, a shiny, bald head, a basketball player's physique, and bow legs. I'd gleaned all of that once he had stopped clapping for Ennis like a hungry baby seal.

Rapidly blinking my eyelashes to filter Achilles out of my line of vision, I concentrated on Ennis as he spoke about his always-pregnant wife who loved to breast-feed, and his five children, and how they had recently migrated from Brooklyn to the base of the Catskills.

"When black folks left their agrarian roots, they lost touch with their humanity. Just as when women departed from their role as child bearers, they lost their souls." To protect myself from an immaculate conception right there in the restaurant that would render me barefoot and pregnant, I cemented my feet to the floor and glued my knees shut.

"If we were really serious, as a people, the epidemic of starving children could be cured in a blinking of an eye, if single women would breast-feed orphaned children. When you carefully consider the plight of our people—our children—we are not using all of our available resources. There are too many single women whose breasts are going unused that could be feeding a child right this moment, anywhere in Atlanta. Man, women could be feeding two. I almost forgot, women have two nipples. Take you, Iris, for example, just think how letting a child suck milk from your breasts could change the world. Now from the look on your face, this is a concept you have never considered. But if you and some of your bitter girlfriends are tentative about it, just last week, as a matter of fact, I invested in a breast milk pump company. And by fall, we intend to sell these pumps to single black women through multi-level marketing."

If Tammy calls me about this bullshit, I'll rip out her vocal cords.

In response to his Neanderthal attitude, I hid my glare behind my linen napkin. Achilles nodded, watching Ennis and I interact.

"You agree, Achilles?" Ennis asked, prodding for support.

I glanced at my breasts to see if they were still there.

"A black man needs a black woman. And a black woman needs a black man," Achilles responded, swallowing his last morsel of steak, his eyes staring at my bottom lip.

Ennis piped in, "The Honorable Elijah Muhammad taught us the importance of solidifying the black family."

"Um, Ennis, your wife is involved in your breast milk pump enterprise?"

"Oh, absolutely," he responded, buttering his bread. "In fact—," Ennis rested his butter knife against his plate, so that he could retrieve his wallet from his vest pocket, and pulled a photo out of one of the sleeves. "Behold, an image of my exquisite queen," he said, holding his queen's photo in front of me. My eyes squinted to focus, making sure that the resolution of the photo was accurate. "Her name is Rebecca...but I call her Becky...she's the best white woman I have ever met in my life."

Blood drained from my face, just when my heart slowed to an abrupt halt and didn't pump blood to an artery for a full minute. Perhaps this was an episode of *Punk'd* and Ashton Kutcher was going to emerge from the kitchen at any moment. I considered reconvening a "Sisters with Steak Knives" summit, announcing that the elimination of Ennis Raspberry was our top priority.

Ennis glanced at his watch, dabbed the corners of his mouth, which I gathered was his cue to end the evening, signaling my freedom. Instead, he dropped from his chair to the floor on bent knees and turned facing east, closing his eyes, and in an eerie, full-throated voice, he intoned, "*Akkahu Akbar! Akkahu Akbar! Akkahu Akbar! Akkahu Akbar!* (Allah Is Most Great.)"

"What the hell is he doing?" I asked Achilles, grabbing the sleeve of his jacket, with my other hand on my pocketknife. Achilles fell back against his chair, slightly intrigued, exhaling. "He is calling the faithful, letting them know it is time for the Obligatory Prayer."

"Faithful? Prayer?" I retorted with my eyebrows knitted together, glancing furtively at the other patrons, who were staring at us.

"We are the New Muslims, although I am a neophyte in faith." Achilles attempted to continue his explanation, when Ennis yanked him to the floor next to him, both of them falling to a prone position, as if searching for a contact lens.

"*Ash-hadu an la ilaha ill-Allah, Ash-hadu an la ilaha ill-Allah*. (I bear witness that there is none worthy of being worshipped except Allah.)" As I was the only one sitting upright and therefore deemed coherent, the restaurant manager galloped over to bring an end to this re-creation of a pilgrimage to Mecca. "Miss, what are they doing? What *are* they doing?" he asked, as his stiff, handlebar moustache twitched under his banana-shaped nose.

"*Ash-hadu anna Muhammad-ar-rasoolullah, Ash-hadu anna Muhammad-ar-rasoolullah* (I bear witness that Muhammad is the Apostle of Allah.)" Ennis responded.

"I assure you, sir, that we, well…they will be done soon. I think."

"Madam, this is not a synagogue."

"I think what you mean is a mosque," I said, trying to be helpful, physically coaxing the bewildered manager toward the entrance to the kitchen.

"If they declare a *fatwa* ("war"), they'll drive us out of business! The *Atlanta Constitution*'s food critic already hates us! I implore you, beg you, to leave this establishment this very instant!"

Now this was the second time tonight I was being asked to vacate a place that I did not want to be in, in the first place. A change in my circle of associates was overdue. Ennis continued, now turning his face to the right, then to the left, reciting:

"*Hayya 'alas-salah*. (Come to prayer.)

Hayya 'alal-falah, Hayya 'alal-falah. (Come to success.)

Allahu Akbar, Allahu Akbar. (Allah Is Most Great.)

La illaha ill-Allah. (There is no deity but Allah.)"

The nervous, but grim, red-faced manager lifted the telephone receiver, threatening, "I will phone the police." Kneeling beside Achilles and Ennis, trying to gain their attention, pounding on their shoulders, I hollered, "Achilles! Ennis! Can't you do this later?"

Achilles broke his stumbling recitation, answering, "*Allahu Akbar!* The *Salatul-Isha*, (night prayer) must be offered after the time for *Salatul-Maghrib* comes to an end, and before the break of dawn, but it should preferably be offered before midnight."

"Oh," I answered, pretending what he said made sense. Achilles bowed, following Ennis, grasping his knees and keeping his back in a straight line at a right angle with his legs. Then they prostrated themselves so that the palms of their hands, the forehead, the nasal bone, the knees, and the toes of both feet touched the ground. Finally, they sat in a reverential posture, keeping the right foot erect on the toes and the left one in a reclining position under their rumps.

Again threatening, with the vein in his neck pulsating, the irate manager waved the telephone receiver in my direction.

Standing in front of Justin's, Ennis conversed with a kente cloth–wearing, pan-handling fan as we waited for the valet to retrieve my Honda. The sweaty manager hovered around the front entrance with a wooden Jackie Robinson-autographed baseball bat to ensure our permanent departure. As theatergoers exiting the Fox Theatre clogged the road a mile down Peachtree Street, Achilles explained that Ennis was his Imam of sorts, guiding him through his conversion to Islam.

"The mosque would welcome a capable, beautiful sister," Achilles ventured.

"Hmmm, sounds interesting," I said, insincerely as he helped me into my idling sedan. "Right now, I'm straight in the spiritual department and much prefer worshipping my business—Image Control."

Achilles leaned into my car window, saying, "My basketball team is playing Southern University this weekend, but when we get back, how about you and I get together? Dinner or something?"

I hated vagueness; hated when men were not precise when making a request. Achilles was attracted to me and I to him; however, since we'd just had dinner, followed by prayer, couldn't he think of a more interesting way for us to get to know each other? Still, I extended my suede business card and responded, "Give me a call."

Achilles examined my card:

IRIS CHAPMAN. PRESIDENT. IMAGE CONTROL, INC.
404-555-4632. YOUR IMAGE IS IN YOUR CONTROL.

Thumping my business card against his thumb, as Ennis rejoined us, Achilles said, "Uh-oh! We got a new millennium, sister. I respect that."

"Oh, yeah," Ennis said, grinning. "Watch out, man. She may be too hot for you to handle."

"An independent woman is just what Allah ordered," Achilles said, with Ennis' arm draped around his shoulder, the two of them grinning like two Cheshire cats. Revving the engine, I changed gears, smiled, and said, "Good niiiight, brothers," and merged into the reluctant traffic as the driver of a lime-green Mazda blew his horn, angry that I had cut him off.

Achilles never phoned.

Six months later, Quincy's Emporium had again defaulted on their account by issuing a bad check. Working late in my office, I accessed the damage when my office telephone rang. "Yes," I barked, annoyed that I would have to incur the expense of a lawsuit by hiring an attorney.

"You don't sound like you're in the mood for a favor," the husky voice said.

"Excuse me. Who's calling?"

"You may not remember me. I met you about six months ago with Ennis Raspberry."

"Ennis? Yes, I remember him. And what was your name?" I answered, feigning ignorance, placing a pile of ignored invoices in the accounts receivable bin.

The husky voice chuckled. "So much for first impressions. Achilles Henderson."

"Yes. Yes. Of course. What can I do for you?"

"My team, the Clark Atlanta University Panthers, plays a community charity game each year. This year we wanted to play the Wheelchair Rebels. When I contacted them, they said you represented them."

The Wheelchair Rebels were among many organizations that Image Control represented pro bono as part of the firm's community service. The teammates consist of Vietnam veterans who played basketball as if their lives depended upon it, leaving many able-bodied opponents with their tails hanging between their legs.

Flipping open my desk calendar, I clicked a pen and asked, "When did you want to do this?" Achilles requested that the game occur on a weekday in January, at the gymnasium on Clark Atlanta University's campus. I listened carefully for any inflections of familiarity, flirtation, and found none. When we hung up, I checked my teeth in the mirror, trying to recall if there was any spinach lodged in them, or if my titties were sagging the night we met.

My walk down memory lane was interrupted by a vertically challenged but determined Dwight, arriving to escort me to the opening of the Alvin Ailey Dance Company and Christmas party at the Alliance Theater. The desk lamp cascaded shadows, highlighting December 15, 2010, as I bent over to kiss Dwight, then carried him downstairs to the car.

One month later. January 15, 2011.

The Wheelchair Rebels rolled all over the Clark Atlanta University Panthers, 116–95. The noisy crowd booed members of the Panthers when they exhibited poor sportsmanship by deflating the wheels on the wheelchairs of the Rebels. Using an air pump, Achilles assisted me in inflating the wheels.

"Sorry about this, Iris. The players know what they did was wrong," Achilles said, pushing the air pump.

"Wrong? It was beyond wrong. It was criminal," I said, twisting the air cap on the last chair wheel.

"They're good kids, but too easily swayed by challenges. I promise you will get a written apology."

"Is that enough? Have you ever tried to push yourself in a wheel-less wheelchair?"

"Point made. How about the players volunteer with the Wheelchair Rebels? Provide a donation, run errands, wash their uniforms, whatever."

"Deal," I answered, standing and brushing the soot off my fingers.

"One more thing. And this is a deal breaker."

"What?"

"Dinner with me. Wednesday night?"

Over dinner, it was established that we shared similar tastes in music, lust for each other, commitment to the community, lust for each other, several similar bad former relationships, and lust for each other. Achilles passed the initial screening and was promptly placed on a ninety-day warranty, where everything, absolutely everything, needs to be hunky-dory, wonderful as peaches, perfect, a dream come true between two people, ninety days after they meet. Protectively, Achilles would take me on long drives, clocking a speedy ten miles an hour, pumping the brakes miles before we reached an intersection.

Day 10. Babbled to anyone who would listen about how fine, how considerate, how spiritual, how tall, how funny, how different, how wise, how supportive, how nurturing, how generous Achilles was.

Day 11. The bank teller abruptly closed her window to avoid my Achilles-themed drone. Sign read: GONE FISHING.

Day 18. Ghosts of boyfriends past were erased from the Rolodex, the memory on my BlackBerry, deleted as a friend on Facebook and from my email buddy list. Old butt-naked photos were replaced with a fresh box of condoms and new lingerie.

Day 35. Abstained. Ignored the advice of Ms. Chickie, I behaved coyly; behaved like the virgin I wasn't. "Don't be goin' around here acting like you no virgin, 'cause there're a lot of these hoodlums around here who could testify differently. I knowed you kids used to call behind my mango tree, the holiday inn. Now just be true to yourself, Granddaughter. And be the slut you are, so in the long run, and we both knowed you have had a long run, he can respect your honesty," advised Ms. Chickie.

Day 49. Held out, though there were many nights when underwear hung around our ankles as we questioned whether we were ready to cross the primal burning sands. This was a bullshit mating dance. I played the role of "Oh, dear me. I couldn't. Not this soon" and he played the Sir Galahad role of "I'd never want to defile your divinity, pure maiden." Celibacy had not been in my vocabulary, as the amount of potential soul mates who had ended up being only one-night stands was enough to fill the bleacher section at an Atlanta Braves game. I was not a slut, but I was in hollering distance.

Day 65. It was Thursday night. Rained all afternoon. Raindrops still peppered my bay windows, paving the way for a new beginning. Doodled love poems to bring Achilles nearer, loved that he called to hear my voice, to hear how I was, and to find out if I needed anything.

"Just you," I whispered.

"On my way."

Achilles' spirit reached me first, setting off a jackhammer between my legs. With moistened, closed eyes, I curled into a fetal position, his spirit warmly spooning, preparing me for its master.

Sweat began.

Entering the shower, I heard Achilles activate his car alarm, his heels clumping up the wooden front steps onto the porch. The hot shower calmed neither the urgency nor the anticipation I felt. We both knew that it was time. Time to dance.

"Hi," I whispered.

"Hi, yourself!" Achilles smiled, kissing me gently, standing outside the shower, watching me with hungry eyes. Water poured over my body, casting an iridescent shimmer. "You look beautiful," he continued, nibbling my neck, unbuttoning his shirt, leaving his clothes in a pile on the floor, lifting his right leg to enter the shower.

"Achilles, how do you feel about me?"

"Huh?"

"I need to hear it. Right now."

This was not fair and I knew it. A black man is weakest when naked or in a police lineup. But I was willing to use this situation to my advantage. Achilles inhaled slowly, gathering his thoughts, and shuddered as the walls shielding his vulnerability dismantled.

"Iris, I think about you all the time. I talk about you to my friends. I—I love you."

"Really!" I squealed. So much for playing hard to get.

"Yes, really," he said, placing his index finger on my nose, stepping into the shower, wrapping his arms around me. Conversation became unnecessary; body language replaced anything words could say. The air became heavy with the lightness of good feeling. Our lips touched; inviting tongues performed a gentle ballet. I lifted my legs and wrapped them around his waist, feeling as though cayenne pepper had been sprinkled, between my legs exploding, then calm. Ignoring the Atlanta rule against running water, the connection between one another strengthened and nothing was lost except the passage of time. The sound of the water in the shower became hypnotic within our created refuge behind the glass shower doors. Mesmerized in the embrace of one another, our eyes became darker, intent on just being. Time stood still as the sound of the shower roared on.

Day 75. Scared. Is this the real thing? Ordered a subscription to *Brides* magazine. Tammy was so delighted with laughter, wanting all of the details, that I exhausted myself and had to hang up on her.

Day 80. Achilles said he was not good at putting his feelings to words. I was kind enough to do it for him, which I think he appreciated. Ms. Chickie called to ask, "…You gonna talk that boy's ear off...are you rockin' his world, granddaughter?"

Day 81. Sent emails to friends announcing that we were in love. Instead of hitting reply, they posted the news of my love life on their Facebook pages. Tweeted: *I chose love over fear.*

Day 82. Attended Laffapalooza Comedy Festival with Achilles. He suggested I change into a brown, more conservative dress, instead of the red jumpsuit and spiked black boots. We held hands under the table, while enjoying the comedy of Benny Charles. Noticed he is not comfortable with public displays of affection. He waited patiently while Benny introduced me to Peaches Henry, a New York comedienne who needed a New York–based consultant. Recommended Cleo. Heart leaped when Achilles said he was proud of me.

Day 85. Heated discussion. Philosophical. Ennis sends his greetings. Achilles asked me to attend an Introduction to Islam meeting. Last-minute schedule conflict. Later. Ms. Chickie's latest recommendation of erotic films arrived.

Day 90. Passion still felt. Tammy phoned about a fantastic business opportunity. Carmen texted wondering if I could purchase her a wholesale bulk supply of Blonde Ambition, the newest shade of blonde at the Atlanta Hair Show. I texted in reply, "Huh?"

[6]

Achilles groaned as I held his head between my hands, kissing him slowly on his eyes, temple, and lips. His lips, his entire body had been waiting, and in one smooth movement he entered me deliberately, frantically removing the police-issued shirt I wore when we played cops and robbers. Achilles waited this time until I was ready, and then with goofy facial expressions, we climaxed, sounding like asthmatic donkeys.

By the way the February mid-morning sun shone through his bedroom window, I prayed that the ice had melted on the roads. Achilles and I had prepared for the "storm of the century," as the raving meteorologist proclaimed, urging metro Atlanta citizens to stock up on firewood, food, water and fuel. "It's gonna be a doozy, folks! Flooding everywhere! Button down your hatches and stay off the roads unless you absolutely, positively have to drive! Noah! Where for art thou?"

Lying next to him, I snuggled, exploring Achilles' extended navel, which seemed like it had an eyeball on top of it, with my warm tongue. The taste of his navel reminded me of the black licorice squares I'd swipe from Ms. Chickie's pocketbook, until I learned it was nicotine licorice, unsuccessfully designed to help her break her snuff habit.

My finger followed the shape of his nose, down across his lips, across his chin, and fiddled with his earlobes. His head was shaped like that of an African aristocrat. Even when he was sleeping, he held his head like a nobleman. His breathing became shallow; his eyelids slowly blinked as I leaned close to his ear, gently nibbling on his earlobe. My lips retraced the journey my finger had made and blew full force like a bugle into his ear. Achilles jumped up, playfully hitting me with a pillow. Not backing down, I grabbed my own pillow and smashed him in the face. Now he was bent on retaliation, so I did the only courageous thing—and ran. One leg extended out of the bed and the other was on its way to meet it when Achilles grabbed me from behind, flinging me like a kewpie doll back toward the bed. Screaming, yelling, and loving it, I didn't make it to the mattress. My torso draped on the floor with Achilles holding my legs with one arm and tickling my stomach with his fingers.

"Don't tickle me!" I cried, and then resorted to what anyone would do in that position. I farted into Achilles' face.

"You crazy!" Achilles howled, laughing, as he reached down, pulling me up next to him to revel in our mutual satisfaction.

Whenever my friends and I developed specific sexual tastes in men, it led to a dastardly, predictable future. Carmen loved men who fucked like they were taming wild bulls in an unlicensed rodeo, escaping out her bedroom window after being detected. Tammy loves the cuddly types who liked to talk about God for hours afterward over ginger tea and croissants, and who later turned out to be gay, interior decorators, or both. Repeatedly asking, "How did I do? Huh? How was it? Huh? Did you come? Huh? Huh?" And I attracted the silent types who, after they came, turned over, hating to be touched. So I thought my karma had changed when Achilles actually wanted to have a conversation. Unfortunately, it was not with me. It was with Allah.

"*As-salatu khairum minannaum,*" he murmured, unthreading himself from around me and sticking each leg into his gray flannel pajama pants.

"What didja say?" I asked, resting on my ashy elbows.

"Prayer is better than sex."

"Excuse you?'

Believe me, I heard, but I was coming down with a bad case of denials. The shock of the statement numbed me into silence. Wondering if I should throw a shoe at him, I reviewed our activities over the past ninety days, to determine, if there was a clue that I missed.

Under the continued guidance of Ennis, Achilles was indeed a Muslim—part-time, practicing at his whim or convenience whenever the season or guilt upon cast him by the faithful. Lying naked in his bed, I imagined myself to be a modern-day Mary Magdalene, tempting Achilles with sexual desire in 15 A.D.; never accompanying him to the mosque, and often watching television while he recited two-and-a-half prayers on the weekend, fewer than that during basketball season.

In the beginning, we had conversations—rather, he had monologues—urging my rapid conversion to Islam. Imagining myself, as the dutiful girlfriend, nodding supportively in response to his diatribes, wrinkling my brow with just the right measure of concern. Rallying on his side, whenever there was a conflict between Achilles' and the Clark Atlanta University administration. His knowledge, his passion, no matter what he was ranting about, was indeed intoxicating.

Achilles explained his own conversion, his own search, during long drives to Lake Lanier to witness cranberry-orange sunsets. The man was internally driven, so very different from men I had known, who did not believe in anything except the conquest and the departure. Achilles believed that he was of America, but not in it. Not much different from what I had heard from start-up revolutionaries who just wanted to get into my panties.

Initially, I agreed to attend introductory meetings with Achilles and was placed under the care of the warm, caring sisters, where I was encouraged to become a Muslim Girl In Training. Under the observation of gentle-eyed, respectful brothers, whose majesty was demonstrated by their carriage, how they expressed their quiet fire and with deft-like salesmanship, sold me subscriptions to the *Final Call.*

As months passed, Achilles continued to push where my compass would not lead, often turning a topic of conversation as benign as toenail clippers into the current mandate of the Messenger. He would leave hints as to where I could purchase a hajib. And what made it worse for Achilles was that he could see that I was not drawn to Islam because I had another religion that abided by one universal rule—do unto others as you would have others do unto you. It was apparent that I was going to the Nation of Islam orientation meetings, with the same enthusiasm, with which I accompanied him to the barbershop, because my presence was expected, not desired.

Achilles ran his hands through my hair, then leaned against the kitchen counter as I turned the bacon strips in the cast-iron frying pan. "What?" I said, glancing at him.

"Your hair," he said. "Why did you change it?" To tell the truth would be to concede defeat and admit that I had crumbled, in a weak moment, under Lee Artist's expectations.

"Just wanted to try something new," I lied, loading wheat bread into the toaster.

"You remind me of those helmet head sisters I see downtown all the time."

"So you don't like it?" I asked, trying to camouflage the hurt in my voice.

"You look like another woman, that's all. A conformist to the devilish nature of this country." Biting my lower lip, I fantasized taking the frying pan, filled with the pork bacon he loved but I thought Muslims were forbidden to eat, and smacking him on his hypocritical head.

Instead, I loudly banged the spatula against the edge of the frying pan and retrieved organic eggs out of the refrigerator. Achilles ignored my stifled tantrum and snapped the elastic on the white Fruit of the Loom panties he had purchased for me because he thought my Victoria's Secret string bikinis were not ladylike.

"Why don't you put some clothes on," he suggested, returning to the bathroom to complete his *ghusl* (the washing of the whole body). By the time he had closed the bathroom door, I was listening to messages left on my voicemail. There was one from Tammy. Another from Lee Artist, who wanted to know if I needed a touch-up.

"Only under anesthesia, Mother," I muttered to myself.

The third message was from Seth Greenfield, the president of the prestigious Public Relations Society, requesting a meeting over cocktails at the Sterling Club, a sequestered, unofficial whites-only dining establishment complete with an atrium health club and a Confederate historical library. Tammy thought she knew the motive behind Seth's invitation.

"You've been nominated for their Peacock Award for excellence in community outreach. Praise the Lawd," Tammy relayed in her Thomasville, Georgia, drawl from her car phone as she swerved through traffic on the Perimeter. "First ever."

"First ever what?" I asked.

"You're the first African-American to get anything from them other than a tip for Old Black Joe, the bathroom attendant. They thought black folks didn't need P.R." Our telephone connection crackled from the lightning illuminating the darkening Atlanta afternoon.

"Oh dear, praise God! Let me make it to the townhouse! Amen!" Tammy exclaimed, terrified by any weather pattern other than sunshine. She watches The Weather Channel for hours, often phoning to warn me of a tornado that is tearing through Oklahoma.

"Oh, Lawd," she would say. "That tornado is gonna kill us as God as my witness, in our sleep! Amen!"

"Not unless it boards a 747 airplane."

"Don't be a smart ass! Remember when—"

"Tammy, the house is on fire. I'll call you later."

When Tammy begins her weather rants, I will say anything to get her off the telephone. The last time, I told her that Marvin Gaye was repairing my garbage disposal. But the time before that, learning that I had spent 2001 in Sierra Leone, she had recounted the details of Tropical Storm Gayle in Florida.

"Gurrrrl, you missed it! Gayle was a hurricane for about a day when it was out over the Atlantic. But, child, it tore up something awful when it became a tropical storm. There were torrential rains and flooding and mud slides! Omigod, I thought I was gonna die!

So, if you know what I know, you'll take your raincoat. Amen!"

"But weren't you in Georgia?" I asked flatly.

"Yeah, but if that storm had even looked this way, I woulda died. I know I would have. Amen."

Her credibility completely deteriorated when a month later, as I prepared for dinner guests, Tammy grabbed my forearm, pressed the tips of her red manicured fingers into my brownish skin, and hissed, "Listen!"

"What?" I responded.

"Listen," she repeated, pointing to the ceiling above. "That noise."

My horrified facial expression matched Tammy's as we stared at the ceiling, trying to find a rhyme or reason for the muffled roar overhead. When the clamor became louder, Tammy pulled me into the dark coat closet, squeezing me tightly.

"Oh no," she yelped under my hanging trench coat. "It's a tornado! Omigod, we gonna die! We gonna die!"

Not having ever encountered a tornado, I quickly agreed with her, and my heart began beating rapidly. But when the roar subsided, then abruptly started again, I realized the "tornado" sound was nothing but an upstairs hungry vacuum cleaner.

"You know Seth is sweet on you, gurl. Amen!"

"Yeah, I know. But he ain't my type."

"Oh, you're not hung up on race, are you?" Tammy had inconvincibly sworn off brothers ever since her drama with Victor, and now when she wasn't praising Jesus she was praising white men. My attempts to convince her that the sin of one does not rest on all, fell on deaf ears. Tammy claimed she was knee deep in her belief that only white men would treat her like an African queen.

"Tammy, Seth is nothing but business. And have you forgotten, I have a man?"

"If that's what you want to call him."

Wrapped in a waist towel, Achilles strode out of the bathroom, continuing into the bedroom. I switched on the television, turning up the volume, as *Good Morning Atlanta*'s cheerful meteorologist issued her weather forecast:

"With the storm now out over the Atlantic, Northern Georgia will remain dry from the west coast of Alabama all of the way to the northern tip of Savannah. The one exception to this idyllic weekend is Hurricane Beryl, strengthening in the eastern Gulf of Mexico. Ahead of a stalling front over the northern portion of the Florida Peninsula, thunderstorms have developed. As Beryl presses northeastward and strengthens, it is forecast to come ashore between Appalachia Bay and Suwannee River late Sunday. Heavy flooding rains and strong winds are likely over the northern and central portions of the Florida Peninsula Sunday, spreading into eastern Georgia and South Carolina Monday."

"Georgia? Did she say Georgia?" Tammy screamed.

"Yep," I answered, with smug satisfaction, knowing that Tammy was about to lose her mind.

"Let me know how the meeting goes with Seth! Gotta run. Amen!"

Knowing Tammy, she had detoured off of the Perimeter, hit small children and elderly women to rush into Home Depot on Ponce de Leon Avenue to purchase lumber, a breaker switch, distilled water, a heat generator, flashlights, and batteries. Lumber covered her windows so often her neighbors didn't know whether she was building or un-building her house.

I smiled at my peaceful BlackBerry as Achilles emerged, jingling his car keys, wearing his Clark Atlanta University Panthers red mesh T-shirt and sweatpants with a letterman's jacket marked COACH under the Nike logo. There's something sensual about the black male athlete ethos. If I couldn't have a first-round draft pick, I'd settle for a man who dressed like one.

Wrapping my arms around his neck, I said, "So it looks like I have a business meeting around five. Do you wanna get together afterward?"

Achilles pecked me on the lips, answering, "Um, why don't I call you after practice." My eyebrows raised. My head nodded.

"Tammy and I are going to Cisco's for happy hour. Do you want to join us?" Standing in the open front door, with the Atlanta sun beaming behind him, Achilles stared intently at my hair. "You really look different."

And he was gone.

After a series of strategy meetings with a car theft detection company and the Southern Christian Leadership Council, I arrived back to the office to meet with the feng shui master, whom Tammy believed was Satan.

In the beginning during slow downs in the business at Image Control, against Tammy's recommendation, I decided to consult with a feng shui master to evaluate the interior design office. Solemnly pacing around the office in white stocking feet, with his arms extended like a weather gale, Master Fuji, a seventy-year-old Asian native of Cincinnati, softly advised that my ch'i was again clogged. Having paid him a hefty fee to unclog my ch'i and change my fortune, I asked him, "So how do I unclog it?"

"Only Jesus Christ can unclog anything. He is the Lord of

Lords and the King of Kings. Amen," Tammy reminded Master Fuji and me for the third time.

"Tammy, I know that. Would you let me do me?"

"With all due respect, Ms. Chapman san, one's ch'i is first unobstructed by taking out the trash," Master Fuji answered, as he handed me a broom and hefty-sized garbage bags. Slightly offended, but trying to save face, I surveyed my office, Tammy's office, coat closets, the walk-in kitchen, and the stairs leading to my living quarters upstairs. Among other things, Atlanta Chamber of Commerce Welcome Information, Dear John letters to former boyfriends, a broken microwave, and a colossal crucifix that Ms. Chickie had sent to commemorate Nicaragua's Immaculate Conception Day and to comment on my sex life still remained on various shelf corners two years since Mr. Fuji's first consultation, after I had officially opened.

Based upon Mr. Fuji's recommendations, a large, red easy chair, responsible for fame and fortune, faced south; a champagne laminated desk with satin black steel accents for creativity faced west; a black credenza influencing my career and business faced north, a shelf with a variety of plants faced east, and clutter faced ever direction. Scratching his temple with his eyes closed, Mr. Fuji stood by his initial recommendation, but felt he needed to add one more. Reaching into his briefcase, he grabbed a purple, feathery dust buster.

"Just dust, Ms. Chapman san. If you dust you can change your life."

"Lawd, have mercy," Tammy exclaimed, shaking her head and plopping herself behind her desk, typing furiously. "Let them seek the face of God. Amen."

❖ ❖ ❖

The Sterling Club is located in Druid Hills, one of Atlanta's affluent residential communities. Driving through the curving, winding roads, circling the two-story Tudor- and Georgian-style architectures, I stopped to surreptitiously collect black lawn jockeys off of the lawns of politically incorrect homeowners. By the time I arrived at the Sterling Club—located next door to 822 Slingback Drive, the house used in filming *Driving Miss Daisy*—I had so many lawn jockeys, it appeared as though a group of black midgets were peeking out of my trunk.

Turning into the long driveway situated on a gently sloped hill surrounded by tall enchanting oaks, magnolias, and numerous dogwoods, I interrupted a skinny, acne-ridden adolescent with a bad case of gingivitis strumming his banjo. As I began to form a question, he interrupted, harshly advising me that the employee entrance was on Highland Avenue. When I advised him that his mother had given birth to someone with the intellect of a housefly, Einstein replied, "How didja know? It's s'posed to be a family secret."

My entrance into the bar caused a tomb-like silence amongst the white middle-aged patrons as everyone stalled their conversations. And if it were not for Seth's bombastic greeting, I would have turned on my heels. "Iris," he exclaimed, popping breath mints into his mouth. "Glad you could make it," Seth shouted over the din of silence, trotting toward me, his outfit pledging his allegiance to the Lithuanian flag. He had spent much of his childhood in Lithuania and wore black pants, a red jacket, and yellow tie, with a yarmulke sitting like an open flap on top of his head. Seth Greenfield had not gained membership at the Sterling Club through the generosity of an open invitation, but through the deep pockets of his father's class action suit. But still, in the year 2011, he remained the only Jewish member, bringing with him a kosher chef, a Puerto Rican man named Rigoroberto.

"Did you eat yet? The dining menu here is fine. So very, very fine. Rigoroberto's T-bone steak is great. Rare, bloody rare! Delicious."

Whatever appetite I had mustered disappeared with Seth's penchant for repeating description, and his fondness for bloody, rare meat.

"Cocktails would be fine, Seth. I'm meeting clients later." The "clients" were the buppie crowd that would be swarming Cisco's nightclub later that night.

"Oh," he responded, a little disappointed. "I was hoping, really hoping, we could make an evening of it."

"Oh that would have been so much fun," I lied gaily. "But duty calls," I continued as I sat down on the black leather bar stool.

Seth sat on the edge of his stool facing me. "This is a swell place—a swell, swell place," Seth said, chomping on salted cashews, gesturing the bored, blue-eyed, Aryan-looking bartender over.

"A martini with olives. Lots of olives," Seth ordered. "And for you, Iris?"

"Martini for me, as well. Bombay Sapphire, straight up, lemon twist—and make it very dry."

"My dear Iris. You might as well have ordered a white zinfandel. A white zinfandel indeed!" The bartender shed his icy exterior upon hearing Seth's comment.

Seth cleared his throat as he refastened the bobby pin on his yarmulke. "You see, Iris. You see, the veerrry dry martini served in those fancy martini glasses is a dangerous trend that must be stopped. And since cultural elites are doing nothing about it, you and I must do our part. What you really want is your martini wet—with the gin thoroughly impregnated with vermouth."

The bartender smiled appreciatively at Seth, and exchanged the white paper napkins in front of us for monogrammed linen.

"I never knew you were a connoisseur of the martini, Mr. Greenfield," the bartender said.

"Clinton, the making of the venerable martini should resemble the Immaculate Conception. For as Thomas Aquinas once noted, the generative power of the Holy Ghost pierced the Virgin's hymen like a ray of sunshine through a window—leaving it unbroken."

Clinton cupped his palms under his chin, listening like a Boy Scout engrossed in a campfire story. Other patrons, many with receding hairlines and plump bellies, eavesdropped on Seth's homily. My deliberate hacking, dry cough finally conveyed to the enamored Clinton that I needed a drink—and now. Clinton coated the bottom of a cocktail shaker with vermouth as he listened. A large assembly formed around us, mumbling moans of admiration. Glancing at my Gucci watch, I knew that Cisco's happy hour was jumping now; the dance floor was crowded, the DJ urging the crowd to leave their woes at the front door. Black folks galore, I am sure, were ordering Bombay Sapphires, straight up, lemon twist—dry, veerrry dry, without receiving an extenuated lesson on the authenticity of a martini.

"The idea of making a martini with no vermouth in it is absurd. It is *contra naturam*. You see, a goodly portion of vermouth rests in its very essence," Seth droned, rubbernecking from left to right, playing to his throng of admirers.

Clinton poured our drinks, and with great aplomb, set art deco glasses before us. When I reached for my glass, Seth held up his hand, indicating that he first wanted to inspect the drink. Slowly, he sipped, his eyes rolling back in his head, shifting the liquor from side to side, and moaning gleefully. I considered phoning a Catholic priest to schedule an emergency exorcism.

"Divine. Absolutely divine. Like an Itzhak Perlman and Yo Yo Ma duet," Seth said, smacking his lips. The throng applauded before drifting back to their dark mahogany tables and their plans for the South to rise again. The martini was different, excellent,

I will admit. But leaning toward Seth, I began, "Um, Seth, regarding the—"

"Here's the thing, my dear. When you move in certain circles, the drink you consume reveals your breeding. For instance, the upper-upper middle class partakes in vodka or scotch, with water or on the rocks, and Bloody Marys before three p.m. The middle-class prefers vodka with tonic, and liquid sludge such as white zinfandel, Riunite, and Tanqueray. And finally the proletariats drown their sorrows in anything with Schnapps, domestic beer, and any wine in a box."

"This is all well and good," I said, the alcohol supporting my frankness. "But I thought we were here to discuss my award. I don't need a lesson in social graces." Seth replaced his glass upon the black oak bar and slowly rubbed his forehead. Clinton, still enamored, occasionally glanced over, giving Seth a yankee doodle thumbs-up signal. Like a squeaky chalk on a blackboard, Clinton was grating on my nerves.

"Yes, you do, my dear. I am afraid you do."

"Excuse you?" I said, with arched eyebrows.

"You are positively delightful. Absolutely delightful. Radiant. With great style. However, you must admit the etiquette of the powerful is mad different, as your peeps would say in Southwest Atlanta."

"You mean black folks?"

"Yes, yes. If you mean to be direct about it."

Steam was percolating in my abdomen like a radiator, clanging, threatening this segregated enclave with an explosion. "Seth, I'm en route to being offended."

"Oh don't be, Iris. Don't be. You know I care for you a great deal," he said tenderly.

The "We come from different backgrounds, but we can forge

ahead into the sunset and create a whole new world" speech. Remember the noble relations between the Jews and the blacks during the civil rights movement, and all that. Imagine our golden-ringlet, cinnamon-colored children, Seth would say, bridging the cultural divide in school. They would come from the best of both worlds and would check off "multi-racial" on their census forms.

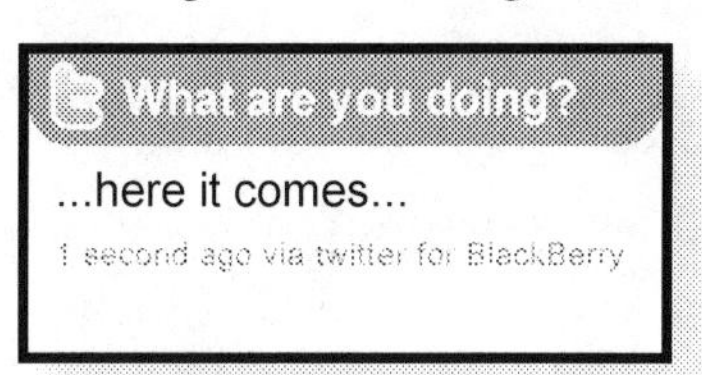

This speech was familiar. As former president of the United Nations Club at Florida A&M University, I had become the love interest for homesick, post-pubescent foreign males. Sven, from the Netherlands, insisted that we wear matching dark blue wooden clogs decorated with windmills that had been hand carved by his father, Sven Senior, who had been court-ordered to stay away from knives. And there was Tomás from Guatemala, who dreamed of us exploring the remote jungles, searching for remnants of Mayan civilization. He wanted me to learn the Dance of the Conquest before his mother arrived for Homecoming Weekend.

"And that's another thing," I inserted.

"What?" Seth asked.

"You have feelings I cannot return. I am in a relationship."

"Excuuuuuse you," Seth said, yanking on his earlobe, giving me his full attention.

"I said, I have a man."

Seth narrowed his eyes, pursing his lips. "Oh I see," he said quietly. "That puts another spin on things entirely."

"You mean this award was a way to—"

"No, no. I just find your situation coincidental."

"How so?"

Seth placed his hairy, stubby hand on my forearm and said, "You see, Iris, I have a man, too."

Silence.

My face froze, and then shattered into a thousand pieces, with the remnants falling to the marble floor. My ego first had to wrap around the fact that another man was not interested in me, as I'd had to fend them off from the time I became a knock-kneed teenager. And I was used to homosexuals, being that my cousin Anthony was out of the closet long before his holy-roller parents had a chance to build one.

When I first met Seth after a public relations seminar, he was thrilled to learn that Ms. Chickie had been a maid for a Jewish family for many years on Miami Beach. His reaction: "My goodness! My family lived on Miami Beach for a few winters. My goodness, we could have been...been..." I thought he was going to say "sisters" or offer some other genetic connection to the fact that my grandmother might have scrubbed his family's floors. But instead, Seth became fascinated with my business life and extended invitations to every Chanukah, Rosh Hashana, and Yom Kippur planning meeting in the Jewish calendar. And when he began emailing me articles from the Ask-a-Rabbi web site, it was Tammy who provided the confirmation. "Uh-huh, that boy is sweet on you." But as with the weather forecast, Tammy was wrong.

"Let's go outside," Seth said abruptly, paying for the unfinished martinis by signing the bill. As we strolled to the exit, Seth's new admirers shouted their farewells, waving over their dimly lit tables hazy from cigar smoke.

Outside, Einstein was still strumming his banjo, singing: "Her teeth was stained, but her heart was pure, and her breath smelled like cow manure..."

Seth grabbed Einstein's attention, causing him to clamor to his feet and run into the gravel-strewn parking lot with a ring of keys.

"The point is Iris. The point is I still had to refine myself in order to move within these echelons. When I first joined the Sterling Club, I actually expected that they would have kosher delicacies on the menu. But I had to ask myself, am I here to have a bar mitzvah or to broaden my business alliances? I chose the latter. And I would suggest if you want to do the same, then when in Rome, do as the Romans do."

"I think I do okay now," I said, teetering on the heels of my stilettos.

"Do you want to 'do okay,' or operate in another stratosphere?" Seth asked.

Einstein screeched around the corner in Seth's silver Alfa Romeo 169, honking the horn. "Dayum, that sho' would put a lickin' on my daddy's tractor," he said, wiping the white saliva off the corners of his mouth, then lurching away to retrieve my Honda.

"See here. I'll introduce you to the heads of Atlanta's top corporations. And you share your connections with black entertainers. We'll help each other, as it were."

Seth, this time, did not repeat himself.

By the time I had threaded myself through the packed, sweltering club, and had heard partygoers spewing self-indulgent lies, I thought I was at a convention for Pathological Liars Anonymous.

"...I don't know why he's paging me."

"...I'm looking for a woman to settle down with."

"...the Bible is my favorite book."

"...I'm a one-woman man."

Tammy, wearing her Christian off-night, signature black mini-dress, was guzzling down a pina colada paid for by two toothy, on-the-prowl brothers who did not realize they were wasting their time. Jason, the shifty but charming owner of Cisco's, blew me a kiss from across the room, where he sat holding court in a brown velvet banquette with a harem of large-breasted wannabes.

Cisco's was a celebrity/groupie magnet and one of the best-known nightclubs in Southeast Atlanta. The bar area catered to an older, professional set. The atrium upstairs featured entertainment for a hip-hop crowd, with the requisite number of hoochies in attendance.

The large, oval-shaped dance floor slowly moved counter-clockwise, occasionally dizzying an overzealous dancer. "You look like you could use a party. Amen," Tammy said, as the two brothers smiled, waiting to be introduced.

"A Tanquer—, um, cancel that. Beck's, please," I said to the plump bartender before hugging Tammy. On the dance floor, dark arms swung in unison to the pounding bass.

When the bartender poured beer into my glass, one of the beaming brothers said, "Hey, my brother! Let me take care of the lady." And then to me, with an affected low tone as if he had been practicing in a tape recorder, "Hi, I'm Antonio." Then he dished a frontal smile.

Even though it was night, I instantly regretted having left my sunglasses on the living room coffee table, because this grinning, horse-toothed brother had the nerve to have gold initials carved into his front buckteeth, and a hoop nose ring as if they needed further attention. The glare bouncing off the ceiling chandelier was burning a hole in my cornea.

"Hey," I replied dryly, and glared at Tammy to get who appeared to be—by his initials on his front teeth—A.J. out of my airspace. Needed a moment to collect my thoughts and develop a taste for imported beer. Considered whether Seth was right. Did I have enough of a wing spread to sail higher, to another professional stratosphere, or would I remain in my comfort zone?

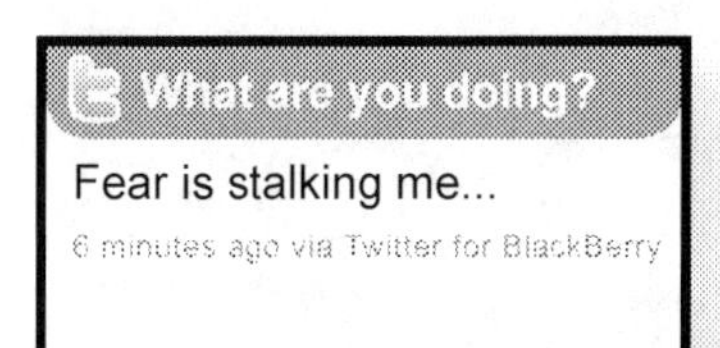

The moment was over soon enough. Dark-suited club bouncers pushed past, whispering on walkie-talkies, heading with serious faces toward Jason, who was now standing on the stairs leading to the upstairs atrium. The bouncers whispered to Jason and rushed up the stairs. Oblivious club patrons continued dancing to Wyclef's latest release to which, the wallflowers released their three inches of territory, revealing sweat stains on the back of their clothes as they rushed to the dance floor.

A.J. extended his hand as if he was Sir Walter Raleigh. "May I have this dance?" Bouncing with Wyclef's pulsating rhythms, I accepted, praying he would not open his mouth. Shortly into the groove, dancers behind me slowed, then stopped moving as they glanced over their shoulders. The bouncers swept past, dragging along a resistant, pint-sized young boy wearing hang-off-the-ass jeans, unlaced work boots, and a T-shirt that read HELL TO PAY; followed by another less-resistant but taller boy wearing a T-shirt that read BORN TO DIE; followed by Colby Woods, their manager, who was pleading with the security guards, and signaling me that he would phone me later.

Panic spread throughout the club when, in spite of the aggressiveness of the bouncers, three large, muscular boys with thick necks leaped onto the backs of the escorted boys, forcing a crush of twisted bodies onto the bottom of the stairs and knocking off the baseball cap of the smaller boy, revealing that he was, in fact, a she, with short, curly auburn hair. Another female voice screamed, "A gun! She's gotta gun!"

A.J. stopped grinning and deserted me on the dance floor, rushing through the kitchen with other frightened patrons. Standing on my tiptoes, I searched for Tammy. Her barstool was empty. There were screams now, orphaned high heels, people, six and seven deep, trying to shove through one door. Trying to exit through this stampede was fruitless, so I dropped to my knees and crawled through legs and behind the bar to Jason's office, loudly slamming the door.

Quickly dialing Achilles on his cell phone, I wished—harder than I had once wished for all of the black and white oxford shoes in the world to be destroyed—that he would answer and come to rescue me from this chaos. Instead, echoes of prayers sounded in the background, when he answered:

Subhanak-Alla-humma wa bihamdika wa tabarakasmuka wa ta'ala jadduka wa la ilaha ghairuka Bismillah-i-Rah-man-ir-Raheem.

Alhamdu lillahi Rabbil-'aalameen ar-Rahman-ir-Rahim, Maliki yaum-id-deen, iyyakt na'-budu wa iyyaka nasta'een; ihdinas-sirat-al-mustaqeema sirat-all-zeena an'amta 'alaihim ghairil maghdoobi 'alai-him wal-lad-dalleen. Ameen!

(All Glory be to Thee, O Allah! and Praise be to Thee; blessed is Thy Name and exalted Thy Majesty; and there is none worthy of worship besides Thee. I betake myself to Allah for refuge from the accursed Satan. (I begin) in the name of Allah, the Beneficent, the Merciful. All Praise is due to Allah, Lord of the worlds, the Beneficent, the Merciful, Owner of the Day of Judgment. Thee alone we worship and Thee alone we ask for help. Show us the straight path, the path of those whom Thou hast favored, not (the path of) those who earn Thine anger nor (of) those who go astray, Amen!)

"Achilles! Achilles! Baby, it's crazy here."

"What are you doing at Cisco's?"

"I told you I was going, remember? What're you doing at the mosque? Look, are you coming to get me or what?"

"Are you hurt?"

Looking over my body for a hemorrhage, I answered, "Not exactly."

"Well, I'll tell you what. I'll meet you at your townhouse in an hour. We're in the middle of *Sajdah*. The Imam—"

Silence.

For the sake of his sperm count, Achilles better not have hung up on me. Perhaps the energy from the chanting caused his cell phone to short circuit. But I knew he did. He continued to place more importance on Islam than *my* life.

Jason found me sitting behind his desk, with my BlackBerry in hand, pondering my next move. Jason assured me that the club was under control, so I ventured through the bottle-strewn, chair-toppled club outside the office, weaving between clusters of onlookers, observing television and print reporters interviewing witnesses from the neighborhood, who for some reason were wearing shower caps. "All you could see was dust. It was surreal," a woman with penciled-on eyebrows said.

"We were right there," lied a skinny teenager, wearing a reverse Atlanta Braves baseball cap. He had leaped over a fence just to get on camera.

"I heard *pop, pop, pop, pop*. And then the shit was on," a woman wearing a blonde wig smilingly lied into the camera, waving to her imprisoned boyfriend, "Hey, Boo!"

The sandy-blonde reporter from Channel 7, summed up his report: "Whether this is another blemish on the reputation of hip-hop, well, that is for the public to decide. But tonight NextLevel

Records rap star Lola Down-lo, and her boyfriend, producer Madd Dogg, have been arrested on charges of suspicion of carrying a firearm and disorderly conduct. Back to you in the studio, Jim."

When I reached my car, Tammy was leaning against it, smoking a cigarette.

[7]

"I thought you quit smoking," I said to Tammy, deactivating my car alarm.

"The Lord is still workin' on me and my nerves are a wreck," she answered, flinging the butt to the ground, mashing out the orange-red flame with her heel.

"You? You were outside. Safe and sound. I was the one trampled under a human stampede," I said, as we entered the car, slamming our car doors, while the news crew from Channel 7 loaded their equipment into their news van.

"You're not gonna light that, are you?" I asked, as Tammy withdrew, and then fiddled with yet another cigarette.

It boggled my mind how smokers automatically assumed that I wanted to join them twenty years hence in an iron lung machine with tubes strung through our noses. Yes, I would say, this was well worth the wait—roaming around the planet with second-hand tar hanging off my collapsed lungs, like a bettor waiting for racetrack results. The anticipation just brings me to sniffles. Maybe I will beat the rush, lock in a lower price and put an iron lung machine on layaway. Everyone knows that fresh air is over-rated. Just like positive thinking, who needs it? The necessity of fresh air is another lie we are sold, along with the advice that wearing black makes you look ten pounds lighter.

"I'm gonna quit. As soon as I finish this box, Amen," Tammy said, smelling before reinserting the butt into the cigarette box.

"Humph, never believe what a man writes in a personal ad," Tammy went on, out of the blue.

"Excuse me?" I responded, stopping at the red light on Campbellton Road.

"Those two brothers at the bar at Cisco's."

"Yeah?"

"I met them online through FlirtingTime.com."

"Do you mean to tell me—"

"The one you were dancing with, his ad read: 'Single Black Male seeks his nubian queen, must be afrocentric, culturally aware, and celebrate Kwaanza.'"

"What's wrong with—"

"Race unimportant.'"

"Tammy, instead of using personal ads to meet a man, why not introduce yourself to the men around you?"

"I couldn't do that. It's unladylike. Uncivilized. Lawd, Jesus, I knew I shouldn't come; I knew it! Amen."

"And hawking your wares on the Internet, isn't? Besides, I thought you weren't into brothers anymore. Looks like you're rethinking your position," I said, clicking on the radio and switching to a local jazz station.

"Being with a man who ignores you is desperate, too," Tammy said conclusively, as Nina Simone's alto voice emanated through the dashboard speakers, crooning "Tell It Like It Is."

The prison fantasy recurred. It was self-defense, my attorney would argue, entertaining the previously catatonic jury with his lyrical closing argument:

"Everybody has their breaking point,
We all have our needs
Yes, my client broke Tammy's joints
But it's my client's heart that bleeds."

❖ ❖ ❖

Achilles' blue-green Mazda was parked in front of my townhouse when I arrived. Tammy recited a prayer before departing in her car which she left parked in my driveway. As was his way, all of the lights in the entire house were on, making it appear as though I was having an open house sale. He would never admit it, but Achilles was afraid of the dark, always opting to do everything under the stark glare of a hundred-watt bulb.

It was apparent that Achilles had been there awhile, as remnants of leftover pasta were on the dinner tray on the black lacquer end table. Wearing a white shirt, olive pants, and green bow tie, with a white kufi, he barely shifted his eyes from the ESPN roundup scores as I entered.

I grumbled.

He grunted.

Dropping my key chain on the brass tray near the front door, I kicked off my high heels and climbed the beige shag-carpeted stairs to my bedroom. As I removed my white silk, scoop-neck blouse and gray skirt, Achilles followed and paused briefly in the doorway before sitting on the bed, running his hand over his head.

"You know, you could have picked me up, Achilles," I hurled, slinging my clothes onto a wooden hanger and stuffing them in the closet.

"You know how I feel about those clubs. Nothing but dens of inequities."

"The same dens of inequities where you were a frequent visitor."

"I don't feel the same way about that part of my past life."

"Yeah, I know how you feel about a lot of things. But do you know or even care about how I feel—about anything?" Achilles shuffled his feet, then threaded his hands together, with his head lowered. These moments were uncomfortable, not knowing what the next would bring—whether there would be resolution or revolution.

My daydreams had always consisted of being with a man who could read my mind, know how to sing love songs, and have good credit. And though it seemed as though Achilles was an answer to my delusional prayers, the more he followed Ennis' urgings to join the New Muslims, a spin-off sect from a spin-off sect, the more distant we became.

Still with his head lowered, Achilles said, "Our relationship—how we do things—has to change."

"Excuse me," I said, snagging a fingernail as I snatched off my pantyhose.

"Tonight, the Imam spoke about male-female relationships. I felt he knew about us. And the fact that we fornicate."

"Fornicate? Fornicate! What the fuck are you talking about?"

"Now see, that's what I'm talking about—"

"Fornicate! Making love is not a science project!"

"Your mouth—"

"You didn't care about my mouth when—" Achilles leapt up and pressed his dry palm over my lips.

"Mmmmmmmmmmm, mmmmmmmmmmmm," I said, squirming under his grip.

"I gotta talk to you," Achilles said, gauging my eyes for my reaction before slowly removing his palm and leading me to sit on the bed next to him.

"The more I hear the words of the Imam, the more my soul craves to hear. And the more I need you there beside me, forming a perfect union with Almighty God Allah."

"Achilles, you know how I feel about religion. I mean, I'm spiritual, but I don't need to have somebody telling me how to live my life."

"It is not 'somebody.' It is Allah, The Beneficent, The Merciful."

"Look I don't want to get into an argument that neither one of us can win."

"Promise me you will consider it, come to a *Juma*, hear the Minister speak—again," Achilles said with sincere doe eyes, as he held my hands gently.

Silence.

"I'll think about it."

Achilles smiled, leaning to kiss me on my cheek, then resting his head on my shoulder. "And there's something else."

"What?" I said, remembering the abandonment I felt over his refusal to meet me at Cisco's.

"The Holy Qur'an states, 'And go not nigh to fornication; surely it is an indecency and an evil way.'"

"Meaning what?" I said, jerking away from him.

"Meaning, no sexual relations without being married."

"Wait a minute. I'm confused. Are you asking me to marry you, Achilles?"

"No."

"Do you want to break up?"

"No, I'm not saying that either."

"What are you sayin', then?"

Achilles thumped his forehead as he exhaled, then sat upright, looking me straight in the eyes. "Until we are unified spiritually, we cannot be unified physically."

My cheeks ignited in a bright flame, though I maintained my quasi-composure.

"So the man who has to have it every night, now doesn't want it at all—no sex, zip, nada?"

Achilles considered the gravity of his statement and realized he had inched out onto the ledge of no return, then said, "No sex."

There were two choices I had. 1) I could stomp out of the house, slamming the door behind me, but then I would be outside of my own house in my bra and panties, to the delight of Mr. Whitaker next door. 2) Knowing my own tendency toward madness without a regular serving of lovemaking, I could throw myself on the floor, writhing, moaning, and wheezing, then show up at the Sex Addicts Anonymous Meetings and announce:

"Hi, I'm Iris Chapman. And I'm a sex addict."

"Hi, Iris. Bend over," the group of pasty-faced curmudgeons would answer jokingly, as they handed me their brochure to memorize: "Twenty Days to Penis Detoxification."

Even in the oddest places, Achilles was easy to arouse, such as during the Batman Ride, the inverted roller coaster at Six Flags over Georgia; or during the television broadcast emergency alert, which always interrupts just when a favorite program reaches the good part. I would use a giant-size bag of popcorn in the case of the former, or a pillowcase in the latter case, to mask his, um, enthusiasm. Knowing this, I opted to utilize the last weapon in my arsenal, my self-respect, and slowly tease him by removing my bra, then turning my back to him, wiggling my behind, turning back toward him and straddling his lap, and tongue-kissing his ears.

With intense eyes, I kneeled between his legs, unzipping his pants, placing my hand to quell his throb. As he entered my mouth I made suckling noises. His breath quickened, his moan signaled surrender. He swayed his head from side to side, steadying my head, loving the sensation as I held on as if scouring the bottom of an ice cream cone.

Achilles breathed heavily, like he was gasping for air. As his eyelashes fluttered, it gratified my ego, and I prayed I was erasing any thought of "go not nigh to fornication," dimming the notion that our lovemaking was indecent, clouding his decision that his happiness could come through celibacy, away from me.

But then, shuddering like an errant jumbo jet, Achilles pulled away, grabbed my wrists forcefully, and lifted me to a standing position. And, like the closing credits in a *Shaft* movie, he strutted into the bathroom, taking a long, cold shower, with the door locked. Achilles didn't emerge from the bathroom until after I had fallen asleep.

Sleeping with a king-sized pillow between my legs, I tossed and turned like a rowboat in a stormy sea, resembling a damp dish towel after a final rinse in the morning.

The whirring of the office coffee grinder and ringing telephones signaled that Tammy had arrived early or I had overslept. The image of the sexy vixen who had attempted to awaken the earthly desires of a zealot boyfriend had disappeared along with Achilles, as I removed the slept-in makeup in the bathroom mirror.

The intoxicating fragrance of Kona coffee, brought back by Tammy from her Hawaiian vacation, permeated the house and wafted up the staircase, along with murmurs of Tammy's voice answering the telephone.

"Iris, you up?" Tammy called from downstairs.

"Barely," I answered.

"Seth is on the phone. It's the second time he has called. What should I tell him?"

"Tell him... Tell him... Never mind. I'll take it up here."

Turning off the brass hot-water bathtub faucets, I wrapped myself in a white, kimono-style bathrobe and flip-flopped to the ivory, upholstered armchair located next to my bay windows, practicing vocal exercises to rid the frog from my throat. "Seth? Good morning?"

"You weren't asleep, were you?"

"Oh no, I was on a conference call to—" I searched around the room for a geographical reference, then instinctively picked up the alarm clock with MADE IN KOREA on the bottom, and blurted, "Korea. I was on a conference call with Korea."

"Wow, you're international."

I chuckled. "So what can I do you for?" I asked, glancing out the window to see the empty space where Achilles had parked.

"You heard of Michael Herman, right?"

"No, I can't say that I have."

"Mickie is only the biggest sports agent in the country. The absolute biggest."

"Uh-huh."

"He's also a friend."

"Okay."

"Mickie needs help with one of his clients. Eba Hamid. You heard of him, right?"

"Seth, until LeBron James proposes to me, I have zero interest in the NBA."

"Well, get re-interested. Eba Hamid is a seven-foot-one-inch Sudanese and the first-round draft pick for the Atlanta Hawks. Mickie is tearing his hair out getting Eba media ready. That's where you come in."

"How?" I asked, fingering the bow tie and unused condoms Achilles had left on the dresser.

"Tonight, my dear, we're meeting Mickie in his private box at Philips Arena. Big game against the New York Knicks. Real big."

An Atlanta Hawks game had been the perfect place to leer during my shallow jock period, shortly after arriving in Atlanta. Being around black men who dribbled, kicked, or threw a ball was intoxicating, with their long limbs, adjusting their jock straps with confidence to their own syncopated rhythm. There is something magical about a man who has no worries other than what time to attend practice, make the team plane, or pretend to enjoy charity events.

Cisco's was also the headquarters for professional athletes, both local and out-of-towners, and their requisite groupies. When brothers over six feet enter Cisco's, all heads turn, the crowd parts slightly, conversations slow to a murmur as bartenders trip over themselves to lavish complimentary drinks until it is ascertained whom he plays for and the amount of his signing bonus.

Sexual favors are often bestowed up in the Cat Lounge. At times, a sister would swallow, then shriek her disappointment after an extended blow job: "Whadda the hell you mean you don't play pro ball?" cueing the bartenders to demand the tab to be paid in full, and the imposter be removed from the prized center booth where legitimate athletes held court. In egregious cases, where the champion team the imposter claimed he played for was in dispute, a groupie would simply Google his ass on her iPhone. If his status could not be verified electronically, he would get permanently tossed from the club.

One steamy summer night, the bartender served me a drink saying, "The brother on the throne sent this over." Over the bartender's shoulder, I met the intense gaze of a caramel-colored, big-forehead brother resembling a sun god, and nodded, raising the glass of rum and Coke for a toast, which gave him permission to join me. The nosy groupies grew fangs and salivated, hovering to see if there would be any leftovers.

Tammy, who had been dancing, returned at the same time, sweating like a runaway slave. Introducing himself as Carlos, the brother gave her his stool and offered to buy her a drink, which she refused, stating, "Thanks, no. I'm fasting."

Carlos wiped his nostrils as he responded in a baritone voice, "That's deep. I fast before every training camp."

"Training camp?" Tammy and I chimed in nonchalantly, as the groupies leaned in to eavesdrop on the answer.

"I play ball for ARIS Thessaloniki in Greece," Carlos said, flashing his European Union championship ring. Since they had never heard of the ARIS Thessaloniki, the bartenders debated whether to request payment in full, but because it was a slow night, the groupies foamed at the mouth anyway, whipping out their iPhones to surf the Internet to determine the salary of their prey.

As I sucked on an ice cube, Tammy and Carlos debated the merits of a coffee or oxygen colonic. Here they did not know each other longer than an hour and already they were discussing how to insert plastic tubes in their asses.

Later, at IHOP, they frowned over the lack of wheat grass juice on the menu as I sipped a glass of canned tomato juice. Tammy and I bid Carlos farewell when the sky began to shift to welcome Sunday morning. Then about a quarter to six, after I had finally warmed the middle of the bed, I wondered aloud who was overworking the ding-dong on the doorbell, interrupting my peace.

When I peered out of the bedroom window, there were no recognizable cars parked outside. Tiptoeing downstairs, carrying a box of Cracker Jacks in case I had to get violent, I peeked from behind the cranberry-colored draperies and saw Carlos preparing to detonate the doorbell again. "Carlos, what are you doing here?" I shouted through the door.

"Iris, I wanted to talk to you, seeing as though we didn't get a chance earlier." My eyebrows knitted together as my eyes squinted at the walnut wall clock, confirming it was now 5:45 a.m. Slowly unlocking the front door, removing the door chain, I cracked open the door and allowed him to slip in.

"Hey," Carlos said, relieved he was now in my foyer.

"Isn't your plane leaving in a few hours?"

"Yeah, but I kept thinking about you. I've been accused of being shy, you know."

"Well, I tell you what, Carlos, why don't you give me a call from Greece, or wherever, and we'll keep in touch that way?"

"Can't I at least have a cup of decaf? I feel so wired," he said, wiping the back of his hand under his nostrils.

"I thought you were into herbal tea. Drinking the earth, and all that?"

"How about a kiss, then," Carlos said, then without waiting for an answer, torpedoed his lips directly toward mine. Ducking, I dove for the door and ordered, "Get out, Carlos!"

"Ah come on, you know you want me."

"Get the fuck out of my house. Whatever you came here for, I am not the one," I said, pointing my index finger at myself, to make sure that he knew to whom I was referring.

Carlos stared at me with dilated pupils, as if I had taken leave of my senses. His look said I was throwing away a world of possibilities: "I could have possibly been the father of your children. You could have slept with a professional ball player, although imported, who could have possibly flown you first class to Greece, and possibly paid all your bills. And you could boast to all the doctors in Atlanta that you have been infected with an extreme case of Grecian cooties, possibly incurable. Then we could have shared precious moments in family court or even with the district attorney, working away at some legal agreement to silence any public statements. Our child could possibly grow up and say, 'Wow, there's goes my sperm donor on television again...the same sperm donor who allows his loins lead him around the planet."

Carlos took shallow breaths; his nostrils flared. He had been determined to come and relieve whatever the cocaine couldn't, but the raised box of Cracker Jacks discouraged him. As he edged out the doorway, he turned, sneering over his shoulder, "Atlanta bitches ain't worth shit!"

"What's up? Trying to make up for not playing in the NBA?" Carlos winced as I stabbed him in the back with an unattainable dream; although surely trying to bed as many women as he could was one he mastered easily.

By the time I had finished dressing and was descending the stairs into the office, Theotis the mailman was chatting up Tammy as she sorted the mail. Theotis often tried to convince Tammy that he was the man she needed in her life. Admittedly, Theotis is nice, but he carries himself as if he had not received the memo that slavery had been abolished. At any minute, you expected Shirley Temple to enter, dancing beside him. Once after assuring him that we were indeed free, he became enraged, accusing me of blasphemy.

When I entered, Theotis was saying, "Nah, I knows you needs a good, Christian man, and I's willin' and I's able to works myself to death for a minute of yo time, Miz Tammy."

"Theotis," I interrupted, "your supervisor, Mr. O'Malley, is looking for you."

"Oh Lawd haf murcy on my soul. He lyball to gib me a whippin' fo sho! I's gonna circle 'round and wade through the swamp to confound the hound dogs. Dat will confound hem fo' sho'. Make him thank I was dere allatime."

"Yeah, well. Do what you gotta do," I said, as Theotis flung his mailbag over his shoulder, ducking out the back door.

"Iris, you wrong! Girl, you know you wrong, Amen," Tammy said, doubled over with laughter. "You'll never forgive Theotis, will you?"

"Look, Mother Teresa, *you* catch Theotis, aka Pissy Man, taking a leak on your hedges and see how you like it. And there's only so much of his Stepin Fetchit routine I can take," I answered, sorting through stacks of mail. "On top of that, the man is dyslexic. I'm tired of my goddamn mail being delivered to 105 instead of 501! And I don't know why you tolerate it."

"Oh, I dunno," Tammy answered, typing a client's press release. "He's kind of sweet. Boy, you and Achilles got your behinds on your shoulders this morning."

"How do you know." I sipped a cup of hot chocolate.

"He came downstairs while I was making coffee. What happened?"

"He wants to stop having sex. Part of his religious training. I'll give up food, cable, but I'll be damned if—"

"He's pretty upset, Iris."

"Wait a minute. He talked to you about this?"

"No, not really."

"Either he did or he didn't. I don't like him discussing our business. I should be the only one talking about it."

"Achilles knows we're friends. That's probably why he felt comfortable talking to me. But even if he hadn't, it was written all over the brother's face that something was eating him up," Tammy said, hitting print on the keyboard, fingering the hemline on her favorite checkerboard, micro-mini skirt. Ignoring her, I continued sorting the mail, throwing out envelopes marked OCCUPANT.

"Do you see yourself marrying him?"

"In the beginning I did. Hell, in the beginning I saw a lot of things."

"You think he'll ever be good enough for you?"

"I never thought in terms of 'being good enough.' Why all the questions? You never liked to talk about Achilles before."

"I dunno. This morning I saw a different side of him," Tammy continued, gnawing on her bottom lip. "You love him?"

"Yes. Yes I do."

"He must care for you, too, 'cause no man would be sulking like he was, if he didn't."

"If Achilles loves me so much, why can't he accept me for who I am?"

"And who are you, Iris?"

I was in no mood for psychoanalysis from a woman who emailed me an invitation to a multi-level marketing meeting for a breast pump product, especially after I had directed her not to. I sucked my teeth and opened an envelope addressed in careful handwriting:

Dear Granddaughter,

How are you? Fine, I hope.

I called up there to let you know I sent you One Night in Paris *— my favorite porn film of all time. Tammy answered the phone. Y'all ain't lesbians, is you? 'Cause that would create a whole lot of commotion. Be careful, 'cause being around ugly girls all of the time is contagious. And like I told you before, she may have a heart of gold but she could scare the flies off of a shit wagon.*

You know you could call or write your family sometime, you ungrateful heifer.

How is the weather? It's real hot here. That's all for now.

Yours truly,

Miss Chickie

"Oh, I meant to tell you, Ms. Chickie called. She's such a sweet old lady. Told me how pretty I am," Tammy bragged, grinning like a Cheshire cat.

[8]
THE QUESTION

If Eba Hamid was Mickie's prize client, the agent had a funny way of showing it. It was the end of the fourth quarter; the Hawks were leading 98–86. Seth and I were waiting in the super agent's skybox, with the host nowhere to be found.

"He'll be here any minute," Seth said, checking his pocket watch nervously for the fifth time. Twin blonde hostesses with tattooed cleavages extended their trays of hors d'oeuvres under Seth's double chin.

"This will really be a coup for you. Really big," Seth said, smacking on lobster shish-ka-bob. "Mickie can't wait to meet you."

"Yeah, I can tell," I droned, leaning forward to focus on the game. The Knicks were in possession of the ball. Knick forward Jared Miller zipped the ball to teammate Nelson Paul, who drove to the basket, too quick for Hawk guard Lorenzo Thomas, for an easy layup. "Are you sure he's coming?" I asked.

Led by his swollen belly, Seth jumped to his feet, pointing down below to the Atlanta Hawks bench. "Look, there he is." Pacing behind the Hawks bench, Mickie, a tall, thin man with a greasy ponytail, was whispering to an even thinner, raisin-complexioned player, who was pouting at the end of the bench. The player shook his head in frustration as Mickie continued to whisper and pat, whisper and pat.

"That's Eba, huh?"

"That's him. Mickie has been babysitting him ever since Eba cleared customs. What the Atlanta organization thought would be a public relations dream has turned into a nightmare. An absolute nightmare."

"What's the problem? Language? Culture? Ego?"

"It could be some of that," Seth said, watching Mickie give Eba a final pat and stride past hot dog–filled security guards and into the restricted players' tunnel. "Eba wants to be an American citizen."

"That's what he wants—to be an American? That's an extensive process, isn't it?"

"You can't blame a man for trying. Eba wants to be red, white, and blue, through and through." The buzzer sounded, ending the basketball game. Atlanta, 105. New York, 90. Atlanta Hawks cheerleaders performed somersaults and cartwheels, celebrating another team victory and a rendezvous with any willing opposing player, while the sound system blasted "Hit the Road Jack."

Entering the room like a svengali, with his trench coat draping his shoulder, Mickie paused to air kiss everyone in the skybox before embracing Seth and me, grabbing my face in his huge, fleshy hands, an unlit cigar clenched between his thin lips.

"Howya doin', honey? Wait 'til Eba gets a loadayew," Mickie said in a Brooklynese accent, swaying his torso from side to side, his eyes scanning my body like an elevator.

"Um, Mr. Herman."

"Stop. Mr. Herman is my fadda. Mickie," he emphasized, kissing the buxom twins' breasts as they served him a glass of champagne. "Did Cindy and Mindy take care of you? Huh? Huh?" he continued, admiring the cleavages of the fawning twins hanging on each of his arms.

"They are extraordinary. Extraordinary!" Seth blustered.

"Ah, Mickie, before I meet Eba, we should discuss your expectations, my fees, make sure there is a meeting of the minds."

Mickie untangled himself from around Cindy and Mindy and

reached into his pant pocket, pressing a blank check into my hand, and again pinching my cheeks until my lips puckered. "Here is a blank check. Write in whadevah you think you are worth. Wadevah! 'Cause downstairs in that locker room, being ignored by the media, is the next endorsement king. I swear on my mutha's grave! Right now, he doesn't understand how to play the game. Oh, he knows how to play the game of basketball, yeah. But the game of corporate endorsements, no. And he won't listen to some Jewish guy from Brooklyn. Dat's why I called yew."

Slowly peeling his fingers from around my face, I said, "How many consultants did you contact before me?"

"Four," Mickie answered quickly. "But you were the only black. He needs to be with his own, you understand? And your pretty face and plump melons don't hurt nuttin'. Ha! Ha!"

What are you doing?

Mickie is a regular Don Rickles. Headlining in Vegas at Yuck Yucks...

45 minutes ago via Twitter

"I've never been to the Sudan."

"Yeah, but you're black. And you're American. Two things he wants to be," Mickie said, as Seth chuckled nervously, gauging my reaction. "And not the wipe-off MAC makeup black," Mickie continued, examining his fingertips which were soiled with residue from my foundation.

"He doesn't bite his tongue, does he, Seth?" I murmured to an uncomfortable Seth, who contorted his face.

"While we're up here yapping, multi-million-dollar deals are being signed with players with less talent, and less charisma than Eba Hamid. I need you to groom him so he can get a piece of that pie. Are you with me? She's with me, right, Seth, you fat fuck, yew." Seth rubbed my shoulder as if he was making three wishes to force the answer he wanted.

Slapping Seth's hand away, I smiled, answering Mickie, "Let's meet Eba." Cindy and Mindy squealed, clapping like appreciative whoopee cushions.

By the time we had reached the hallway outside the locker room, the player interviews were completed and the press was leaving, rushing out to meet their deadlines for the eleven p.m. sports roundup. Each time the locker room door swung open, the fumes of sweat, soiled jock straps, and donated cologne filtered into the hallway, along with the residue of canned answers given by the players.

"So, Jamal, how is the team going to prepare for the Lakers on Thursday?" the cub sports reporter asked.

"We just gonna come out and play at the level we capable of playing at—night in and night out."

"And what will you do defensively to hold off their full-court press?"

"Practice, then I'm just gonna go out and play at the level I'm capable of playing at—night in and night out."

"Let me see what's keeping Eba," Mickie said, leaving Seth and me leaning against the lime-green wall in the hallway as he entered the locker room. Various lanky basketball players, now dressed in bright-colored, three-piece zoot suits, exited the locker room, barely acknowledging Seth's greetings. "Great game, Steve."

Elbowing his ribs, I corrected him, "Um, I think that was Todd."

At which he would yell as Todd rounded a distant corner, "Great game, Todd."

"Seth, you're salivating," I teased.

"They are not my type, my dear. Not my type at all."

"Oh really," I quizzed. "What is your type?"

For the first time revealing a tiny bit of femininity, Seth dangled his pinky finger and said, "Oooooold money, honey. The kind that likes to grab me by the hair and slam me against the wall! Oooooolldd money, honey!"

Seth quickly regained his masculinity when Mickie opened the locker room door for Eba, who wore huge Bose headphones, extending the width of his face and dark sunglasses. As he walked, his head brushed against the hallway ceiling. Following Eba were four felonious-looking young men, all with their pants hanging off their asses exposing red striped boxer shorts, with red handkerchiefs tied around their tiny peanut heads at different angles, and limping like one leg was stepping in a ditch.

Emanating from Eba's beat box were the excruciating hip-hop screams of an anguished soul who pleaded for a bullet to relieve him of his suffering. Because of the deafening volume of the, er, music, Mickie pantomimed an introduction with Eba, explaining that I would be his media consultant. Eba, wearing aviator sunglasses, bobbed his head in rhythm with the soul sufferer and flashed a peace sign, then limped down the hallway surrounded by the four thugs as though they were balancing him, like a giant float, down Peachtree Street for Atlanta's Thanksgiving Day Parade.

Mickie scribbled Eba's address on the back of his business card and said, "Eba is having some people over. That will be a good time for youse two to tawk. See ya at the house." Mickie trotted down the hallway after his multi-million-dollar client, while I searched for Seth, who was congratulating yet another man on the game. "Seth, let's go," I huffed impatiently, pulling on his lapels. "That was the scorekeeper, dammit."

❖ ❖ ❖

My 2000 Honda seriously clashed with the rich ambiance of Heaven's Gate, a gated community for the filthy rich located in Forsyth County, north of Atlanta. From the security guard's facial expression as he surveyed my car, he probably thought that the Beverly Hillbillies were relocating—here—tonight. The tree-lined, winding entrance split off into smaller roads leading to tennis courts, man-made lakes, bike trails, and walking paths. Each luxurious home was set on multiple acres, nestled among majestic live oaks dripping with Spanish moss.

The circular drive, with a twenty-five-foot water fountain flowing in front of Eba's breathtaking mansion, contradicted the image of the limping, sullen basketball player and leeching entourage whom I had observed earlier. Seth apologized for not accompanying me. "My lover Basil is introducing me to his parents. Isn't that delicious?"

A petite, smiling girl with a short Afro answered the doorbell, gestured for me to remove my shoes and escorted me into the expansive, sunken living room, barely decorated except for the seventy-two-inch plasma flat-screen television mounted on the center wall. The petite, smiling girl returned shortly thereafter serving, what she called a *tabribana*, a fruit drink. Mickie, in his black socks, walked into the room, waving, but continued to bark into his cellular phone: "Phil! Phil, are you listening to me? I'm telling you dis kid is the perfect image for Nike. He'll bring you fucking Africa! Africa! When has any athlete since Olajuwon and Mutombo brought you Africa! Can he tawk? What kinda question is zat? Would I screw you ovah? Huh? Huh?" Mickie said, winking at me. "Okay, okay, get back to me," he concluded, disconnecting the line, and stuffing his iPhone into his jacket pocket.

The felonious entourage emerged from the rear of the home like oil from an oil tanker, followed by Eba, who had changed into a floor-length caftan. Opening the eight-foot-high front door for his retinue, Eba said, in a husky, Moses-parting-the-Red-Sea voice, "I'll git wit you muthafuckas later."

"Awright, man, awright," the entourage chimed, like a Wu Tang chorus, as they boarded their bicycles, chained to a bicycle rack outside, and pedaled down the circular driveway.

The petite girl stood on the edge of the living room, still smiling, glancing repeatedly from Eba to myself. Mickie filled in the silence. "Eba, you remember Iris."

"Of course, welcome to *nyumba*, my home. Please meet my Hanifa." Hanifa cautiously stepped toward me, then shook my hand with such conviction, as if finding a lost twenty-dollar bill between paychecks.

"Jina lako nani? Wewe nani," Hanifa asked sweetly.

"Hanifa wants to know your name," Eba said.

"Iris. My name is Iris," I answered, confounded by her warmth.

"*Unasemaje nafurahi kukona?* (How do you say it is nice to meet you?)" Hanifa asked Eba, tugging vigorously on his caftan.

"It is nice to meet you," Eba replied slowly.

Hanifa practiced, "It's nice to meet you. It's nice to meet you," under her breath as she shuffled through the dining room, to another expansive area beyond it.

"Dinner awaits, Iris Chapman." A gentleness emerged from Eba as comfortable as a bed during a badly needed sleep, though I intermittently expected the reappearance of the self-absorbed athlete.

The dining room, scented with the delicate fragrance of sandalwood, had dark beige carpet, with low, bare walnut tables and cushions decorated with ostrich feathers neatly stacked underneath. Following Eba's lead, I removed my heels and gingerly squatted, my skirt rising dangerously up around my hips. Mickie's iPhone rang; he checked the caller ID, then answered, rushing out of the room.

Hanifa reentered carrying a shiny copper *ebrig* (pitcher), and a copper basin. Beginning with Eba, she poured water over his bony, ashy hands, catching the water in the copper basin, then handed him a towel and placed a large cloth over his knees. She repeated the procedure with me, as I sat trying not to appear unnerved, not knowing whether she was going to bathe or baptize me.

"My sister is a good girl. Our parents were killed ten years ago, attacked by a band of tourists from Uganda because we wouldn't give them a ride on our camel, leaving me to take care of Hanifa. After that, we moved from sand dune to sand dune depending on which way the wind blew, selling sand sculptures for pennies in Khartoum," Eba said, patting Hanifa on the head.

"Omigod! You poor, poor thing," I exclaimed, clutching non-existent pearls to my chest. "Your names are so beautiful. What do they mean, pray tell?"

"*Eba* means acquirer, earner. *Hanifa* means true believer."

"How did you come to the attention of the NBA from the Sudan?" I asked, noticing his deeply engraved tribal scars fanning out like whiskers on both cheeks.

"Ah, one hot afternoon, at the market, no one would buy our sculptures. At that time, we had no water, no clothes and nothing to eat. Because I was concerned about her welfare, I gave Hanifa a piece a cloth to cover herself, because I had to leave her alone for long hours as I worked in the marketplace to sell enough rice, so that I could one day buy a cow, so my sister could have something to eat and maybe if God heard our prayers, send her to school. In America, you are blessed with free education, but in

Africa, the costs are very expensive, almost fifty cents a month. And no one can afford that. So that we would not starve to death, I was going to kill our camel that evening, after we played Fetch the Frisbee. I really didn't want to kill our camel. His name was Joe, and really good at catching the frisbee. I had gone to sharpen the knives, when a white man from America approached Hanifa, asking about our sculptures. Because she was so young, he asked her about her family.

"In Africa, we are normally very wary of approaching white men, asking questions. Either they want you to star in their documentary for the Travel Channel, they are some movie star, who wants to connect with their inner Tarzan or they try to smuggle our babies out of the country in their suitcases. Hanifa, being able to read the soul of people without melanin, told the white stranger about me, her seven-foot-tall very good-looking brother.

"Fortunately, God blessed us because the white man, with the kind blue eyes, was the trainer for the Atlanta Hawks. He was kind to smuggle us here in a large barrel and now here we are. Living large in America." Eba smiled broadly, exposing his reddish-blue gums and his white teeth extending far beyond his jaw line.

"That's a beautiful, heart-wrenching story," I said, wiping tears from my eyes. Seth wept, too, resting his bulbous head on my shoulder. "Have you ever thought of turning your life into a movie and getting a major star, someone who understands what it's like to be and live as an African? Someone like George Clooney, to portray you?"

"That's a brilliant idea, Iris," Seth said excitedly, tapping me on the shoulder, with me giving him a high-five. We realized that in just a few short seconds, that we were going to be movie producers.

"And that's what it is, a story," Eba said, as Hanifa carried a tray decorated with beaded doilies, with what Eba explained was *shorba* (soup). She handed Eba and me large spoons, then placed a stack of eight *kisra* (flat breads), a bowl of salad, and a platter of *maschi* (white rice) before us. Eba did not warn that the red stuff was *shata* (red hot spice) until after my face had turned purple. This sent Eba tumbling over with thunderous laughter.

After downing a liter of water, I found my strained voice to ask, "What do you mean, a story?"

"You see, Iris Chapman, you Americans love a white man rescues the uncivilized African, rags-to-riches story. If I were to tell you my parents were professors at the university, you would not have been so quick to waste your tears on me," Eba explained, sopping his *kisra* in the *shorba*, and licking his enormous dark lips.

"You mean, you concocted the whole thing," I said, a little perturbed.

"You must admit, Iris Chapman, I am right in my evaluation of you and your country." Eba smiled, gulping *tabrihana*.

"I think you've got it all wrong," I said, waving my spoon.

"Survey your social landscape, and you will see I am correct."

"Meaning?" I asked, placing my spoon on the table.

"Look at the black people who make the most money. All whom have fame; they are not your professors or scientists. Instead you uphold athletes and entertainers. So I surmised, if that's what America wants in order to pay me millions of dollars so I may take care of Hanifa, then that's what I'll give them."

Hanifa entered, pouring *guhwah* (coffee) from the *jebena* (coffee pot), placing a platter of *creme caramela* in the middle of the table, becoming aware of the rising tension. Concluding his phone call, Mickie flew back into the room and clumped down on the cushion between Eba and me, unaware of the previous conversation.

"So. Youse two. How we doing?"

Hanifa flipped through *Ebony* magazine, giggling behind her hand.

"No, no, no, no, no, look at it this way, if he wants to be a thug, that's his life. So what? He's paying you a lot of money. Amen," Tammy said, totaling up checks to deposit in the bank.

"If I ever do anything just for the money, it's time to hang up my press releases," I said, spinning my Rolodex, searching for talk show bookers. "Anyway, I faxed him his appearance schedule and we are going to meet again to discuss some interview ground rules."

"Does Mickie support your strategy?" Tammy asked, stuffing her rain hat and umbrella into her tote bag on this sunny morning.

"Mickie would support Hitler if it would increase his bank account. And at this point Eba isn't listening to him, so what does he have to lose?"

"What makes you think Eba will listen to you?"

"I told Eba, with Mickie sitting right there slurping the *creme caramela*, that unless he was willing to drop the thug act, then they could throw their money at someone else."

"Ooooooh! Amen! Go on wit your bad self, Iris! A-Men!" Tammy exclaimed.

"Hanifa was looking like she was about to be deported or something. And Eba kept staring at me, with these intense eyes he has. And I stared back at him in case he was about to jump kuh-razy. And when he saw that I was not going to look away, Eba burst out laughing, rattling the terrace windows. And of course, Mickie laughed because his money client was laughing, but I wasn't cracking a smile. Finally, Eba calmed his ass down, and said, 'You are strong. I like that. Like a lioness. I can tell by the shape of your ankles. I like that in a woman. Maybe you can show Hanifa how to be like you.' And then, Tammy, Hanifa abruptly stopped flipping through *Ebony* and gave me the look of death."

"Oh no she didn't," Tammy said.

"Oh, yes she did! Then Eba didn't ask, but told me: 'Iris Chapman. To be perfectly honest, since honesty is what you American women say you require, you need to know that Hanifa is not my sister. She is my wife. Now I have made another decision. And you will be my second wife.'"

By the time I finished updating Tammy, and she had left to pick up her breast milk pump marketing materials and attend a "Freedom from Fibroids" seminar, Eba had flooded my townhouse with deliveries of yellow roses.

[9]

"Let me put it in a language you can understand. Rolling your eyes and sucking your teeth is not attractive to anyone except a bunch of horny orangutans." Neither my directness, nor my tapping the right heel of my Giuseppe Zanotti slingback pumps, seemed to impress Lola Down-lo, real name Lola Rochelle Peters, as she dug into the pocket of her leather Pierotucci jacket for another piece of Wrigley's spearmint gum.

"And must you sound like a Tito Puente percussion section when you're chewing?"

"Who? Does he get down with Kanye?"

"Never mind."

It had been a distracting and infuriating day. My brother Victor phoned at the crack of dawn, alarmed that he'd discovered that Ms. Chickie was corresponding with prison inmates—and with one violent lifer, in particular.

"Well, what's wrong with Ms. Chickie making new friends?" I asked. "Probably a better caliber of people than those rooster murderers you hang around with."

"...that's the other thing I wanted to rap with you about, ya feel me?" Whenever Victor announces that he wants to *rap* with me, it's concerning a scam that he's been chewing on for quite a while or he wants me to part ways with my money. "Um, yeah, um, see Avril, the spirit of Ezruil and I have gone our separate ways, so I moved back to the house to, kind of, you know, help our parents take care of Ms. Chickie, since they're gettin' older themselves. And since a nursing home is out of the question, I thought the next best thing was to move back in, ya feel me?... By the way, how Tammy doin'?"

Now, ain't that a blip.

First of all, Rule 101 of black folks, is that we don't do nursing homes, because black folks don't have nursing home insurance. And the last thing black people are willing to do is to go into debt, when all you have to do is to conduct minor home renovations. That's why Uncle So and So or Auntie Nay Nay have been living in that back room, that black families will not freely admit to having, with the door locked since Truman was president.

If there is a God in the universe, a beneficent supreme being will enable me to reach through the telephone, and wrap all ten of my fingers around his free-loading, sociopathic throat. Barring that urgent, but noble request, a supreme being could lighten the bad karma in the Chapman gene pool, by electrocuting Victor the next time he touches the handle of my parents' refrigerator. Another ingenious idea would be of arranging for a j-o-b to show up at the front door, so he could die of a heart attack.

According to the Book of Victor, Ms. Chickie had pushed her lifetime friends over the edge of death's doorway and thus, needed another social outlet, other than threatening the new Bishop at Mt. Herman Tabernacle and Judgments of the Blessed and Highly Favored. Apparently, Ms. Chickie responded to a request for a pen pal in the *Miami Herald*. In a lovingly, but extortionist manner, Ms. Chickie coerced my father to drive her up *yonder*, to visit with her new special friend.

"Shadrack and I want to sit together for a spell and fellowship. And as a good Christian woman, that's what I gonna do and you're gonna help me, unless you want Lee Artist to know that you've been out in the front yard grinnin' like a coyote at that skank Janette, while she was hunched over in the middle of Napier Avenue with no draws on," Ms. Chickie shared, spitting out a mouthful of tobacco juice on the side of the front porch.

The Florida State Prison was located in the countryside of Bradford County, surrounded by a long, narrow highway and barbed wire fence. Police units, driven by muscular women with crewcuts, patrolled the twenty-acre complex in unmarked squad cars. The reception center was anything but welcoming, more like military barracks for shell-shocked soldiers returning from war. Stern, broad-chested corrections officers with skinny legs wore sunglasses, guarding the outside of the rusting, gray building. Located in a remote area of the prison, and away from the rectangle dormitories with tiny barred windows, the entrance was in close proximity to a brothel, a liquor store and a Greyhound bus depot. According to their website, prison officials considered these amenities as a support system to reduce recidivism and to enable discharged inmates to easily readjust to society.

Shadrack had completed his ninety-day stint in solitary confinement, for boiling feces, naming it chili and serving it to corrections officers, with a dash of oregano. When he was placed back into general population, Ms. Chickie was granted permission to be added to his visitor's list, as his spiritual adviser. Shadrack, who was a three-strikes-out felon, was serving a life sentence for stealing a crate of active GPS devices.

While my father waxed his Oldsmobile out in the steamy parking lot, Ms. Chickie hobbled, gripping her favorite Bible, through the visitor's entrance, and presented her social security card as her identification. She underwent three metal detectors, a body scan and a cavity search, which she didn't seem to mind. "Y'all sure you don't want to look again?" The corrections officers melted their harsh demeanors and chuckled with the elderly woman, who was clearly there to visit Shadrack to bring joy to his bleak life and provide him with desperately needed spiritual sustenance.

Ms. Chickie continued, hobbling around the corner, through the steel doors, which clanged shut behind her, and into the visiting room, where the waiting Shadrack stood, warmly greeting her. They shared a mutual, warm hug. Shadrack had adult acne, chapped cracked lips, wore fuzzy cornrows and was built like a compact refrigerator. His short-sleeved, orange prison-issued jumpsuit made him appear to be waiting for a flood. A grim reaper and a skull with cross bones were tattooed on his angular face, but he possessed a beautiful smile. Prison officials often remarked, "If Shadrack hadn't almost entombed himself by trying to steal quicksand, he might have had a lucrative career as a toothpaste spokesman."

The two souls stood facing one another; Shadrack and Ms. Chickie's eyes glistened, holding each other's hand. Both acknowledged the blessing it was to finally meet in person, and the void that writing letters could never fill.

Other visitors entered the reception area, some with screaming, prison-bound children, others, mostly women, visiting their boyfriends and trying to masturbate under the graffiti-ridden metal gray table. On the far side of the room, a corrections officer arrested a gothic-looking gentleman with a purple mohawk for trying to slip an aluminum-wrapped packet of cocaine into the anus of an inmate, without being conspicuous.

"Ms. Chapman, your letters have meant so much to me and remind me so much of a mother I never had. And I want to thank you for your friendship," Shadrack said sincerely.

"Oh, bless you, son. You're a blessing in my life, too," my grandmother replied.

"You probably remember that I didn't want to hear nothin' about no Bible, but your friendship has changed that, Ms. Chapman. I want to straighten out my life and get closer to God."

"Oh, praise, Jesus! That's so beautiful, son," Ms. Chickie replied distractingly, staring at the other inmates around the room, while sniffing and wiping her watery eyes.

"Since we only have a few more minutes, would you like to read a few Bible verses together?" Shadrack asked, reaching for the pocket-size Bible in the front pocket of his jumpsuit.

Tears fell down Ms. Chickie's cheeks. Using her handkerchief, she tried to wipe them away, but they were spritzing from her eyes too fast. "Is the spirit of the Lord moving your heart, Ms. Chapman?" Shadrack asked.

"Not exactly, baby. I'm just confused, that's all. Is y'all havin' a soap and water shortage? 'Cause that policy of just washing your stankin' ass every other day, ain't realistic." Shadrack was crestfallen. After playing find-the-homo all morning, he knew his ass and his armpits stank, but he thought washing up in a paper cup would suffice.

Wrong, Phone-a-Friend.

"Well, I guess you're doing the best you can, with the Lawd's help. But how come most of these boys in here got puny little pointy heads? That may be the reason they do bad things 'cause their brains is mashed together and they can't thank straight.

Look at that one. One part of his head is squashed higher than the other side. And Shadrack, see how your eyes don't blink at the same time? See what you just did? First, the left side blinked, then three seconds later, the right side. I bet if you get that looked in to, a gynecologist would tell you that both sides of your brains ain't coordinated. And then that'll solve all of your problems. Then maybe you can get out, after you get that shit off of your face, and enjoy the Florida sun like the rest of us blessed and highly favored people."

"Females? Sounds like something you'd dissect in biology lab."

9 minutes ago via Twitter

It should come as no surprise that Ms. Chickie was removed from Shadrack's visitor's list. And according to Victor, she refuses to discuss the matter.

My entire schedule was disrupted as I waited an hour and a half for Lo-Down, or whatever she calls herself, to arrive. Then I observed while she purposely irritated five newspaper reporters and one nervous brunette producer from *Entertainment Tonight.* Lola and I were to meet to discuss an imaging plan. Instead, Lola was focused on whether her rapper/producer/boyfriend Madd Dogg, a.k.a. Seymour Reynolds, was flirting with other women.

After introducing myself, I had explained to Lola that the mission of Image Control was to assist the client in putting their best foot forward. Even dropped the names of former clients I had worked with, but to no avail. Ms. Lola was not impressed. Rising out of her apathetic state, Lola hurled, "I ain't changing for noooobody." My weary eyes bore into this young girl, not much older than nineteen, trying to reconcile her delicate features, her brown saucer cup eyes, and adolescent frame with the fury that raged from within her.

When my impatient BlackBerry rang yet again, I moved into a corner of Next Level Records' conference room. Lola swung her legs on top of the mahogany table, lit a Newport cigarette, and clicked the remote, turning on the television to BET's *106 & Park*. My index finger pressed the antihelix on my right ear to drown out the angry railings of a one-hit wonder coming from the television, and I mentally kicked myself for tapping my foot to the hypnotic beat.

Lola increased the volume by remote. "Would you turn that down!?" My voice cracked from strain as a smiling voice greeted me from the other side of the cellular divide.

"I see you met Lola." Colby Woods' mellifluous voice was unmistakable and annoying at this perilous moment.

"Colby, this isn't going to work—"

"You're not afraid of a little attitude, are you?" Colby challenged as my fingertips dug into the beige wall, causing the blood in my fingers to escape to points unknown. Colby was backing me into a corner; he knew that, and he knew me. He knew I had garnered a hard-earned reputation for taking on difficult cases, transforming clients into refined human beings or at least individuals who upheld the corporate brand.

No one thought Gil Cooper, the cantankerous, long-winded, Emmy award-winning Atlanta television anchor, would ever be in danger of termination. But in a last-ditch effort, I had been retained by his thirty-something news director to try to pry Gil's Sears plaid jacket off him and drain the Texas oil slick from his head. The news director felt he owed his aging anchor one last hurrah, although the ratings indicated it was time for Gil to clean out his stall. But still I was intrigued, knowing his background. Gil Cooper was a Tuskegee Airman, flying in the 44th Fighter Bomber Squadron in the Philippines and the 7230th Support Squadron in Italy, returning with scrap metal lodged in his calf after his P-51C Mustang Red Tail took a hit from enemy fire. The limp he incurred didn't weaken his feisty spirit, nor dampen his resolve when American racism, at that time, ignored his achievements against Nazi imperialism.

Nearly a month passed before he would even meet with me, and then only by way of a gruff order from the network president barked into the telephone late one Friday afternoon. Dressed in a lavender Ralph Lauren suit dress, I arrived at Gil Cooper's office, located behind his flagship restaurant, Daddy Cooper's, one of many that he owned.

Gil Cooper was ready for me. Ready to go night fishing.

I asserted that I had a business meeting—albeit with Achilles, but that was my business—but to no avail. Cooper's wiry frame rounded his walnut desk, dressed in an olive mesh fishing vest that covered his red plaid shirt, black pants, tall black rubber boots, and a mossy oak–colored bonnie hat complete with a chin strap, and carrying a bucket and a five-foot-tall aluminum rod and reel. Before locking his office door, he reentered, grabbed a red rain poncho from the clothes tree, and tossed it at me.

"What the mosquitoes won't bite, the chill will," Gil Cooper cracked, teetering away, humming, sounding like Billy Eckstein. Only mildly comforted, I winced, and heel-clicked behind him to his dented Ford pick-up truck, parked next door in the municipal garage. The Indian garage attendants stole glances at my crotch as I hoisted myself into the truck through the driver's door, since the passenger-side door was…well, Gil Cooper never explained, other than to say, "Everything in life don't work, you know, take a look at that news director." He lurched the truck forward, the tires spinning on top of the gravel-strewn pavement. There's a mysterious relationship between old black men and their vehicles. Between my father and Mr. Cooper I haven't met any black man over sixty years old, who owns a working, fully operational automobile. And the more quirks, the more obsessively in love old black men are with their piece of junk. If you probe deeper, most old black men, have pet names for broken-down vehicles. Just ask Willie about *his* Lena. "You wouldn't catch me in a car built after 1974. Anythang made after that, it costs you an arm and a leg to fix. And why should I do that, when I can get a stud and a few washers out of my toolkit and have Lena runnin' good as new?"

En route to Lake Lanier, I finally reached a sullen Achilles, who was sitting in my living room and didn't appreciate being stood up. His accusatory tone was that my career must be more important than our relationship.

"This world that you're so devoted to, will it provide you with a family, your history, your connection to Allah?"

"I never said that I was trying to have a connect—; look, can we save this conversation for later—"

"If I'd known that you weren't gonna be home, I wouldn't have wasted my time comin' out here—."

"Isn't Tammy still there? Didn't she let you in?"

"Look, I don't appreciate you being deceptive about your whereabouts..."

If I wasn't mistaken, Achilles had just called me a liar, a noble characteristic that Ms. Chickie had taught me with aplomb. When the nice people from the Opa Locka Kingdom Hall would routinely try to visit early Saturday mornings, Ms. Chickie would run and scoot underneath her bed. "Tell those people that ain't nobody's home," she would instruct. Now explaining to a six-year-old that no one was home was practically impossible, when I knew that that wasn't actually true. When the doorbell had initially rung, my father peeked through the sheer curtains, then ran and squeezed himself into the hallway closet. Lee Artist, who was already in the bathroom, bolted the lock, and chained the door.

"Good morning, little girl," the smiling nice ladies with wavy hair yanked back in a French chignon would say. "We're Jehovah's Witnesses from the Kingdom Hall on Nineteenth Avenue. We would like your family to be amongst the four hundred-thousand saved souls to meet Jesus Christ when he returns for us. There's only room for four hundred-thousand saved souls and spaces are very limited. And there's quite a demand for this type of opportunity as you, as young as you are, can imagine. Is there someone that we can speak with to make sure your family's souls are saved, little girl? You do want that, now don't you? You don't want your family left behind with all the hell, fire, brimstone and damnation that'll be going on, now do you?"

Sprinting to Ms. Chickie's bedroom, I flattened myself on the floor to give her the urgent news. From under the bed, squashed against her dusty church hat and shoeboxes, an angry Ms. Chickie whispered, "Tell those people that it's too late, 'cause everybody in the house is dead. Now, stop lookin' stupid and go on and tell those people, that everybody just died."

Armed with a coherent message, I ran back to the door where the nice ladies baked on the front page in the Florida sun. "My grandma said that it's too late for us to be saved, 'caused everybody just died."

❖ ❖ ❖

Whispering, attempting to create some privacy, was futile, as Gil Cooper sat two feet away from me, gnawing on an unlit pipe and hanging on to my every word. "I promise, I'll come to your house when I've finished here," I replied to a display which read "Disconnected" on my BlackBerry screen.

The truck lights illuminated the tar road, which led to a grassy embankment where other fishermen had parked their trucks and recreational vehicles.

"Here, use these," Gil Cooper said, handing me knee-high black rubber boots.

"Mr. Cooper, I-I d-don't think that'll be necessary. Why don't I wait here in the truck until you come back." Yes, I sputtered those words, but Gil Cooper didn't hear me as he was already at least twenty feet away, replenishing his tackle box with bait. There were two choices: I could either follow Gil Cooper through a grassy marsh to an eerie swamp, er, lake and use the opportunity to persuade him here to upgrade his image; or I could sit here, in a dark, beat-up truck, avoiding the leers of a crusty, weather-beaten fisherman from the nearby trees.

"Omigod! Omigod!" I shrieked in a lyric soprano, scrambling to remove my right leg from my boot, as a tiny brown snake tried to slither down my leg. I caused such a ruckus, the snake fell onto the floor of the truck, and I took the floor pads and tossed them and the snake out of the window. The snake remained still in the mud, before moving to secrete itself under the wheel of a nearby Land Rover.

Hearing me screeching from the inside of his truck, Gil Cooper narrowed his eyes as he no doubt questioned his decision to bring an unmitigated fool on a fishing trip. "You alright there, Ida?" he said, rushing over, holding my flailing arm as I balanced, stumbling out the truck, yanking on the other boot.

"Oh sure, I'm fine. Just great. And it's Iris."

"That's good." Gil Cooper beamed. "Here's your bait, Ida," he continued, stuffing mucky night crawlers, squirming for freedom, into my trembling hands. My intestines somersaulted.

"And a flashlight."

"A flashlight?"

"Sure, how you expect to see in the dark?"

"But... but..."

But it was too late; too late for my date with Achilles; too late for my sheer lavender Anne Klein stockings; too late for a pearl earring that had disappeared under the torn leather car seat; too late to appeal to Gil Cooper, because he had lumbered away, whistling, "You're Not Gonna Make a Fool Out of Me."

When we reached the bemired bank of Lake Lanier, a bullfrog choir heralded our arrival. There were several bullfrogs, with voices resembling moaning, whining, announcing, and one deep Barry White bass. Gil Cooper stroked his precious rod as he set the tension to a maximum, holding the spool with his thumb, and pressing the release. He baited his line with two night crawlers, then loosened the tension as he waded into the dark water, while I kept a paranoid eye out for any serial killers lurking nearby. Crickets contributed their own opera, competitively trying to outshine the bullfrogs.

Trembling from the night chill, I tied the collar of the poncho snugly around my throat. A light haze hung over the water as winking porch lights from beachfront properties pierced the cloudless sky. I cleared my throat. It was time to address the business at hand so I could return home to drown my body in calamine lotion.

"Mr. Cooper. WGHC has retained me to offer any coaching you may need to enhance your on-air delivery, to improve your broadcast ratings." The aging media veteran was silent; his stubborn back faced me as his line hung out into the murky distance. The frog choir quieted, eavesdropping on my soliloquy.

"My firm, Image Control, assists clients in handling commercial copy, delivering effective speeches, connecting with an audience, et cetera."

Arching his arms over his head, Gil Cooper snapped the rod, propelling the line beyond my vision. The fishing line plunked a quiet echo against the water surface. "So, Mr. Cooper, I will be more than glad to coach…refine, or—"

"You can't know about something until you wade into it. See how it feels." I had been babbling so long, it was strange to hear a voice other than my own.

"Pardon?" I ventured, aiming the flashlight at Gil Cooper's narrow profile.

"You got to read the water, see how it feels. That way you know which direction the current and the tide are moving. You can't know that on a boat."

"Mr. Cooper. That's all very well and good, but—"

"How old are you? Twenty-five? Twenty-six?" Though I hadn't seen twenty-five since I turned thirty, I couldn't prevent a crimson blush from erupting across my face. Being in the boondocks was suddenly not so catastrophic. And since lying was beneath me, I merely became creative with my answer.

"Uh-huh."

"Come on out here, little girl. Let me talk to you," Gil Cooper said, extending his hand to me.

"I'm okay, Mr. Cooper," I managed as my hands tightly clutched the flashlight, my jaw rattling from the chill.

Gil Cooper moved backward, wading wide ripples in the shallow water until he reached me, then gently inched me in until the water peaked near the black rim of my rubber boots. If a snail moved two feet in three minutes, on this night, the snail would have beaten me. When he was sure I was steady, Gil Cooper pried away his hand, massaging it, restoring circulation, and then turned his attention back to his lifeless line.

"My nephews got shit for brains."

"Excuse me?" I said, distracted by cold water sloshing in my boots.

"Take after my wife's brother. I ain't never met nobody ain't good for nothing. Most people good for some things, but not them."

"Well, I'm sure they have their good—"

"They think I got old all these years being stupid."

"Oh, I'm—"

"There are ways of doing things."

"Sir?"

"Like I said, I didn't get old being stupid. See, I'm the one who interviewed Martin Luther King, when Martin wouldn't talk to anybody else in Atlanta. When the Kennedy brothers came to town, who did they call? Me, Gil Cooper. And I built Cooper's Restaurants 'cause a man can't rely on one source of income. Started selling sandwiches to factory workers out of the back of the pickup truck you rode here in."

"Well—"

"I hope and pray you never get to a point in a life where everyone is trying to put you out to pasture."

"Everyone?"

"My nephews don't want me to be the spokesman for Daddy Cooper's anymore. Now, WGCL management wants me out; they want me to change to suit their style. And maybe I would have a long time ago, but they didn't serve it up right, you know what I mean?"

"No, sir. I'm not sure I do."

"You wouldn't know how this water felt unless you were standing in it, am I right?" His intelligent eyes studied me closely. "So how does management expect me to like the idea of anything unless I was standing in it, feeling it? And how do my nephews expect me to feel just kicking me out?" When my face registered that I saw his point, he nodded, taking out a handkerchief, wiping his forehead.

"Neither one of them served the idea right to me. With respect. Respect that I have earned. So how am I supposed to like it?"

"That was only one of management's concerns," I began, moving into fragile territory.

"They want me off the evening news, huh? They want me to leave a program that I built."

"Mr. Cooper, have you considered producing a public affairs program? With your valuable history and relationship with historical figures, living, of course, you—"

"You think they will do a show like that? No one can deny my standards of journalism. But if they want me to alter what I do, then they will have to come to me with respect. These gray hairs have earned it. I deserve that respect."

A loud silence hung as Daddy Cooper and I fixed our gazes on his now-animated line.

"I deserve that respect," he repeated, yanking a two-foot trout out of the water, then tearing it from the hook.

Wincing from the splashing water, I chuckled. "Yes, you do, Mr. Cooper. Yes, you do."

Gil Cooper accepted my recommendations for his makeover, which transformed him into the revered media darling and executive producer of "Rallying Cry!" As for his nephews, they begged Gil Cooper to be their on-air spokesman, changing their restaurant motto to "At Cooper's, everybody gets respect."

"Iris, Lola is my next breakout star, but she's made enemies in the press," Colby loudly bragged, on the other end of my phone.

"She'd piss off the Pope," I whispered, flashing Lola an insincere smile.

"She just needs somebody to work with her."

"Yes, I have that all arranged. She'll be assigned to Tammy."

"You can't pass her off to a subordinate. Look, Iris, Lola has had a rough time. But hopefully she will change when she realizes people care about her."

"Care? In the music industry?" People imagine that the entertainment is one, long laugh track. Filled with care-free, creative geniuses, whose sole purpose is to illuminate the magic, and the beauty in the world; to put to music the longing of our souls. That would be a beautiful concept, if only it were true. Behind the scenes of the whimsical lyrics and heart-tugging music, is a world of heathens bent on self-destruction. When you think about it, music geniuses are mad, in their own peculiar way, and are strung out on cocaine or heroin, because some roadie handed them a needle and syringe on the tour bus from Portland. Then the hanger-oners who pledge their love and their loyalty are the same ones who cop the dope and alert the paparazzi that their beloved genius is high on blow and playing in traffic on Sunset Strip. Following the publicity script, the same people that bought the drug of choice, hire a publicist to craft an apology that admits no responsibility; apologies to the genius' mother who has been on the celebrity's gravy train, and of course, the fans, who frankly think you're funnier, a better actor, and a far better songwriter, when you're strung out of your mind.

"Lola may be a little standoffish at first but I assure you, she's just a baby."

Glancing over my shoulder, I saw the *baby* light another blunt. "Colby—"

"Thanks, Iris. I owe you one."

"You owe me more than one—!" Before I could launch into a muttering tirade, Colby was gone, leaving me alone with a drug-addicted, scowling post-adolescent who wants to be a star.

I leaned against the wall studying Lola. When she noticed I was eyeballing her, she merely gave me the finger and mouthed, "Fuck You!"

"Lola." There was no answer. "Lola." Her head turned, gazing at me with wide, cold, brown eyes. "Lola, let's set some ground rules." She turned back to the television. I snatched the remote control, snapping off the television.

"Lola, it's obvious that Colby has a great deal of confidence in your talent, otherwise he wouldn't have invested in you the way he has. Perhaps we got off on the wrong foot today. I'm tired; you're tired. Let's start again tomorrow. But for the future, when you and I are scheduled to work together, I expect you to be here on time. The next time you're late, don't bother showing up, *capiche*?"

Lola did not show up the next day. Nor the day after that. Colby's retainer check remained in the bottom of the desk drawer; un-cashed. Returning it now would create another debate I wasn't ready for. Let Lola tell Colby she was irresponsible. Not that I am unable to stand my ground, but Colby needed to respect my policies.

Late one evening a few days later, Achilles appeared at the townhouse—appeared as in showed up, which he never does, as he learned early on that I am liable to be entertaining a client, or drumming up business for new ones. After finally returning my telephone calls, Achilles informed me he had been out of town attending an athletic training conference at Bethune-Cookman College.

From my office, I could hear his voice as his bass rose over Tammy's confidential tone. She didn't believe in raising her voice, so usually I was the one who ended up screaming to get her attention. Their voices rose and threaded, cascading up, then down, finally punctuated by laughter. When I heard him turn the corner and walk back toward my office, I quickly reapplied my red lipstick.

Tammy was an associate and close friend, but what encouraged their conversations in my absence, though they both claimed to dislike each other, was always a mystery.

"Who loves you, baby?" Achilles said, peeking around the corner into my office.

"Um. Telly Savalas?"

Achilles chuckled, swooping me up into his thick, muscular arms, dotting my neck with slow kisses.

"Telly Savalas, huh? I'll give you some Telly Savalas," he said, pushing his pelvis into mine, conveying a warm sensation.

"Hey. Hey, slow your roll." I was still annoyed by Achilles' decision that we remain celibate. "How was the conference?" I asked, using my propped-up arm to prevent him from sprawling me out on my own desk, though I had been there before.

"It was alright," he answered bluntly, avoiding my eyes.

"Just alright?"

"They didn't teach me anything I didn't know. I don't even know why I go to them things."

"Hmph, according to you, you go so the Wolverines can reach the conference finals. At least that's what you say."

Achilles' eyes calmed down, leveling so they could return my gaze. "Lord knows, I don't feel like talking about no basketball, as fine as you look." Achilles—though ridiculously handsome, with perfect bow legs, washboard stomach, rich chocolate skin, a perfect work of African art—could be self-centered, a religious hypocrite and super critical at times and I knew that. But somehow, when his curvaceous, ample lips got hold of mine, all of that was forgiven.

"Give me about an hour; I'm polishing this proposal for a new client." The words were not even out of my mouth before he frowned in disagreement, his eyebrows furrowing.

"When are you going to give *me* time? I'm not used to playing second fiddle, Iris." Achilles rammed his hands into his pockets.

There was a time I would have pleaded my case, begged for forgiveness, even though I had done nothing wrong.

"What am I supposed to do? Just drop everything because you've come back a day early? You didn't return my phone calls, remember? You weren't trying to get with me—remember?"

"I-I didn't know what I was saying. I need you, need to be with you, baby."

Trying to lighten the moment, I said, "Look, go home. As soon as I finish, I'll be there—with a few surprises." Achilles raised a bushy eyebrow and clucked his tongue.

"Surprises?"

"Surprises." I smiled, rising, wrapping my arms around his neck.

"I like your surprises."

"Uh-huh, I know you do," I murmured, kissing his forehead, bonding with his ears, his erogenous zones. The intercom signaled another interruption. I was glad I had gotten a French manicure that afternoon as I pressed the talk button.

"Tammy?"

"Colby Woods is on line one. I told him you were in a meeting, but he said it was important."

"Thanks. Tell him to hold on. Sorry, honey," I said, returning to Achilles, rubbing the sides of his shoulders. "But this won't take long, then I'll finish the proposal and see you later with those surprises."

Achilles' eyes became dark and serious again. Nodding, he said, "Okay, do what you have to do. But don't be too long. There's so much I want to make up to you."

What are you doing?

...something has got to give...the network proposal, Achilles.

1 second ago via Twitter

"I'll be there soon," I replied, as he spun around and walked back down the hallway. Pausing, clearing my thoughts, readying myself for Colby, I remembered my tear-stained pillow, when the man I loved had pushed me away. Hoping that Achilles and I were only experiencing a rough patch, I froze, listening to Tammy's cackle as Achilles tickled her funny bone.

"Colby. Tammy said it was important," I said, sounding official.

"Hey, Iris, I need to see you."

"Okay, now tomo—"

"Tonight, Iris. Tonight." Colby heard my hesitation. "Come on, you owe me! I'm calling in all favors."

Everyone used to call Colby—a Louisiana native—"Country" because of his bayou drawl. We would always joke, asking him, "So where's your banjo?" because of the stone-washed overalls he always wore. Colby knew music, though often asserting that jazz was America's classical music. Instead of overdosing on funk and rhythm and blues, Colby listened to everything from Bach to B.B. King. His program on WFMU made it one of the top-rated college stations in the South. And Colby was my inept, cheap lover.

I kept that information under wraps until we reached the middle of junior year. Initially, he was just a friend, meaning he wasn't "getting any." He was mainly an accomplice during our cafeteria raids. But when one of our raids yielded real food that we could actually digest and became a disciplinary action spearheaded by the dean, and Colby took the punishment, denying my involvement, I knew then, that he was more than a friend.

The news that we were a couple came out when his blabbermouth roommate, who was supposed to be at the library, caught Colby and me playing naked Garden of Eden.

But as our senior year ended, when talk of the future dominated, Colby and I knew that marriage wasn't our next move. However, we loved each other for being there through the loss of our virginity, all-night study sessions, and his crossing the burning sands into Alpha Phi Alpha fraternity. We never broke up. We just stopped having sex. I moved on. And readied my thighs for the graduating valedictorian who was headed for West Point. So much for loyalty and foresight. Years later, he was seen at a Quincy soup kitchen. And Colby had signed a letter of intent to acquire NextLevel Records.

At the Black Entertainment Lawyers Symposium, a tap on the shoulder returned the blast from the past. "Hey, Eve," a familiar voice said. Of course, I thought this was clearly a case of mistaken identity until I whirled around and saw Colby. We made sincere promises to stay in touch and have lunch, but none of that transpired until my phone rang, with Colby on the line wanting to do business.

"A return to the days of Motown. That's what NextLevel is about. Remember when every Motown artist knew how to walk, speak, dance, greet the public? Well, that's what I want to do here. And I need your help." And his first client was Lola.

"Okay, where?" I said caving in.

"Hosea's Chicken and Waffles. Forty-five minutes."

Colby loves these kinds of joints. Close to the streets. In the community. Close to the pulse where he could discover the next music phenomenon. And cheap. Colby likes to quote Pablo Picasso, "I'd like to live like a poor man with lots of money." Cheap men always justify their cheapness by quoting people they've never met. And Colby's cheapness reminded me of my father, Willie.

"You kids throw some clothes on. Let's go for a ride." Victor and me would be hanging out with our friends in our front yard, playing Spin the Bottle or some other neurological advancing activity that child prodigies play when they are not accepting the Nobel Peace Prize. By saying, 'Throw some clothes on,' you would think we were prancing buck naked around Napier Avenue. What Willie inferred was that, 'we're going to probably cross paths with some white people. And I don't want them thinking that I raised a couple of pickaninnies. So run in the house, wash your face, iron your clothes and let's take a ride over yonder."

"Where we going, Daddy?" I'd squealed, with promises of a butter almond ice cream sundae, a brand-new pair of black patent leather shoes or something sparkly dancing in my head. Our friends dripped with palpable envy, as they wished their dad, their mother's new lover, or even a psychotic killer, would take them on a ride to buy something shiny. But that day and that moment, Victor and I were the lucky-lucky kids. Drunk with the anticipation of a surprise grand adventure to a destination we had seen on television, we jumped in our dad's Oldsmobile, like trained hamsters in a cage, eager for barley. What added to the excitement was the fact that my father had vacuumed the inside of the Oldsmobile, which he never did, unless Willie planned to go somewhere truly special. Willie even permitted Victor and me to hang our heads out of the car window, and let wind blow on our faces, as we merged onto 95 North from the Palmetto Expressway, headed toward Fort Lauderdale, the destination which bestows magnificent trinkets on children. Lee Artist would have had a coronary if she knew her husband had her children out gallivanting with wind blowing on their faces.

Stifling the urge to do a triple jump somersault in the middle of B.J.'s parking lot, I instead did the "lucky-lucky" dance behind my father's long strides. Entering the football field-sized warehouse, my eyes were big as saucers, thrilled with the huge portions of everything I loved, touching everything I saw.

Willie, who clearly wanted to show Victor and me a good time, even let us have samples of wiener sausages with saltine crackers and anchovies served from a giant, plastic hot dog by a red-headed lady with a peg leg, dressed in a Seminole Indian outfit. Following my father up and down aisle one, then aisle two, we paused at all that, for me, was holy, like the enclosed ten-foot long trampoline, the Schwinn twenty-one speed bike, and the Super Water Soaker CPS 200 squirt gun. My father asked detailed questions of the salesperson: "You think this trampoline would be a good idea for my kids?" "What are the safety guidelines and the warranty? Sure wouldn't want my kids to get hurt. Hey, partner, you sure are a mighty good salesman. You could sell a drowning man a glass of water." My father would chuckle, patting his wallet. And when the salesperson had answered his questions to his and my satisfaction, Willie would move on to the Pelican Monaco paddle boat, with me still doing the lucky-lucky dance behind him. "Now the women that I live with ain't high on watercraft and we have a small circular driveway in the front of the house, but would it be okay to store this here paddle boat in our backyard?" Again, the next salesperson would answer Willie's questions to his and my satisfaction. "You sure are a good salesperson. You could sell sand to a desert," Willie complimented, patting his wallet.

Customers with rapturous gazes on their faces waited in the cashier lines, which snaked around the front of the store. I relished joining them with a shopping basket full of treasures. The sheer urgency of my wanting to be just like them grew, causing me to breathe in short spurts. After two hours of my touching all that I loved, and listening to my father interrogate every salesperson, now I needed my father to, at the very least, get a giant shopping basket so we could load it up with something. Anything. I had grown desperate, willing to settle for five hundred rolls of two-ply toilet paper, one hundred rotisserie chickens and a giant box of Skittles. There was no way that I could return to our neighborhood without something to prove to my jealous friends that I was the lucky-lucky girl.

In my mind, Willie and I had a shared fantasy to buy me anything my insatiable heart could want and that he would be delighted to do it, but that was not to be. By aisle seventy-two, it began to dawn on me that, even though my father kept patting his wallet, he had never once reached into his pocket and taken it out. The fact that he was merely window shopping was, to me, tantamount to child torture and the ultimate betrayal. My lucky-lucky dance came to a slow painful end. With the acceptance of this reality, Victor and I groaned our disapproval, as we sulked empty-handed out of the warehouse, through the crowded parking lot of happy-go-lucky shoppers, piled with goodies in their shopping baskets to the Oldsmobile, which in my mind stuck out its tongue singing, "You're not so lucky..you're not so lucky."

Reacting maturely, I flung my body onto the back seat and repeatedly slammed the back of my head against the headrest, until I was interrupted by the delighted squeal of a little girl, around my same age. In the gray Dodge Caravan parked next to us, this little girl was doing my lucky-lucky dance. Her handsome, philanthropic dad had his wallet open, with cash peeking through his hand, promising, "Contessa, my dear precious child, today, we're gonna buy you an enclosed trampoline and a Super Water Soaker CPS 200! And by doing so, you'll see that I am expressing a father's ultimate love."

On the drive back to Opa Locka, my father happened to notice the continuous sighing and flowing snot, emanating from the back seat, sounding as if Victor and I had suddenly become asthmatic. Being the ever empathetic humanitarian, Willie scolded, "You kids ain't got nothin' to be pokin' your lips out about. Here I am tryin' to be nice, makin' a day out of it, having fun. Shoot, there're kids in Africa that would have jumped at the chance to walk through the aisles of B.J.'s; touching stuff, and looking at food that they'll never eat. Nosireeee, you wouldn't have seen their lips poked out. You kids don't appreciate nothin'! That'll be the last time I try to do something nice. Since y'all don't know how to act, you can forget about going on a tour of Parkside Memorial Cemetery."

Victor and I were humbled. Prior to our father's one-thousandth reminder that there were children in Africa, who would have jumped at the chance to stare at food that they would never eat, provided us with an entirely enlightening perspective, which, thanks to Willie's life instruction, my brother and I had never considered.

"Now if y'all want something to drink, there's a canteen of water in the glove compartment."

Hosea's contained ten red booths with silver railings that lined the far wall. In the middle of the room were small, round cafe tables. On the walls were photos of entertainers and politicians from Harlem. Our waitress, a thin, pregnant woman in her late forties, hobbling on a bad bunion in run-over flip-flop heels, and exhausted from a hectic dinner hour, gruffly took our order.

"They treat you like shit, but the food is slammin'," Colby drawled, looking forward to the all-you-can-eat Hosea special consisting of baked chicken smothered in bell peppers, onions, herbs, and spices with butter-drenched waffles. From the way a stocky man at a nearby table panted over his own Hosea special, spread out over three plates, the man must have had a tapeworm.

The thought of chicken and waffles on the same plate struck me as odd, and I'm not an odd eater, but I decided to walk on the wild side, ordering just one chicken breast and one waffle. An hour later, I had pilfered another succulent piece of chicken and a delicious waffle off Colby's plate, having depleted mine. I was stuffed and Colby still had not revealed to me what was so urgent.

"Hmmm, I like your hair like that. Finally gave up the scruffy look, huh?" A wall of bricks fell around me as I weighed whether his comment was a compliment or a criticism.

"What is so important, Colby?"

"Lola. Lola is important." He smacked his lips.

"How's that?" I navigated my tongue to remove a food particle out of my wisdom tooth.

"Look around you. This is where Lola comes from." Colby handed me a toothpick.

"Colby, I fulfilled my responsibility. I made the appointments. She didn't keep them. What else am I supposed to do?"

"All her life, people have been telling her she's nothing. Only now, since they smell she's gonna bring in some loot, do they pay any attention to her." I leaned back in my chair, absorbing what Colby was saying, wondering what the fuck he meant by "scruffy."

"So you want me to do what?"

"Remember when we were at FAMU, those late nights we'd talk about helping our communities, giving back to our people."

"So you want me to be like a big sister to her?"

Colby nodded enthusiastically. "Now you're getting it! Look, she is going to test you, see how long you'll stay around, see if you're like all the others."

"But what about her image work? Oh, I still have your check, you know."

Colby smiled. "You know I know where my money is." Then he became serious again. "As far as NextLevel Records is concerned her image is a priority. But her becoming a star don't mean nothing unless she's got her head together."

"And we can't have any more incidents like the other night at Cisco's."

"Agreed."

Colby and I sat in our booths, staring out the window, watching police cars speed by. Vagrants swarmed passersby, hawking stolen dresses for ten dollars. Our waitress, now behind the counter, turned up the volume on the television, signaling the eleven o'clock news.

"Eleven o'clock? It's eleven o'clock?" I gasped, sliding out of the booth. "I'll call you tomorrow so we can schedule a meeting with Lola."

"Iris," Colby said calmly, as I inspected my clothes for grease or syrup stains.

"And sleep on some strategies, okay?"

"Iris."

"Yes, Colby?"

"Your part is five-sixty; seven dollars including tax and tip."

Achilles was not answering his telephone. Bastard. He had caller ID. He knew it was me. He was expecting me. I stepped on the gas pedal, my engine knocking, doing seventy miles per hour on 20 West, vibing with WVEE's Vernon Blackwell doing his "Quiet Storm" show and thinking about Lola, her sadness, and wanting desperately to slap some sense into her.

Vernon's broadcast was interrupted by breaking news: "This just in. Atlanta rapper Lola Down-lo has been arrested. The eighteen-year-old woman is alleged to have purchased narcotics from an undercover officer. In other news—"

Finding an emergency median, I swerved to a stop. And then phoned a priest.

[10]

The knocking in the engine was not a symptom, but the final deathblow to my beloved Honda. Maintenance has never been one of my strong suits; gas is all I think about until, well, the knocking starts, the steering wheel shudders, and next thing you know, I am in search of another automobile.

It would make sense to have AAA on speed dial; due to the amount of service I have needed. I know many of the tow truck drivers so well, they send me get well cards if they have not been paged in a given month. Stanley, the driver assigned to the Greenbriar Mall region, rattled up in his bright red Autocar Tri-Axle heavy-duty tow truck, greeting me with his usual I-told-you-sos.

"Ms. Chapman, how many times do I have to tell you to put oil in the engine? You could have had another year or two with this car, but there ya go, destroying a perfectly fine vehicle."

"Thanks for the advice, Stanley," I said, climbing into his truck as he loaded my dead Honda. I phoned Achilles, asking him to meet me at the service station. In Stanley's world, ignoring the majestic beauty of an automobile is tantamount to murder. Any automobile. And the punishment for that, I have learned, is having to listen to Stanley gush over his tow truck. Don't get me wrong, everyone should take pride in their work, but the cash-paying public does not need to be burdened with the intimacies of your tricks and trade.

Once, I made the grave mistake of asking to borrow a pencil

from an overly helpful librarian. Instead of handing me the sharpened No. 2 instrument, allowing me to finish the letter of revenge I was composing to an ex-boyfriend, this public servant said, lowering her reading glasses to the bridge of her nose, "You know, the pencil is a national treasure. To leave home without one is unforgivable. If folks like you knew the effort that goes into making a pencil, you wouldn't have such a devil-may-care attitude. The pencil that you're holding in your grubby hand was made from a block of cedar, then cut into slats. The slats were then stained, and grooves were cut into one surface. Prepared leads were placed into the grooves and a second slat was placed on top and bonded with the first. This pencil sandwich was passed through a milling process to separate the individual pencils. The pencil was painted and finished, a ferrule crimped onto the end, and finally, an eraser crimped into the ferrule. Now, maybe you will think twice before leaving the house without your own writing instrument, won't you, missy?"

Stanley, the tow truck driver, acted as though I was the first customer he'd had since the new moon, as he was yapping more than usual about his pride and joy: "Named her Bertha. Yes, indeedy, Bertha, the tow truck."

My mistake had been asking, "How are you, Stanley?"

"This baby, she's got 11,000 original miles. Last time I towed you, she had 10,500. I added a forty-five-ton Challenger boom and my brother-in-law sold me an extra drag line winch; the sonabitch, he shoulda gave it to me for nuthin', all the business I have steered his way. Did you check out the forty-eight thousand rears and the heavy-duty front axle? Bet you didn't see the Cummins diesel, didja? Yep, this baby is like new inside and out. 'Cause I keep her inside a heated garage year round. My old lady thinks I treat Bertha better than her. And you know what? She's damn right. Hell, when she's worth two hundred sixty grand, I'll pay her more attention, too."

Lying in bed next to Achilles felt comforting, alive, and was just what I needed. I felt used up and needed healing. Needed him. Instead of being critical, he understood, saying, "My boy got a dealership. He'll give you a deal on a rental."

But when my hand traveled over his washboard abdomen, coming to rest between his legs, he rolled over, locking the silk sheets around him, saying, "I'll call him in the morning about the car."

"What do you want done with all of these flowers? It looks like a greenhouse in here," Tammy exclaimed from behind a vase of white roses when I returned to the townhouse later that morning. "And Colby has been calling—something about Lola getting arrested? And we need to talk, Iris. I want to talk to you about something."

Without acknowledging her, I entered the kitchen, tossing my rental car keys on the counter, pouring a glass of orange juice. "What's the matter?" Tammy asked, quietly following behind me.

"Nothing."

"You haven't been this down, since…since I don't know when. And look at you. Your hair. Your perm is growing out." Tammy's brown eyes searched my poked-out face for a glimmer of my old self. She seemed altered until I realized she was not wearing makeup, and was dressed in a long, black skirt. None of the usual black eyeliner to outline her lips, the silver lip gloss or her sideburns were present. For the first time, I noticed how radiant, how innocent she looked without cosmetics.

Instead of telling her this, I merely grumbled, "Arrrrrrgggg," trudging up the stairs in low spirits, unable to shake the rejection I'd felt from Achilles and not knowing what to do about it. Achilles left for work earlier than usual. And as I later drove away from his house that morning, I remained stunned that the man who had courted, pursued, and made love to me had changed the game plan without compromise.

Dialing Colby, I ran hot water in the shower and sat on the toilet seat, head in hands, finding the voice to pretend that all was well with me. "Iris Chapman handles her business," the Atlanta *Daily World* had written in their feature on Image Control.

"Eba Hamid signs with starmaker Iris Chapman," the *Atlanta Constitution* profiled. The Georgia Black Chamber of Commerce award committee said I was "a mover and a shaker," destined to create vistas of opportunity in the new millennium.

Tweeted that.

If that was so, that I was able to make an impact in the lives of so many people, answer the call to resolve any dilemma, then why did my closest relationship feel so alien, leaving me intimidated, vulnerable?

"Colby, it's Iris."

"Yeah, you heard about Lola?"

"How is she?"

"I bailed her out. And sent her ass home."

"Where's home?"

"I put her on a plane to New York to stay at her mom's crib. With distance from all of this bullshit, maybe she'll finally get back into the studio."

"Colby, clients get the best results when they know they need the help. And nothing you have told me indicates that Lola is reaching out," I said, testing the water temperature under the faucet.

"You can have the kind of influence on her that will make her want to change."

"Why are you so sure?"

"I've made millions from gut instinct. Except for that Peaches & Herb reunion concert, I haven't been wrong."

"Okay, I'll see her, 'cause you won't quit nagging me if I don't."

"Solid. What you got planned tonight?"

"National Organization of Black Mayors is having an art auction. You should go, too, Colby."

"Oh yeah? Why?"

"When these mayors want your music banned from their cities, you can say you've been introduced."

"Funny."

"When Lola gets back from New York next week. In the studio, recording, I'll definitely reach out to her."

When I walked into Sports Zone in Buckhead, I fully expected Eba to be wearing one of his earth-toned tailored suits designed from the Steve Harvey collection. Instead, as he signed autographs at the bar surrounded by a crowd of giddy white teenagers, he was wearing a bright yellow, wrinkled, cotton suit, looking like a giant banana. Cotton. As in Old Man River cotton.

Shooing away the teenagers, I asked Eba, "Why didn't you wear one of the suits that I rushed to have designed for you?"

"Everyone! It is Iris Chapman," Eba said to his subjects. "She has consented to be my wife!"

The giddy teenagers said, “Wow, gee, super.”

Then I thundered, “Hold up, Eba, slow your roll!”

“You didn’t like your flowers?” he said sadly.

“They’re very nice, but that’s not the point.”

“Ah! You do like them.” Eba laughed loudly. “This pleases me a great deal.”

The teenagers, sensing an opening, renewed their requests for autographs. A producer, whom I had met at a Metro Journalists award dinner, interrupted. “Iris, is Eba ready?”

“Hi! Ready to go,” I said, giving him the thumbs-up, when in reality, I wanted to strip that yellow traffic signal off of Eba. And Eba wanted me to strip him, too.

Hanifa no longer smiled when she greeted me. She sat with her knees drawn to her chest under one of the Kentia indoor palm trees that littered their mansion.

“Have I offended Hanifa?” I asked, after she slammed a glass of ice water down on the coffee table in front of me during a consultation.

“Nonsense. Hanifa will soon understand that my having a worldly second wife will be better for her. Hanifa is better suited to bear my children, while you will run my empire.”

Breaking all the rules that say to be pleasant toward a client, I blurted, “Eba, are you out of your cockamamie sand-particled mind?”

“Ah, a fiery disposition is a rare commodity in Sudanese women, which makes you all the more suitable.”

“The children’s ward at Grady Hospital appreciates the flowers I donated in your name. The gesture, whether you know it or not, upped your public standing, but that is all that it did, because you and I will never, n-e-v-a-h, become involved romantically. Am I making myself clear?"

"Very well," Eba said softly, returning his attention to the notes I had made of his interview with the *Atlanta Journal-Constitution*. That was easy. Far too easy.

"Now, Iris Chapman," he continued, refusing to call me plain old Iris, "you say here that I must look a reporter in the eye during the interview. That is unreasonable."

"How is that?"

"In my culture, it is considered a marriage proposal to stare into the eyes of another." The night of our first meeting flooded back to me, when Eba stared into my face before announcing I was to be his second wife.

"With all due respect to your culture, you are now in America. What goes on in the Sudan, thank God, does not go on here."

"Very well, Iris Chapman; I understand."

"You did well at the Hawks Charity Golf Tournament. Didn't even frighten the Japanese corporate sponsors."

"Yes, Mickie negotiated a very good deal with Nike."

"To wear their sneakers?"

"No, golf shoes. They want to build golf courses in the Sudan."

"Well, you definitely have the land for it," I said, giving the evil eye to an approaching teenager. "You've done really well making yourself marketable, Eba, which was our objective. So your ESPN interview tomorrow will be my last consult." Eba had mastered his destruction of the English language from "Yo! MTV Raps," but gradually he had returned to the properly educated Sudanese-American man that he had been in Khartoum.

"That is very disappointing, Iris Chapman." Not knowing whether Eba was disappointed or being polite, I smiled, handing him the proposed interview talking points.

❖ ❖ ❖

"Good evening, everybody, and welcome to *Up Close*! I'm your host, Gary Miller, and tonight, in studio, we welcome first-round draft pick and starting center with the Atlanta Hawks, Eba Hamid. Welcome!"

The television lights softened Eba's yellow suit, making it appear more manila, giving his already jet black complexion a richer, less ashen quality. A brunette production assistant handed me a cup of black coffee as I relaxed, leaning against the wall behind one of three cameras, proudly watching my soon-to-be ex-client reveal my handiwork. Handling Eba had been a coup, and had brought in referrals of other professional athletes, including the center from the Los Angeles Lakers.

"So, Eba, how does America differ from the Sudan?" Gary asked, his eyelashes blinking incessantly.

"You have such tall buildings." The studio was filled with smiling people who wanted his autograph, to shake his hand, to touch him. Cleaned up, Eba was indeed charismatic. Even I hung on to his every word, laughing at his unfunny jokes.

"Moving to America must still be quite a culture shock. With your mansion and all."

Eba stared past the studio cameras and into my eyes, and grabbed his crotch. "Man, niggas be posted at my crib all night long, smoking like Cheech and Chong. And I always bounce with my heat or chrome. Strapped right here, like a beeper on my hip, ready to flip when the heat is on!"

By the time the studio technicians finally scraped me out from under camera one, Mickie Herman had canceled our contract and withdrawn his referrals, telling them that I was more hype than substance, clearly unable to deliver. Seth was on his honeymoon with Basil. Eba Hamid, who could have rallied to my defense, used the opportunity to have the last word, leaving a cryptic message on my voicemail. "Only Eba walks away. Only Eba."

I plowed through the rest of that overcast day, completing errands with tears collected behind my mascara-lashed eyes, a wave of grief sweeping me, causing my bottom lip to quiver. I wanted, needed to weep. Loudly. The kind of bawling where you display all of your cavities. But the traffic on Highland Avenue was highly opposed, so I drove blindly along Peachtree Road, searching for solace, summoning up a game face to put on for tonight's dinner. Achilles had agreed to pick up his Jhane Barnes tuxedo and my Carolina Herrera orange silk taffeta duster with sequins and an orange crème halter mini dress, purchased during a shopping spree in New York last year.

Mr. Whitaker paused while watering his lawn, watching as I walked up the steps to the townhouse. Sensing that I wasn't sashaying with my usual snap, crackle, and pop, he held his usual appraisal and refocused on a forty-something widow who had just moved across the street. Her determination to gain the attention of the men on the block was comical; reminding me of Ms. Janette in Opa Locka, but had her beat on an entirely different level. My new neighbor strolled up and down the block half-dressed in cut-off shorts and a sheer halter-top, pretending to pick up trash and pull weeds. When the Georgia Power utility truck, filled with a crew of horny electrical workers rumbled onto the block, she made sure she bent over in that high-ass, kangaroo-gathering-for-berries type of way. After the workers had sufficiently leered, she would resume the posture of a normal homo sapien, satisfying whatever low-feminine-esteem kick she was on.

❖ ❖ ❖

Tammy left my messages on the desk with a note that she would phone me Saturday morning, which was unusual as Tammy spent most weekends with her new boyfriend, a brother, having decided to give black men another chance.

A water glass had been left on the kitchen counter, which indicated that Achilles had been here, probably to drop off my dress, and would return to pick me up at eight as we had discussed. It would be good to have a night on the town, hanging with the black bourgeoisie, who only let their rhythm hang out when George Clinton's "Flashlight" propelled everyone out of their pretentiousness. That song would even have the Polish waiters tapping their feet. Achilles and I had not been out since the Wolverines won their division, and that was only for pizza and soda with the team.

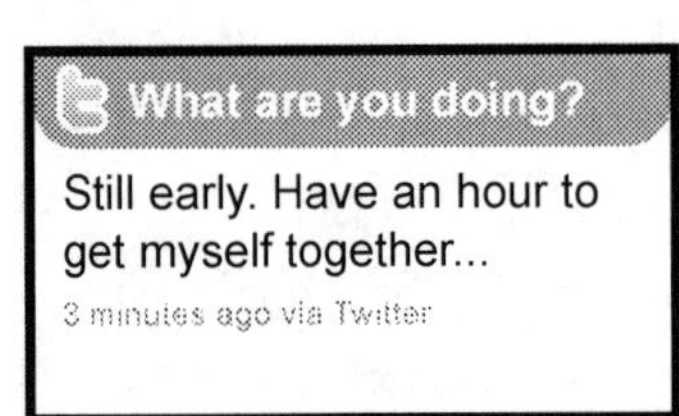

I climbed the stairs, and upon entering my bedroom, I felt as if a sword had been driven through me.

There, strewn about the room, on the bed, on the floor, was my makeup, MAC loose powder emptied out onto the carpet and Iman lipsticks broken and smashed. And my dress. My exquisite dress had been cut into a thousand tiny pieces. In the middle of my bed, black scissors anchored a handwritten note:

"O, Children of Adam! We have indeed sent down to you clothing to cover your shame and clothing for beauty and clothing that guards against evil, that is the best. These are the communications of Allah that they be mindful."

❖ ❖ ❖

Dried tear stains, creating a white ash, haunted my face. I could feel it as I swooped past Achilles' house like an LAPD SWAT team and saw his empty parking space, past his health club, past any place I thought he could be. I slowed in front of the mosque. Gallant bow-tied brothers courteously greeted humble, beautiful sisters. Continued to drive.

More tears. Flipping off other drivers. Called Tammy. No answer. Shit. Screeching brakes. More tears. More dried tear stains. Red eyes turning into slits. Eight-thirty p.m. Attendees of the dinner dance were entering the Atlanta Marriott now. All smiles. Mayor Kasim Reed, elegant, charming, greeting attendees.

Using my key to unlock Achilles' front door, I decided to wait as long as it took for him to get home. Dangling me on a string, wanting me one day, then hiding behind Islam the next, destroying my dress... I fantasized, re-creating the scene in *Waiting to Exhale* when Angela Bassett destroys her husband's wardrobe. Her husband was fucking around. Achilles fucked with my wardrobe. And my makeup. Far more serious. And how would that look? Image consultant in a cell next to rapper Lola Down-lo.

Achilles had been home since basketball practice. His funky sneakers were strewn near his bathroom door; the bath towel was wet; he had taken a shower. His apartment felt foreign, as if a stranger lived there. The man standing proudly holding the trophies, with his arms around his players, who in a love-drenched shower belched that he loved me, was not the man I was waiting for.

[11]

As I plotted my revenge on Achilles—planning to disconnect his telephone, order a Mafia hit, post his name on a gay personal ad web site—I had dozed off in his living room, later awakening to muffled giggles, chanting, humming, a harmony of voices. Wiping the dried saliva off my face, I looked around his still-darkened living room, and out the window. Lights were on inside the houses across the street, cars passed. I flicked on the lamp, looking at my watch—10:15 p.m.

Silence returned. I was probably dreaming, I thought, too many *National Geographic* specials. But then the voices returned, questions, humming.

Living in a self-contained house, Achilles did not have upstairs neighbors to tell to turn down their television, so the chanting must have been coming from inside the house. Achilles must have come home. But he would have seen me slack-jawed on his sofa, holding the retribution list. When I'd entered his house, I had gone into his kitchen, bedroom, bathroom, closets, where? The recreation room in the basement. The staircase to the basement was adjacent to the entrance to the backyard. A yellow light pierced through the crack in the barely opened door. As I tipped down the staircase, Achilles' voice was recognizable, but I could not place the female voice until I peeked around the corner.

"Alhamdu lillahi Rabbil-'aalameen ar-Rahman-ir-Rahim, Maliki yaum-id-deen, iyyakt na'-budu wa iyyaka nasta'een; ihdinas-sirat-al-

mustaqeema sirat-all-zeena an'amta 'alaihim ghairil maghdoobi 'alai-him wal-lad-dalleen. Ameen! (All Praise is due to Allah, Lord of the worlds, the Beneficent, the Merciful, Owner of the Day of Judgment. Thee alone we worship and Thee alone we ask for help. Show us the straight path, the path of those whom Thou hast favored, not (the path of) those who earn Thine anger nor of those who go astray, Amen!)"

"What prayer should we offer as a follow-up, Achilles?"

The bitch was on her knees. Spread eagle. Prone. And Achilles was next to her, bending her over, holding her hands, then bending her over again. Her face was euphoric as he guided her, over and up, correcting her pronunciation patiently, with care. Between them was an invisible bond, an eternal connection, a trust that united them, a circle that had to be broken.

"We continue by reciting some passage from the Holy Quran, which should not consist of less than three consecutive verses. For this purpose, any one of the small chapters may be selected, for instance, the Unity."

"Last night, at the mosque, we recited: 'He is Allah, the One-Allah, the eternally besought of all! He begets not, nor is He begotten. And there is none comparable unto Him.' Then we said, 'Allahu Akbar.' Then I bowed down in Ruku."

"Sister Tammy, that is excellent."

Achilles said her name with such a reverence that it cut me cleaner than a Thanksgiving turkey. And Tammy's brown eyes exuded a loving trust that could only be expressed by someone who knew him, or wanted to know him intimately. Math was never my strength, which prevented me from adding up why my business associate/friend was in a prone position, in the basement of the man who joined with me in a variety of sexual escapades on the exact same treadmill she was kneeling beside.

As far as I knew, Tammy did not even like Achilles, nor did he like her. But somehow, there had been a shift, and I had missed it. Perhaps it had occurred when she wanted me to be more understanding of him when he decided to abstain from making love. Maybe it was their roller coaster laughter; secret snickers that I considered, then dismissed, particularly when I was knee-deep in work. And when did Tammy become interested in Islam? As far as I knew, she was a blessed and highly favored Christian, peppering everything she said with an "Amen" or a "sweet Jesus." But the way she was now praising Allah, perhaps she had flip-flopped like she changes multi-level marketing businesses. And perhaps, Tammy had concluded that being "born again" required her to be too happy.

Achilles attracted women. That was a fact, but I never suspected him of stepping out on me, bending someone else over, as it was my belief that my love was as precious and rare as gold in Fort Knox.

"What the hell are you doing here, Tammy?"

"Iris, I—" she stuttered, gathering her long skirt, which contradicted her preference for mini-skirts, and stood.

"Iris, my ass!" I exploded, hurtling toward her.

When Achilles intervened, jumping between us, protecting her, my tears, this time angry and bitter, erupted like a flood. "Are you protecting her? Against me?" Achilles calmly folded his arms across his chest and gazed at me with such contempt, I struggled to remember the reason for my outrage, my feelings of betrayal. Tammy, whose eyes were popping out of her head, cowered behind his right shoulder.

"You want *her*?" I screamed, daring either of them to answer, knowing that Achilles at any minute was going to order her out of there and throw his arms around me, begging forgiveness. *Any minute.*

"Iris," Achilles began in a tone that was infuriating, "Sister Tammy has come to me for Islamic instruction, seeking a path of righteousness in her life. Unlike you, who seeks to wear Satanic garments, run the streets, soil your hair, and choose to live in unclean ways, I—"

My arm cocked back, slapping Achilles like the clap of a lightning bolt, across the face with all the fury I could muster.

"How dare you? How fucking dare you?" I heaved in short breaths as if running a four-hundred-meter sprint.

Achilles felt his reddened face to see if I had drawn blood or if it was broken. "After everything I have done for you, been to you. Wearing what I hated, cooking what I hated, sitting at your boring-ass games, listening to your dumb, country ass go on and on about everything under the fucking sun, how black people are supposed to live, how I am supposed to be, when you yourself are the hypocrite—"

"Iris, I cannot in good faith have a future with a non-believer, an infidel. The Holy Qur'an states: 'And do not marry the idolatresses until they believe, and certainly a believing maid is better than an idolatress woman, even though she should please you.'"

"Oh is that what you are, Tammy? A maid?" I said accusingly.

"I should leave," Tammy said, shrinking toward the stairs.

"No, I think you should stay," I said.

"Yes, stay, Sister Tammy. Please," Achilles said, grabbing Tammy's hand, holding it. "Yes, Iris. The answer is yes."

"What the fuck are you talking about?"

"You asked if Sister Tammy is what I wanted. I didn't know until now. But the answer is yes. Yes. Look at her. She is appropriately adorned. She is Earth. And she knows that I am a god. She is beautiful. Reflective of the correct teachings." Tammy squirmed, not wanting to leave Achilles, not knowing how to explain to me, fearful that I would kill her dead.

"I-Iris, I'm sorry. I think I'm gonna die," she whispered, lowering her head.

"Oh, don't worry about it, *Sister* Tammy. 'Cause a cold front is about to swoop down on your ass." I sneered. "Stay right where you are. Because after tonight, this is how I want to remember you. On your knees." Wheeling around, and climbing up the basement staircase, I turned, screaming, "Your shit will be in my front yard in one hour. Pick it up or the goddamned garbage truck will!"

A sheet of tears glazed my eyes during the drag race against myself home. I parked haphazardly, half on the sidewalk, half in the street. With my front door wide open, I threw everything that remotely reminded me of Achilles and Tammy on the front lawn, as promised, decluttering like my feng shui had advised weeks ago. I did not want to break promises to God and Earth. Even though I felt like a landfill. Needed a shoulder to cry on. Too numb to reach out. I could have called semi-friends in Atlanta, but they would have secretly rejoiced over my misfortune, spreading the word that Achilles had kicked me to the curb. And stood around for the crumbs to see how they could benefit. Vultures always wait.

Opening the latest package from Ms. Chickie sent me spiraling down into the depths of depression. I could never reconcile how this woman, who had obviously been on the planet for a few decades, could think that I had any use for a plastic miniature hammer and screw set, a ping-pong ball (without a paddle), or a package of pink barrettes (perfect for a toddler). But in spite of my depressed state, I scribbled off a thank-you note:

Dear, Ms. Chickie:

How are you? Fine I hope.

I received your wonderful gifts today. I am so lucky to have a grandmother who is so thoughtful and knows exactly what I need. Right now, I am bouncing the ping-pong ball on my desk and the pink barrettes are in my hair. Everyone in the neighborhood says I look beautiful. And when I feel bored, I hang photos of you around my townhouse using the plastic miniature hammer and screw set. That really, really cheers me up. And just this morning, I used the plastic hammer to install a chandelier in the living room. Quite handy.

Well, that's all for now. How is the weather there?

Sincerely,

Iris.

P.S. You were right. Tammy does look like Redd Foxx in a dress.

But then I reached an all-time emotional low by phoning Achilles multiple times and slamming down the receiver, then chopping all the relaxed hair off my head. This was long after he and Sister Tammy had rented a $19.95-per-day U-Haul to nervously retrieve their bullshit belongings from my lawn, as I hovered in the doorway of my townhouse, modeling Virgin Mary outfits.

Achilles insisted that Sister Tammy remain in the locked truck as he picked up, with lowered, shamed eyes, her multi-level business products, his boxer shorts, her CDs, her weather almanacs, his Hawks jersey, her kona coffee, her Jesus Walks memorabilia. My neighbors peeked from behind drawn curtains, witnessing my rarely used talent for conjugating the word "fuck." I still wanted to beat Tammy's ass badder than a rented mule. As their tires screeched, sped away, blasting the Fugees, I threw rocks, trash barrels and pine cones against their U-Haul truck. I lost it. Needed an escape. Start spreading the news.

A kettle of vultures chuckled, trailing my flight to New York.

NEW YORK CITY

[12]

"New York City? Whatchu mean, you in New York? Up North? Ain't nothin' up there but a kettle of vultures. I knows New York, and that's why I ain't never goin' back. Peoples move too fast and ain't goin' nowhere but hell... those people be so mean, wouldn't smile if you paid 'em. And make sho you stay outta Harlem, with all the race riots going on…" Ms. Chickie warned, after I received her messages, proving that she was hallucinating, when she couldn't reach me at home.

Despite my protestations, Ms. Chickie believed that the Harlem race riots of 1935, still continued today. "The Sapersteins, the Jewish family I slaved for on Miami Beach, had me live with them in the summer of 1934 in New York City. They had a big, beautiful, clean apartment on Fifth Avenue. I knows it was big, clean and beautiful, 'cause I'm the one that kept it that damn way. Well, my friendgirl, I thank her name was Lucinda, or maybe it was Lucy, cleaned for the family down the hall. Well, we just had ourselves a good old time." Ms. Chickie chuckled from her bedroom in Opa Locka, with *Judge Judy* barking in the background.

I stood outside the Times Square Brewery, near the entrance of the subway station, next to the man wearing only a diaper which read: "Advertise on my ass." Before ducking into the subway, my plan was to briefly chat with Ms. Chickie. The *brief* part was my plan, not hers. "...and I liked going up to Harlem to see all the fine, fine Negroes, not like how these fools dress today. At night, Lucinda and me would stand across the street from the Cotton Club and watch the rich, white people goes inside for the show. The rich white ladies wore fine silk, long furs and the rich, white men folk drove up in Packard Phaeton and Alfa Romeo. We likta died when this rich, white couple drove up in a Auburn Salon Speedster. Lucinda and me fell out. And then we start talkin', you know how friendgirls be talkin' 'bout leavin' whereever they at. Nothin' is ever satisfyin' when youse young. If I never saw the Sapersteins and their floors again, it woulda been too soon for me. Next thang, I know, Lucinda, she up and decided she wanted to be a Garveyite, and next thang I know she went to live in Africa. And I mean Africa Africa. Not Detroit, which is Africa-light. She wanted me to go and all, but I told her that ships and Negroes never work out. But after she left, I gots ta thankin' how is Ms. Chickie going to change her own life. And sometimes, Iris, a voice tell you to do something. Like one time, a voice told me to pour sugar in the tank of Ms. Janette's car across the street. But this time, the voice said, 'Chickie, go up to the Cotton Club and try out to be one of they dancers.' I was tall, light and young; that was a winning combination. Shoot, I was the Jitterbug and Lindy Hop Queen—one time in a row!"

Droves of commuters were brushing past me, and the sun had set. A cool breeze was blowing off the Hudson River, dipping the temperature, causing me to button my jacket around my throat as I squeezed my BlackBerry between my ear and shoulder. "The son-of-a-bitch manager told me that I didn't kick my leg high enough. But that night, after Ms. Chickie rocked his world, he came to another goddamned conclusion." Funny, how Ms. Chickie referred to herself in the third person, when sixty years earlier, she slept with some man to prove her *dancing* prowess.

"But that long-tooth bastard still didn't hire me, and that taught me a big lesson, Granddaughter."

What amazed me was that my grandmother was about to admit that she struggled for her self-worth, when faced with the casting couch. "That man really hurt my heart. I thought that was gonna be my ticket to get away from cleaning floors for the Sapersteins. But it turned out for the best, 'cause that's where I met your granddaddy. He parked all of those rich, white folk cars for 'em."

Family rumor had it that, a former valet and a woman who bore a striking resemblance to Ms. Chickie, ran down the manager of the Cotton Club in a speeding 1935 Studebaker, after which the police were distracted from investigating the sudden death of the Negro manager, when race riots erupted.

According to my father, the Sapersteins boarded Ms. Chickie on the next train back to Opa Locka, where she eventually married Woodrow and continued to work for the Sapersteins for another thirty years, until the couple died. Though a nice, tidy rumor, no one truly believes that Ms. Chickie has a murderous proclivity in her body.

Despite Ms. Chickie's bias, New Yorkers love and trust one another. In what other city, can you stand three inches away from someone's ear lobe, and not whisper a sweet nothing? Not in Opa Locka, and definitely not in Atlanta. Back home, you'd better start announcing yourself from across the street.

Sights and behaviors that would have had someone run out of Opa Locka, are just ignored here, I thought, sauntering past Bellevue Hospital and noticing an outraged woman, measuring a penis, absent its owner, yelling, "He said it'd be longer! He said it'd be longer!" No one else on the sidewalk gave her or the penis a second glance. A police officer stood in the middle of the intersection continuing to obstruct traffic. And a woman pushing infant twins in a stroller continued on their way, as if the ranting woman was reciting Shakespeare. In New York City, her outrage was as commonplace as a bluejay chirping in Central Park.

The rules in New York City are quite different, as it's perfectly acceptable that your crotch is within inches of some pastor's face. However, the trick, is that neither one of you must utter one word nor meet each other's eyes. The other Big Apple rule, is that the phrase, "Excuse Me," only alerts the blockers that they should *not* move out of your way. Only when you stick your umbrella point, albeit accidently, in their kidney, is it likely that others will permit you to pass. Once everyone is clear on the rules, New York City is the most cordial city in the northern hemisphere.

City planners obviously had a specific ambiance in mind when zoning Manhattan. Just for your convenience, on every city block, you can witness, if you hang around long enough, someone spitting, cursing or a maiden milking a cow. Certain neighborhoods are specific in providing various amenities. In Harlem, though in a racial flux, one can find a storefront church, a Chinese food take-out window and a check cashing store on every block.

It's like an early Christmas.

If you're looking for a terrorist, the obvious place to begin your search would be on the New York City subway, a so-called *rapid* transit system, which always seems to be stuck due to rat congestion. Your experience never gets any easier when the lithe troike dancers from Russia want to entertain you on a crowded subway car with the Day of Conception celebration.

If you think the subway conductors exist to serve and protect the traveling public, well, then you must have been sniffing the same glue as the graduate student nodding out in your lap. Subway conductors are your reincarnated abusive parent, designed to serve two purposes: one, to scold you on what not to do with your body in a subway car. "Attention, please!" a conductor cajoled, on the rickety loudspeaker. "This is your conductor. It is a violation of the law to lick the emergency cord. Please refrain from doing so. We apologize for any inconvenience this law may cause. Thank you in advance for your cooperation. And thank you for riding with the MTA."

Now, he tells me.

Other subway conductors believe it's their duty to scare the living daylights out of you. "Attention, subway passengers, this is your conductor. Please ignore any loud ticking sound that you may hear. We've ruled out that it's a mechanical watch. I repeat. The ticking is not a watch. Investigators are on the scene and we should be moving shortly. Should any passenger choose to take their lives in their own hands by leaving the train, please exit through either door on the far end of your car, climb down onto the tracks, making sure to avoid the one-hundred Kv third rail voltage, ignore the fifty pound rats and just wade through the bubonic-plagued sludge, until you can find a sewer hole that will open. Unfortunately, there are no MTA employees to assist you, as they have been laid off due to budget cuts. Thank you for your patience and cooperation. And thank you for riding the MTA."

If this woman, with a scab on her lip, steps on the back of my Cole Haan slingback pump one more time, I'm gonna knock her into a vat of penicillin, I thought, as the woman in question, hoisting mannequins of Sonny and Cher on her back, pushed ahead, disappearing into the waiting cross-town shuttle to Grand Central Station.

New Yorkers have an aversion to silence, believing it to be tantamount to Chinese water torture. These resilient urban warriors scream within inches of the intended listener, loudly honk at a feeble senior citizen crossing the Brooklyn Bridge on a trapeze, and scream into their communication gadgets. Within days of my arrival in Manhattan, I had been hustled by "entertainers" who expected financial contributions, and cornered by complete strangers who wanted to spend the holidays together under a stairwell.

The Spanish accordion player: "*¿Ya se que estoy calato; sólo quiero saber cómo volver al hotel?* (I know I'm naked, but could you just tell me how to get back to the hotel?)"

The French one-legged polka dancer: "*Mais ce n'est pas tout! J'ai encore deux autres albums de photos!* (That's not all! I have two more photo albums!)" And her twin: "*Est-ce que quelqu'un a un remède pour un mauvais cas de phlegm?*" (Does anyone have a cure for a bad case of phlegm?) The German tourist: "*Ihr würdet diese Ghettos nicht haben, wenn ihr wirklich arbeiten wolltet.* (You wouldn't have these ghettos if you people were willing to work.)"

It was Friday night, after evening rush hour, but the subway was still crowded nonetheless. I was being herded, nudged, and shoved through the Times Square station, making my way downstairs to meet Cleo on the platform of the IRT No. 3 subway train to Harlem, en route to the All Jokes Aside comedy club. Over the past few days, I developed wind burns trying to keep pace with Cleo, a former full-sized model and media consultant for the NBC Radio Networks who walked like a swan in motion, fluid, regal. She often attracted curious glances from strangers who wondered which celebrity was in their midst.

It was early October. New York was experiencing an early fall, and at night, the temperatures would suddenly dip. Running from obsessive urges to arrange a mob hit on Achilles and Tammy, ducking lies that Eba circulated, which slandered my ethics, I needed peace and to be redirected back toward myself again. And there was no better sister-friend to walk me through the fire than Cleo Elliott.

When my telephone rang, 'round midnight, hours after the confrontation with Achilles, I started not to answer, as I was in a criminal state of mind and ducking the whole world. Let the answering machine pick it up, I thought. Then because of the lateness of the hour, I thought maybe it was an emergency in Opa Locka, so I lifted the telephone receiver on the fourth ring.

"Girl, you been on my mind all week. You okay?" Cleo had asked. Earlier that evening I had anonymously sent a barrel of chitlins to Achilles' house.

"Same bullshit. Different day." Cleo and I could each sense when the other was in a crisis, and would not give up until we could verify our intuition.

"What's going on?" Cleo was the only friend with whom I could be vulnerable, share my dreams, my fears, and not be judged. Listening quietly while I had given her regular Achilles updates, Cleo had been initially encouraging, until she later felt that I was defending his benign neglect and ignoring his passive aggressiveness.

"Iris, men are like laxatives—they irritate the shit out of you!"

"It's serious this time, Cleo."

It took that all-night telephone call for me to accept Cleo's demand that I board an airplane the next day.

"Iris, you better get outta dodge before Achilles files a restraining order against your ass!"

"Maybe you're right. Though I was thinking about going home, eating some of Ms. Chickie's crunchy sweet potato pie."

"Now I *know* you're delirious. Text me later. Let me know what time your flight arrives. Get ready to hit the ground moving, girl. No grass is gonna grow under your feet."

Except for the time Cleo and I had had a lengthy layover at John F. Kennedy International Airport, en route from a vacation in Paris, I had not spent much time in the bustling Big Apple. Cleo loved Manhattan, a decade ago, falling in love with its energy, the museums, and a dreadlocked Bajan brother named Delroy.

Cleo and I grabbed two seats, elbowing two Girl Scouts out of our way just as the subway car lurched to a stop at 72nd Street and Broadway, swaying the entire row of late-evening commuters. "The best thing about the subway is that it gets you there fast," Cleo said, removing lint from her rust-colored blazer.

"And the worst?"

"Knowing how many nose hairs the stranger seated next to you has."

"Ain't that the truth." I scooted away from the drooling Yorkshire terrier held by a humming Dr. Love.

Cleo and I had begun the morning with a Bikhram yoga class, where I thought I had entered the gates of hell, followed by the joy of maxing out our credit cards at Moshood, an eclectic boutique in Brooklyn. "Moshood is one of the few reasons I come to Brooklyn. This and jerk chicken," Cleo remarked, twirling in an elegant midnight blue sarong dress that accented the bright lock of red hair near her front temple and the freckles sprinkled across her nose and cheeks.

Our shopping spree was followed by an afternoon of luxury at Gazelle Fly Away Day Spa, where we enjoyed a therapeutic seaweed wrap, body polish, facial, pedicure, and manicure. It was not until we were feeling no pain during the hydrotherapy underwater massage that we spoke about what had transpired in Atlanta.

"Achilles wanted you to be someone you're not. But the pitiful thing is that you almost went for it," Cleo said, sliding into the Jacuzzi.

"I was trying to compromise, that's what I was trying to do. Make things work."

"And that was your first mistake."

"What do you mean?" Streams of water shot out of the tubes, swirling, creating bubbles in the ivory-colored Jacuzzi.

"My family always told me I was beautiful, but when I got out in the world, some people needed to let me know that a full-sized woman wasn't their cup of tea. But when I let them know that I didn't give a damn what they thought, they left me the hell alone."

"Good for you, Cleo."

"So when I meet a man and the first thing that comes out of their mouth is 'You need to lose weight,' they get kicked to the curb. If he wants a smaller woman, then that's who he should be with, instead of plucking my damn nerves. People who don't accept you as you are, are trying to control you. Point blank."

"That's right, girl. Don't be taking no shit off nobody."

"Yeah, but *you* did."

"Yeah, I guess I did."

"That fool knew when he met you that you were ambitious, sex-crazed, couldn't cook worth a damn, slightly spiritual, and the best thing that ever happened to him."

"He did, huh?"

"And you knew he was a part-time Muslim. You shoulda left his ass at the mosque."

"Don't kick me for saying this, but I thought I could change him."

"And he shouldn't expect you to change. Give him the same

respect. Take people as they are, I always say. Life is too freakin' short." The spa attendant completed washing our backs, moderating the water temperature. "Mama's death drove that home for me."

"How do you mean?"

"When she found out she had breast cancer, the doctors said that she had six months, seven months tops, to live."

"She inspired so many people, Cleo."

"Mama taught me to live as if I had only six months. Who knows how long we really have? And I will be damned if I go through this life jumping through hoops for other people."

"I thought I believed that, but somehow I got derailed."

"Derailed by the dick. Don't worry, it's the death of most women." Cleo laughed. I joined her.

"I was going to set the world on fire. Make my rules. And have a man and career that proved I could do it. Is that still even possible?"

"Of course it is, girl," Cleo said, climbing out of the tub, wrapping herself in a plush white towel. "You, Iris, have to know, really know, that you are perfect as you are. See I'm always going to be full-sized, big-boned, fat, whateva people want to call it—but I'm still perfect. Some people call me fat. That's okay, I'm perfectly fat. I have never dieted. I just eat what's good for me. I'll be damned if I let some skinny chick or a man tell me what my body needs. Every roll, every inch is a work of art, a tribute, an extension of my beauty. My daddy always told me I'm as cute as I can be. And you know what? I believe him. And you know I have never, ever had any problem in the man department."

❖ ❖ ❖

All Jokes Aside was packed to the rafters. Latecomers who couldn't get in for the first show loitered out front, or looped around the block to wait on line for the second show, content to be in the midst of whatever might happen. Automobiles of every variety double-parked with flashing hazard lights while drivers inquired whether tickets were still available. Buppies from downtown took the trip uptown to remember what it was like to be in the 'hood. White folks, having heard about the spectacle of the black side of comedy, came in clusters, before scurrying back to the security of what was, to them, familiar—their brownstones in Central Harlem. Asian tourists, after digesting their soul food dinner from the local rib joint, came to witness an element of American culture that wasn't in their travel brochures. Hordes of young men overloaded with testosterone rubbernecked for an opportunity to affirm their maleness with Lil' Kim lookalikes, who were poised to attract any penis with benefits.

Industry types, prowling for the next Chris Rock, sat alone with pen and paper, alternately taking notes and monitoring their vibrating BlackBerries. When talent scouts arrived, word spread backstage like a California wildfire. They were easy to spot. Usually it was the white guy with the receding hairline, humming "Hey Jude" under his breath, nursing seltzer water in the rear of the club.

Friday was New Jack Night and Cleo said this was the place to be. Everyone jockeyed for attention, even celebrities who loved being seen in the place where everyone wanted to be. The club sweltered with ambition and loathing. Time to take out frustrations accumulated from earning a minimum-wage salary, or facing a corporate downsizing on some wannabe comics.

The stripper/doorman, wearing an eighties-style fade and moisturizer on the top, came over to give Cleo a peck on the cheek, before later ejecting a woman who insisted on bringing a handgun in the club. The woman couldn't fathom why she couldn't have a gun at a comedy show. No matter how bad a comic can be, shooting them, although understandable, is a little drastic. The stripper/doorman carried the woman outside, while she cursed every branch of his family tree. A mature woman whom had been counting dollar bills, moved from behind her tattered, wooden podium to greet Cleo, hugging her the way an alcoholic embraces a bottle of gin. Colby stood backstage talking to a short, middle-aged white man, wearing a brown and beige cardigan sweater and brown corduroy trousers.

Comedian Peaches Henry peeked from the wings, watching the crowd grow rancorous with the first two comics, reducing them to a pulp of snot, debunking the myth that men don't cry.

"How long will you be in New York?" Peaches had asked when Cleo and I had slipped backstage before the show to visit with her.

"Day after tomorrow. My life is waiting for me," I said, chuckling. Cleo profusely apologized to Peaches for not having the time to meet with her as promised, explaining that personal representation was really not her specialty.

"I would love to talk with you both. How about after the show tonight?" Peaches asked.

Cleo and I nodded. "Sure. So you get ready and we'll see you later."

Since briefly meeting Peaches in Atlanta, she had been working New York comedy clubs, polishing her act. Peaches was immediately likeable, and I wanted to protect her. If my father had not been one of the loyal types, I would have thought he was a rolling stone, as Peaches reminded me of many members of my family. Her blunt haircut framed her delicate features, except for her nose that was reminiscent of Cherokee ancestry.

With the audience now almost full to capacity, Cleo and I reluctantly sat in the front row next to two sinister-looking homies, looking like fugitives from a rap video. On the other side of us sat a conservative-looking couple who introduced themselves as being from Woodbridge, New Jersey, and were the parents of one of the comedians. The mother, adorned with diamonds, continually stroked her fur, as if verifying it hadn't been stolen. Her facial expression mirrored that of a toddler trying spinach for the first time. The father was a plain sort, clutching an obviously seldom-worn hat, and his crumpled, off-the-rack, brown suit matched his sullen demeanor. The Woodbridge parents nudged Cleo, pointing out their son Joel, who was lip reading his material, pacing in the backstage doorway like a caged cougar.

"He looks nervous," I mentioned to the mother.

"Oh, Joel will be wonderful. We've been practicing for weeks."

We? I thought, as Joel's parents did not look like bastions of comedic thought. As show time drew near, the audience became restless, already intoxicated, anticipating the bloodletting. When his name was announced, Joel bounded toward the stage like a black Jay Leno. The half-hearted applause died before he grabbed the microphone. Dressed in an Izod LaCoste shirt over-creased Eddie Bauer khakis and mahogany brown wingtip shoes, Joel was primed to re-create the routines he had seen on *The Tonight Show with Jay Leno*. Little did he know that this crowd had never heard of Burbank and didn't give two shits about Jay Leno. Except for his parents' expectant gazes, Joel stared into a sea of nonchalance as he cleared his throat and creaked, "Hi, everybody! Don't you hate people that end their sentences without ending their sentences?"

The crowd looked like an unabridged edition of the *Encyclopedia Britannica* had struck them. When the sinister-looking homies recovered, realizing their brains had been force-fed a question of grammar instead of a joke, they jumped to their feet, wailing, "Boooo! Boooo!" The crowd followed their lead with a chorus of verbal assaults. "Get off the stage, Richie Cunningham!" yelled a woman in the middle section wearing a weave and a hat. "Take your ass back to Mayberry!" said a man in a gray Harve Bernard suit. Each heckle fed into the crowd's amusement. The plump host shook his head as he waddled slowly to the stage, forcing the microphone from Joel's frozen hand. When Joel emerged from his daze and scurried off the stage, the plump host added to the crowd's delirium, with: "Interesting concept, professor. But how about a fuckin' *punchline*?"

Joel's mother was inconsolable, her eyes filling with tears as she scolded the Lil' Kims beside her who had erupted with hyena howls of laughter, displaying six jagged rows of teeth. Joel's father pleaded with God to intervene. Cleo and I slid down in our seats, in case any chairs were going to be thrown.

Joel and his parents fled, exiting through the backstage holding area. The other comics, snickering at his misfortune, parted like the Red Sea in case Joel's failure was contagious. In the middle of the frenzy, my BlackBerry vibrated, signaling there were messages waiting. One urgent. As I had forwarded my business phone to my cell, I surmised the urgent message could only be from someone out of town. I rose, quietly tiptoeing to the lobby.

When Jamal, the next comic, a loud, obnoxious mouth-breather, was introduced, he stamped the stage, yelling like a hip-hop Ed McMahon. With the exception of his cut buddies, the homies sitting next to Cleo and me, the crowd stared at him with curious amusement. *At least he's louder than the hecklers*, they probably thought.

In the crowded lobby, I entered my password to receive my voicemail and listened for the urgent message, which was from a cloaked local telephone number. Whoever it was, was calling from the street, as there were the sounds of police sirens, loud voices. The person started to leave a message, sighed, then hung up.

As I walked toward my seat, I saw that Jamal had begun his routine. "...so I was fucking this big, fat bitch last night. She was so fat she used a satellite dish as a beeper. And when she rubbed her thighs together, I smelled bacon." Cleo puffed, giving him a death stare. The audience grew uncomfortable, started to murmur, becoming restless. Sensing his impending doom, Jamal desperately searched for a life preserver. And I was it.

"Hey, baby!" he called, rubbing his hand along his chin, collapsing the audience into an embarrassed hush. I was halfway back to my seat before I realized he was talking to me. Jamal continued, "Oh, so you want to ignore me, huh? You weren't saying that last night, nowhatumsayin'?"

Jamal's socially retarded friends were energized, salivating, "Get her, Jamal!" A verbal war between the sexes is something they lived for.

My deadpan face was devoid of any fear as I retorted, "How could you hear what I was sayin'? You were in the bathroom getting a drink of water and the toilet seat fell on your head!"

The crowd, relieved I could stand up for myself, erupted with laughter. Even Jamal's ignorant cohorts laughed. One heckler drew a line with his finger across his throat. Audience members high-fived Cleo and me. Cleo had forgotten that I had won many campus championships playing the dozens. Jamal dropped the microphone dejectedly and scampered backstage through the comics, who parted again to avoid contagion. He retreated to a rear corner, flailing himself furiously against the wall.

"Girl, if that hadn't happened, I would have dragged him off the stage myself." Cleo laughed, shaking her head.

"What's wrong with him? 'Victim' is not written nowhere on my forehead."

The plump host returned to the stage, commending my skills, encouraging the audience to give me a round of applause, snapping on Jamal, "If you had thrown yourself into writing your material instead of against that wall, maybe you would have done better."

Cleo grinned, nudging me, then read a note that was passed to her over my shoulder. "Oh Lawd," Cleo whispered, glancing back at the author.

"Problem?"

"Delroy. I'm surprised his red velvet cake franchises could survive without him."

"I remember you telling me about him."

"Ever since I dumped him, he's been singing a different tune, showing up at all my haunts. Begging."

"Stalking."

"Naah. I love the brother. He just needs to sweat a little more. Know how to appreciate a good woman, the first time around. Had to let 'em know that he couldn't treat me like his customers at the bakery; while they decided what to select, he decided if they deserved what they asked for."

"Nothing can ever be like the first time."

"If he really wants me back, he better make me feel like it's the first time. I want to feel as pure as the driven snow."

The plump host asked the audience to give a rousing applause to Vernon Blackwell, the syndicated radio host. "Hmmm, I listen to him in Atlanta all the time. I thought he would look like he sounds, with more of that Teddy Pendergrass thing, yelling, 'Close the Door.'"

Vernon rose slightly from his seat, waving and acknowledging the audience.

"Okay, he can sit down now. He's always waving like he's Nelson Mandela." Cleo chuckled.

"You know him?"

"He's interviewed a few of the actors from the network. He eats into a lot of the time with his long-ass questions, but he's nice enough." Vernon pointed at Cleo, nodding at us, before resuming his seat, flashing a wide fluorescent smile. His dark, almond-shaped eyes crinkled in the corners and thick eyebrows warmly framed his eyes. He wore a brown T-shirt under his dark brown blazer, and crisply ironed jeans.

When Peaches danced on stage to a Mary J. Blige remix, she tripped on the third stair step. The plump host stifled a chuckle as he handed her the microphone, while the audience took a visual inventory. Some looked at her like it was her fault they were kicked off welfare. Wearing what she thought would be an appropriate comedienne outfit, blue jeans, a gray T-shirt and worn sneakers, she instead blended in with the low-rent audience members, causing them to be repulsed by her.

She told her first joke.

Cleo and I laughed louder and longer than anyone, daring anyone with our dagger glances to mess with our girl.

Though Peaches' lungs slowly deflated, a ferocious tension still clung to the air like icicles. The glare from the spotlight created a Mojave Desert haze, magnifying every gesture, every movement for heightened inspection. A mop string was wedged between two floor tiles about a foot away from the stage. It's funny what you notice when you are scared for someone.

Don't show your fear, Peaches, I thought, noticing her right kneecap jiggled. A police siren pierced the cacophony of the comedy club, its presence imperative, then disappeared like a thief in the chilly, fall night.

Help her, Cleo's face silently pleaded, biting her lower lip, as Peaches joked about women and orgasms, which got a laugh from two people: Cleo and me. Again laughing louder and longer than the joke warranted.

Peaches canvassed her memory to retrieve her next series of jokes. Finally remembering them, she fired her best shot, but they sunk into a silent abyss. Our nervous cackles could not save her. We could see jokes three and four roll down the runway and fly over the heads of the audience, while the plump host rolled his eyes, trying to instigate a response. Reacting to him, Peaches sneered. "Whatchu rollin' your eyes at, fat boy?" The crowd inhaled. Cleo and I inhaled

A man in the rear section muttered, "Boo," under his breath.

"Boo your momma," Peaches retorted, returning the microphone to the stand and leaving the stage. My intestines rearranged themselves, watching the comics again part with averted eyes, bludgeoning Peaches with silence.

"Let's get out of here," I said. Cleo rose, following me to the backstage entrance, searching for Peaches as the club disc jockey played "Another One Bites the Dust."

Cleo and I found her in a corner talking with Yusef, the club owner, who wore baggy sweats that camouflaged a massive body, and rubbed the coarse bristles on his chin. As Cleo and I approached, he was saying, "Everyone has a bad night. You just keep at it. You'll be okay."

Peaches turned, saw us, and winced. "Sorry y'all had to come up here for this. I just couldn't get my rhythm together, couldn't remember the material I worked on all week."

"Don't worry about it, Peaches. That other idiot put the audience in a bad mood, because his material sucked." Just then, the idiot in question sauntered past, overhearing my comment.

"Hey, fuck you!" Jamal hurled.

Yusef, without hesitation, leveled the heel of his boot against Jamal's jaw with a swift, roundabout kick. A loud thud sounded as Jamal hit the floor, his eyes blinking rapidly as he wiped the trail of blood dripping down the side of his mouth. Yusef serenely hovered over Jamal as if he had merely requested a donation for the Red Cross, and in a raspy whisper that reached everyone's ears snarled, "If you disrespect a woman, *any* woman again, I'll bounce you harder than government cheese. Is that crystal clear?"

Cleo, Peaches, and I cowered, moving away from this ghetto Bruce Lee as Yusef continued, "I said, is that clear?"

Jamal nodded.

Yusef extended his hand. "Cool, man. Let me help you up."

Not sure whether to trust Yusef's sudden charity, Jamal knew he had no choice but to allow himself to be hoisted to a standing position, rechecking his mouth for blood.

"Nice meeting you ladies." Yusef winked before he lumbered back inside the theater to check out the comic onstage. Cleo, Peaches, and I hurried out the door and rushed to the corner of 125th Street and Fifth Avenue to hail a taxicab. Vernon Blackwell called out to us, rushing to catch up.

"Cleo!"

"Hey, Vernon," Cleo replied, sliding into the now-waiting taxicab next to Peaches and me.

"Hey, Peaches! You hang in there."

"Thanks, Vernon," Peaches answered sweetly.

"Cleo, did my producer set up that cross-promotion with your office yet?" Vernon asked Cleo but stared at me, which Cleo noticed, and relaxed into a smile.

"Yessss. You and I spoke three times yesterday, remember? We opted for the last week of November sweeps. Vernon? Vernon?" Cleo looked at me, then back at Vernon, whose brown eyes were glazed over. "Vernon?"

"Huh?"

"Your pants are on fire."

"Huh? What?"

"Her name is Iris. Iris Chapman."

"Ah, ah, I'm sorry. Vernon Blackwell," he responded dreamily, leaning across Cleo and Peaches to shake my hand. "I love the shape of your head."

"Huh?" Now I was dumbfounded.

"What I mean is—a short haircut becomes you."

"Excuse me, sir, are you going to ride in the window or get out?" the impatient driver yelled. Cleo gauged my reaction to see if I wanted to stay to marinate in more of Vernon's compliments.

"Nice meeting you," I said.

"Situations erupt like that all the time around All Jokes Aside. In fact, if someone *doesn't* get into an altercation, then that's breakin' news," Peaches said, over drinks at Mikell's, an upscale bar, which served warm *tapas* on Columbus Avenue. "Yusef never hesitates to resort to violence to get his point across."

Delroy had convinced Cleo to let him join us, with no strings attached, drinks only. And since he was buying, I didn't mind.

But judging by his body language, and the way he entered Mikell's, the brother walked as though there was a ray of hope of him resurrecting their relationship.

"All Jokes Aside can't be the only club you can work out in, can it? Comedy shouldn't be a violent profession."

Peaches explained that she was beginning to make inroads at the mainstream clubs, but it was hard breaking through the perception that all black comics use profanity. "And it seems like all people expect female comics to talk about is men, like we don't think about nothing else."

"You can hold your own. I saw how you handled Jamal," I said supportively.

"Comedy is no stranger to me. My family is full of comedians," Peaches replied.

"Professional?"

"No, but they should be. So what did you really think about me tonight?"

"You win some and lose some."

"Oh," Peaches said quietly, hoping I would tell her that she was the next big thing.

"But don't take that to mean that I think you're a loser. You have great stage presence. A crowd without a chip on its shoulder would appreciate you more. And I would lose the nickname. Isn't Audrey your real name?"

"Jamal told me that everybody has a nickname. He was the one who gave me the name Peaches, 'cause he said it matched my complexion."

"Cute. Forgive me for a snap judgment, but Jamal is an idiot. Ten years from now he'll still be working in chitlin'-circuit joints in remote parts of Brooklyn."

Peaches inhaled. "You think so?"

"Historically, comedians move into acting, both in television and films. Very few comics continue to perform standup after they break into movies. So if I were you, I'd take some acting and writing classes."

Bored, Delroy blocked Cleo's view of Peaches and me, and tried to plead his case. Cleo rolled her eyes, and pushed his back against his chair.

"And one last thing, may I call you Audrey?"

"Sure." She smiled. "My sister thinks I should use my real name, too."

"Right! When you get famous, your relatives want to know that you're part of their family, that they can google you, and reach you when they need to borrow money."

"That works!" Audrey laughed.

"And always, Audrey. Always dress better than your audience," I stressed.

"Even at All Jokes Aside?"

"You never know who's in the audience. Like tonight, there were two talent scouts. The other thing is the audience always wants to feel like this was a special occasion for you, even if they look like hell."

"And most of them did look like hell."

"Well, ladies," Delroy interrupted, speaking with a clear West Indian accent, his dreadlocks cascading over his slim shoulders. "Give me the honor of escorting you home." Cleo shrugged.

"Cleo, give him some. He's so pitiful," I whispered, chewing on a cherry, just as my BlackBerry rang again, the call coming from an undisclosed telephone number. "Iris Chapman."

Silence.

"Hello? Iris Chapman." The silence continued, until I moved the speaker closer to my ear. Suddenly the sorrowful voice leaped out at me.

"I'm losing it."

[13]

Buddha and King were their names. The two bristle-coated, mastiff-type Rottweilers stared unabashedly at the arteries in my neck. Reminded me of that flatulent bitch Cocoa from when I was a child.

"You wanna get your dogs," I said through clenched teeth to the apathetic receptionist as I squeezed through the smoked- glass interior doors. My movements were monitored on the telescopic cameras, droning whirring sounds, following my approach through yet another glass door, which opened onto a full-scale, stone-cold, verbal war.

"I ain't mad at the boriqua for tryin' to come up, but she need to stick to the radio mike, 'cause she ain't doing nothing to hip-hop but polluting it," said the stocky Puerto-Rican man, swiveling in his black leather chair before an engineering board with scattered blinking lights. "And I don't give a shit if she was givin' Lola's joint mad play. Ol' girl popped that 'nigga' word. In the words of Kyle's mom on South Park, '*What what what?!*' Somebody needs to smack her. And quick. Fo' real. Fo' real. Fo' real."

Madd Dogg, Lola Down-lo's skinny boyfriend, exploding a gust of marijuana toward the fluorescent white lights in the plush recording studio, said, "Who the fuck are you, tryna say Lola fucked up a track? She'll say 'nigga' when I tell her to say 'nigga.' Do you know anything about hip-hop? You must still be on a contact high, Serebral. Listen to other niggas' shit, otherwise you'd know what the fuck I'm talkin' 'bout."

"Muthafucka, you buggin'. Only peeps who wanna get a cap popped in their ass call themselves 'niggas.' You saw how Melvin caught a bad one? Running that fake thug life shit? He ain't never been in a ghetto. And why would you cloud the collective history of your people by perpetuating some shit like that?" asked Serebral.

"And why you keep coming at me wit some lame-ass excuse for why Lola shouldn't be keepin' it real? Come on, Serebral, hip-hop is about emotion, survival, people's struggles, not about some clown-ass fools trying to make some dough on some straight and narrow bullshit—"

I cleared my throat. All eyes were on me. Serebral glared with creased eyes, his lips pinched around the marijuana butt, smoke spiraling down over his *The Bitch Set Me Up* T-shirt. Lola cowered in the corner, her arms wrapped around her knees. When she recognized me, she sprung up, hurtling toward me, with eyes that pleaded to let her do the talking.

"Aunt Iris! Momma said you were going to meet me here. Sorry I didn't meet you at the bus station," Lola said, desperately hugging me around the neck.

"Um, sure," I responded, smiling as if I, too, was glad to see a long-lost relative. "Long bus ride." Madd Dogg and Serebral maintained their stern gazes, circulating their eyes over my frame.

"Where's her luggage?" Madd Dogg demanded.

"In a locker at Port Authority," I answered quickly.

"We got work to do, Lola," Madd Dogg said in a hostile tone, taking a puff from Serebral's joint, his gold teeth as bright as a night game at Shea Stadium.

"Baby, Iris came to see momma, being that she is sick and all."

Irritated, Serebral collapsed into his chair, exposing his navel. "Take five minutes. Not ten. Five. I'm not trying to pull another all-nighter."

Still wincing, and not knowing what circumstances Lola had

gotten herself into, I asked, "Where's the ladies room? My kidneys are screaming." Serebral adjusted knobs on the engineering board, replaying tracks they had recorded earlier featuring an angry, violent-sounding Lola. Quite different from the vulnerable, fresh-faced young woman that was now leading me down the hall toward the bathroom.

Both puzzlement and fear draped me upon hearing Lola's words over the phone: "I'm losing it." Her voice was unrecognizable, altered from that of the arrogant, uncaring girl I had met in Atlanta. She offered no details—no answers as to why she had called me, how she had gotten my telephone number, or how she knew that I was in New York. She rattled off the address, 715 West 54th Street, StarTyme Recording Studios, and begged me to come quickly, before leaving me to hurl questions at a disconnected telephone line.

Cleo and Delroy had insisted on coming up to the sixth-floor studio, but then we thought that if necessary, a getaway car with the motor running was a better option.

Lola peeked into the hallway before closing, then leaned against the bathroom door, and attempted to light her own cigarette. Without hesitation, I plucked the unlit butt from between her lips, flinging it into the silver trash can under the towel dispenser. "Lola, what's up?"

"Shhhhh," she replied. "Don't talk so loud. He'll hear you."

"Who will?"

"Madd, I mean, Seymour."

"What the hell is goin' on?" I whispered.

"Seymour. He's drinking. I don't like it when he drinks. He bugs if I don't do what he wants," Lola said, stroking her upper arm.

"What does he want you to do?"

"Score some coke."

"What?"

"Out in East New York."

"Nobody can make you—" Lola jerked up the sleeve of her sweater, exposing a blue-purplish bruise. "He did this to you?"

Lola nodded, slowly pulling up her pant legs, the back of her sweater, pointing out her pinky finger, revealing other bruises and swellings.

"I'm tired of dressing like this, covering my bruises, hiding what he did to me."

"Is that why you didn't do any of those covers I had arranged? For *Vibe* and *The Source* magazines?"

"Those folks peep my body, and my shit would be on front street," Lola replied, the corners of her lips turning under. Lola's hard image clearly had been manufactured. The tomboy swagger was still there, but more so was the essence of a flower screaming to be revealed.

"Lola, how did you know that I was in New York?"

"Colby. He said he couldn't get here quick enough. Another one of his clients was taken to the emergency room."

"What for?"

"Losing weight too quick. Then he said to try you. That he would be gettin' back with me. Only momma knows I'm in New York, 'cause if anyone else found out they'd be blowin' up my phone, askin' for all kinds of bullshit.

"Okay, you want me to get you home? Pretend you're sick or something." Lola closed her eyes, and rested her head against the door.

"Wait a minute. You can't leave." Lola shook her head, staring down at the white tile floor. The wooden door suddenly rattled from pounding fists, then pushed open, and Seymour stepped in, causing Lola to jump out of her skin.

From his steely facial expression, Seymour was not pleased that

I was still on the premises. He stared through me to Lola to see if his merchandise had been tampered with. Satisfied, but now testing, he said, “Gotta get back to work, baby girl. Time is money.” Lola’s eyebrows knitted together.

In response, I bent over, holding my abdomen, pretending to be in writhing pain.

“Ooooohhhhh! Oooooooohhh!” I moaned. “My, um, my ulcer. That’s it, my ulcer is hurting.” Lola handed me a Kleenex, placing her hand on my back. “I need to lie down.”

“Why don’t she go to the hospital?” Seymour said, in a tone as cold as a Chicago wind.

“No! No hospital. No insurance. Just need to get to the house.”

“Come on, Auntie! You know how you are when you don’t take your medicine.” Not really. Since I did not know what medicine I was supposed to be on. And I hoped that Seymour did not ask.

“What medicine she take?” Seymour asked, before I had completed the thought. Lola and I searched for an answer.

“Aspirin!” Lola volunteered.

“Aspirin and partially hydrogenated cottonseed! Ohhhhhhh! Ohhhhh!” I added, remembering a cereal additive I had decided to stay away from. I held onto the edge of the bathroom sink.

“Seymour, I’ll make up the session. Deduct Serebral’s costs from my advance, like you always do. Got to get my auntie out of here.”

With my eyes closed into half-moons, I limped around Seymour, opening the door, aware of his reluctance to let his paycheck out of his sight. When Lola and I reached the lobby, Buddha and King barked furiously, awakening the receptionist as we dipped into Delroy’s waiting car.

❖ ❖ ❖

Cleo's four-story Strivers' Row brownstone was decorated with sculpture, artwork, and literature from her travels around the world. Lola got comfortable in a third-floor bedroom, which Cleo had decorated in pink with hundreds of antique African and Native American dolls placed on the dressers, bed, and the windowsills overlooking her collard green and herb garden. With a quick stop at Lola's mother's apartment in the Abraham Lincoln projects, I was reminded of the phrase: "You are a reflection of your environment." The broken elevators; the darkened stairway reeking of urine; the narrow, shadowy hallways; sudden slamming doors; a distressed, wailing infant; then the random gunfire made me wonder how Lola's mother could open her door and her heart so wide, exuding warmth that embraced not only her daughter, but captivated two strangers, Cleo and me.

"All Momma needs to know is that y'all are friends. You just came with me to get the rest of my stuff."

While Lola threw her clothes and money in a satchel, Cleo and I smiled away the fears of a mother who wondered why Lola was leaving so suddenly after she promised to stay until Thanksgiving.

"In this business, sometimes you have to hurry up and wait, for something today," Cleo said.

"Right, and appearing on *Soul Train* will help Lola's CD sales," I added, knowing that Don Cornelius was not even in production.

"I suppose you're right," her mother said, wringing her hands. "It's just that I rarely get a chance to see my baby anymore. She's alright, isn't she?"

"Oh yes, ma'am! Yes, she's great!" Cleo and I chimed.

"That mad fool called here looking for you," Lola's mother yelled over her shoulder toward a rear bedroom. That piece of information silenced Cleo and me, and brought Lola stoically out of the bedroom, carrying a fur jacket and a caramel-colored satchel. "What didja tell him?"

"Told him I thought you were with him. What was I 'sposed to tell him?"

"Oh nothing, Momma," Lola, said kissing her mother on her moled cheek. "I just don't think he needs to know everything. Women don't need to be telling mens everythang."

"That's what I been telling you. I never liked him anyway. Always bossing you around, like he owned you. I am the only one that owns you. And what kind of name is Madd Dogg for somebody."

"If he calls again, tell him you haven't heard from me, okay?" Lola said, faking a smile toward her suspicious mother.

"Lola exaggerates sometimes. Madd Dogg ain't that bad," Colby said from Atlanta, having finally responded to my text messages.

"This sister trusts her instincts. If it isn't that bad yet, bad is right around the corner," I replied, as Lola snoozed upstairs. Cleo had already left for work at dawn, preparing for a series of budget meetings, hoping she could squeeze out a few million dollars to promote a fledgling Asian comedy set in Little Italy.

When we arrived at Cleo's brownstone, Lola fought her exhaustion, needing to talk, to tell someone about her life and express her feelings of powerlessness. Cleo excused herself to get on a conference call with the network's Japanese affiliates.

"As soon as my royalties come in, I'm gettin' my momma out of there."

"Shouldn't you wait? Accumulate a nest egg first?"

"I promised I would buy her a house when I signed my record deal, but then Colby wanted to recoup the money he put out. Then seem like everybody in my family wanted something, needed something. Peeps I hadn't heard from in years. Or never knew."

"Why did you give it to them?"

"I dunno. I figured I owed them. How many of them are going to get the chances that I will? Make the kind of money that I'm making?"

"Personal responsibility. Everybody has to have some."

"I don't want nobody thinking I ain't down."

"Lemme tell you something. If you're ever in a bind, the folks that are checkin' for you now, as they say, won't be nowhere to be found." Lola stretched her petite frame on top of the frilly pink satin bedspread. This room could have been her bedroom if her parents had had the opportunity.

"I'm tired," she said, yawning.

"Okay, I'll let you—"

"No, not that kind of tired. I mean, I'm tired. Tired of everybody stepping to me with their hand out all the time. Whenever the telephone rings, it's somebody wantin' something. Money, clothes, time. Everybody pullin' on me. Nobody comes to me just to say, 'Hi, Lola. Howya doing?'"

"What about your girlfriends?"

"Don't got none. They trippin' 'cause they thought I flipped, when I'm still Lola. Yeah, I wear the bling, I'm always gonna do that, 'cause I earned it. I work hard."

"I know you do."

"But right now I feel worse than when I used to wait all night for my momma to come home."

"What about Madd? I mean—"

"Call him Madd Dogg, 'cause that's what he be actin' like."

"Then why stay? Do you love him?" I asked, resting my hands on my knees, feeling like a naïve schoolgirl.

"What's that? Only something to sing about. Ain't nobody who makin' any cake, singin' about love and, really, it ain't nothin' I'm feeling."

"Wow! Love songs don't sell? Look, I think—"

"I didn't ask you what you thought," Lola snapped, bristling. The hair on my arms rose like that of an irritated feline. Lola's eyes turned cold.

"Then why did you call me?" I asked defensively, taken aback by her directness.

"Because I thought you would... I don't need a motha. I got a motha. I just need to get my head together. And for people to stop tellin' me what to do. Squash this, I'm leavin'." Lola reached for her orange Timbs.

"Lola, you misunderstood."

"Whatever." Lola gave me the hand as if we were betrayed guests on *The Jerry Springer Show* I felt like—but I didn't.

"Look, I won't push. Promise. Both Cleo and I want you to take all the time you need."

Lola paused. No longer tying the laces on her boots, she looked me squarely in the face and said, "Why are you being nice to me?"

"Because believe it or not, we are in the same boat. Back in Atlanta, and even with my family, everyone wants me to change to suit their comfort level. My mother. My grandmother and my man. Ex-man. Tryin' to tweak me into their version of perfection. And frankly, now I'm not trying to hear that. Take me as I am. And you should...oops! Sorry."

"That's okay," Lola said quietly, smiling. "I'm listening."

Needing very little encouragement, I continued, "You should know, Lola, that you are perfect as you are. And if anybody, particularly Madd Dogg, wants you to do something immoral or illegal, you need to distance yourself from him. You have too much to lose."

"Because of my record deal?"

"Fuck the—sorry, forget the record deal! The boy is draining you. He's a vampire who wants to suck your blood, your body, your spirit from you. Basically, he wants you dead. Straight up. If you don't feel good around him, and I mean like the Queen of Sheba, really adored, then he needs to bounce. Especially with him putting his hands on you." Tears welled up in Lola's eyes.

"Thanks, sista," she said, lacing her arms around my neck.

---Original Message-----

From: Coby@nextlevelrecords.com

To: Iris@imagecontrol.com

Sent: Thu, Oct 6, 2010 3:46 pm

Subject: LOLA

Yo! Lola better get back into the studio. I'm losin' loot every day she's not recording.

---Original Message-----

From: Iris@imagecontrol.com

To: Colby@nextlevelrecords.com

Sent: Thu, Oct 6, 2010 3:50 pm

Subject:REPLY/ LOLA

Coby,

Just give her some time. In the state she's in, Lola couldn't record a lyric if Jay-Z was her daddy.

Trust me on this one.

Iris

"Can you hear me now?" I said into my phone as I strolled along the wide corridors with several office doors and photos of entertainers, some infamous, others dead. The plush hallway carpet leading to Cleo's office in ABC's corporate tower near Lincoln Center harbored secret company strategies reeking of money and competitive programming, no matter how much the celebrities in the photos were grinning. Giving up on the telephone connection, I gathered myself, shaking my head, deciding to get a new wireless provider.

The ample waiting area for corporate sales was decorated with four brown leather chairs and there were copies of the *Hollywood Reporter*, *Variety*, and the *Wall Street Journal* strewn across the walnut coffee table. The receptionist, an Asian girl with a short pug nose, was on a telephone call when my phone sprang back to life. "Iris Chapman."

"Gil Cooper here."

"Mr. Cooper, how are you?" I said, glad to hear from him, as the only time I saw him now was smiling down at me from billboards. "Did you try to reach me a minute ago?"

"I'm not surprised you couldn't hear me. I don't believe in those things…you can't hear the person you're calling and you're likely to come down with cancer."

I giggled, repeating, "How are you, Mr. Cooper?"

"Fine. Fine. Your neighbor told me you were up in New York."

"Oh really, who?"

"The woman walking around with half her ass hanging out. Scandalous. Listen, I don't want to run my telephone bill up. Let me tell you why I called," he replied, reminding me of my father who was always mindful of his telephone bill. When the receptionist completed her call, I whispered that I was there to see Cleo. She nodded, keying in Cleo's extension on the switchboard console.

"Clarence Fisher. You heard of him?"

"No. Can't say that I have."

"Clarence Fisher is my nephew. And he is a bumbling idiot, but he's family, so I guess I got to help him."

"And where do I come in?"

By way of blatant cronyism, Clarence had gotten on the ballot for the New York State Assembly. Now, to the Democratic Party's chagrin, he had caused a citywide uproar. While seeking the endorsement of the *Daily News*, he told the board of executive editors, "I sympathized with NATO's decision to bomb Kosovo only because it was justifiable retaliation for the shitty professional basketball players Yugoslavia insists on exporting to the NBA." And he defended his remark to the Asia Society, saying that he thought "Jackie Chan was all that and dim sum!"

"Clarence needs to see a surgeon as soon as possible," Gil Cooper explained.

"Oh. What's the problem?"

"He needs to have his foot removed from his mouth. That is, if you will help him. Write his speeches. Shut his face. Cure his diarrhea of the mouth."

"Mr. Cooper, I'm actually in New York on vacation."

"I wouldn't ask if I—"

"There are other consultants who know the New York terrain far better than I," I added, following Cleo into her office.

"My wife is about to drive me crazy over Clarence. He's her sister's child. I always thought the boy was a little slow. But if you can stop this woman from nagging me, I'll sure appre—"

Smiling, I interrupted him. "Mr. Cooper, I'm scheduled to return to Atlanta day after tomorrow, so I'll have to see him tonight." I hated hearing a man, particularly Gil Cooper, whom I felt affection for, beg. After I hung up, now seated on a red leather sofa in Cleo's expansive office, she shook her head, sadly, saying, "I thought we were going back to Gazelle's for one last day of luxury. I'm not sure you're ready to be in the same city or in the same state as Achilles so soon."

"Cleo, everything happens for a reason. And if I can help other people, in a way I feel like I'm getting my stride back. Come with me to meet this Clarence Fisher. At the Sugar Bar on West Seventy-Second Street."

"We can cab it. And what's up with your girl Lola? She was still 'sleep when I left," Cleo said, draping her purse over her shoulder, standing and pushing her red leather swivel chair under her desk.

"God was still 'sleep when you left. I left Lola pulling weeds in your garden. Said it was therapeutic getting her hands dirty, although she didn't use that word. She said it was 'dope,' and that later she was going to go back to bed, maybe do some writing. And get this: Lola promised to cook dinner for us."

"I hope she can throw down, 'cause my stomach's talkin'." Cleo stepped around a pile of marketing reports, flipping off the office light switch.

Two white senior citizens stood near the curb in front of the Sugar Bar, smiling at the beautiful people entering the restaurant. The decor was reminiscent of an African art gallery. Exquisite African masks, sculptures, and paintings were sprinkled throughout and a straw roof had been built over the bar. A giant mural entitled *Power* was hung on the main wall, depicting two African women offering a baby to the sky, surrounded by zebras, lions, and tigers running in the opposite direction.

Clarence Fisher was easy to spot. But one needed to exercise some restraint in response to seeing him. Whatever problems I had encountered exorcising Gil Cooper's plaid jacket would be magnified with his nephew. The chatty, ass-kissing bystanders standing around him who were smacking on crabmeat and avocado wraps apparently chose to overlook the fact that their candidate was dressed like a modern-day vampire, with the touch of a rural undertaker. They wanted to be in close proximity to power, just in case Clarence won the assembly seat, and they needed a job.

I checked my calendar. It was too early for Halloween. But there he was, a tall reed of a man with high cheekbones and long, wide sideburns. His avuncular laugh shocked the room when he would "Har-de-har-har, Har-de-har-har." Campaign workers paused to see if an earthquake had occurred before returning to their conversations of bullshit and backstabbing.

"Mr. Fisher? Iris Chapman," I said, extending my arm to shake his hand. It felt damp and clammy. The two male bystanders shrugged annoyance that their attempts to secure a government contract in exchange for a campaign contribution, had been interrupted.

"Uncle Gil said you would stop by. How do you do it, Iris?"

"How do I do what?" I replied, looking instinctively over my shoulder for Cleo, who I then remembered was having an appetizer at the bar, not confident that she could wait until we got home to eat.

"With your bald head, people must think you're a lesbian or prefer white men. I bet you get that all the time. Har-de-har-har, Har-de-har!" The two bystanders waited for my answer as if Clarence had asked my opinion on double-digit inflation. Instead of being enraged the way I often felt under the interrogation of my family, or the humiliation felt with Achilles, I pitied poor Clarence, who had somehow gotten through life without shock treatments and a confirmed diagnosis of severe Tourette's Syndrome.

"No. What I do with people who make inappropriate comments is to double my fees. That way, my bald-ass head can laugh all the way to the bank." The two bystanders, including Clarence, smiled sheepishly, nodding as their knees dipped. A waiter glided past serving marinated shrimp, which I heartily availed myself of.

"Cleo said you were in here."

I turned in the direction of the baritone voice, with a piece of crabmeat no doubt hanging from my mouth, taking a step back lest this person breathing within an inch of my nose inhale my next breath.

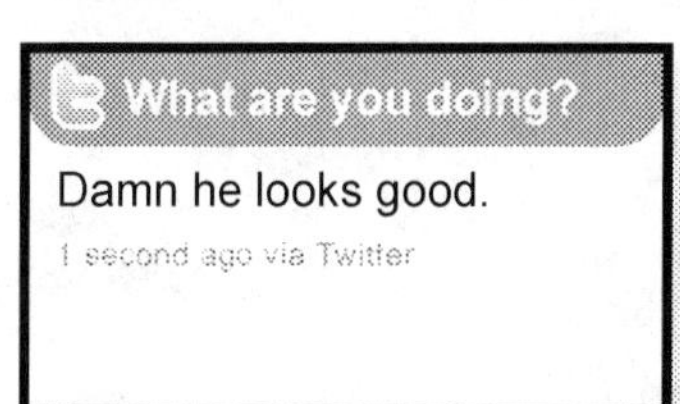

"Oh, hello, Vernon, right?" I said nonchalantly.

"You remembered my name. That's a good sign. What's up, Clarence?" Vernon Blackwell was even more handsome, but in an ugly, rugged way, than I remembered. He was freshly shaven and coifed, with the slight aroma of musk. He scooted close to me to shake hands with Clarence, also making room for a roaming waitress, but remained there after she had long since passed. Still at the bar, Cleo threw her head back in a loud yuck-yuck after a tall, bearded brother whispered in her ear.

"Vernon, my man, you do get around," Clarence said tersely between tight lips, after his ass-kissing bystanders had left.

"And Clarence, you do have your damn opinions," Vernon replied. The two took a dueler's stance, their eyes darkening, surrounded by the flirtatious smiles of various women making it their business to pass close to Vernon.

"Iris and I were discussing business," Clarence said rudely. Vernon looked at me for confirmation.

"We were talking—" I began hesitantly, placing my hand in my pocket.

"I've retained Iris to be my press representative," Clarence interjected, still glaring at Vernon. Vernon again looked at me for confirmation.

"No, you haven't," I said, surprised I was opening a can of worms, being so forthright. Both men waited for me to finish. "Clarence, your uncle asked that I represent you as a favor to him. I love your uncle. Gil Cooper is one of the most honorable men I know. But he'll have to understand that I couldn't possibly work for someone as pompous and insensitive as you." Shoving my empty plate into Clarence's outreached hand, I marched toward Cleo, who was still being entertained by the tall, bearded brother. I abruptly paused and turned back. "Vernon, take care. Nice to have seen you."

Surprised, Vernon smiled.

"Sorry to keep you waiting," I said, reaching Cleo.

"I was about to eat the wax off this bar." Cleo introduced me to her companion before saying her adieus. As we headed toward the front door, I glanced around, noticing that Vernon had been joined by a woman who looked like a Las Vegas showgirl. I could feel my pantyhose unravel as Ms. Showgirl stroked Vernon's forearm, and he blushed.

Go ahead, Ms. Thang. Mark your territory, I thought. *Mark your territory.*

Cleo praised me for standing up to Clarence and deciding against working with such an asshole. "You know how I feel. Life is too short to let people drain you. Toldja coming to New York would do you good."

"Yeah, 'cause if it was three months ago I would have caved, feeling guilt-ridden, not abiding by what I wanted or how I felt."

"In a minute, I'm not gonna recognize you," Cleo said, unlocking the heavy oak door to her brownstone.

A reasonably lit house is what we expected, with the scent of a hot-cooked meal greeting our noses, stifling our hunger pangs. But what we got was silence. Our search throughout the brownstone yielded no trace of Lola. It was as if she had evaporated, never existed. The bed in which she had slept was perfectly made, the dolls neatly replaced, their eyes glazed and expectant. The kitchen sink was cleaner than it had been since I had arrived, the faucet crying a slow drip. When Cleo returned from the backyard garden, the expression on her face provided confirmation. Lola was indeed ghost.

[14]

"Who the hell do you think you're talking to, Colby? I'm not one of your goddamn flunkies!" I screamed back into the telephone, while Cleo sat in her living room staring at a muted television. "Lola needed a safe place. We gave it to her. But I never signed on to be her babysitter or your doormat, for that matter."

Colby had been screaming longer than I was willing to allow. Suddenly his voice took on a low, bludgeoning tone devoid of respect for anyone who did not harbor his viewpoint. "I told you to look out for her."

"You don't *tell* me to do anything. Look, I told you that she called, and that I would look in on her. If she was that valuable, seems like you would have your fat, cheap ass up here." The line went dead. Colby had hung up.

Oh Lawd, I thought, *why did I go there*? Before I could take it back, Cleo had scrunched up her face, giving me a funny look. "Sorry," I mouthed.

It was early Saturday morning. Outside Cleo's kitchen window, children were riding their scooters up and down the sidewalk. A young black woman was sweeping the sidewalk in front of her brownstone. I was bleary-eyed. Cleo and I had been up all night, brainstorming about what to do about Lola. We felt connected to her, more than we wanted to admit. And we felt she'd given us her ass to kiss, leaving without so much as a goodbye note, a text message or a telephone call.

Delroy, seeing a window of opportunity with Cleo, came over with a box of beef patties, the night before and waited patiently for her; then made his move to slip back into Cleo's arms. Now, he was snoring gently upstairs in her bed.

We had considered filing a missing persons report, but Lola was grown, sane (*we thought*), and the last thing she needed was more negative publicity. But as pissed as we were about Lola, we, at least I, felt she needed me.

"Maybe we should call her mother?" Cleo said, walking barefoot into the kitchen.

"I did. Made up some tale about it was nice meeting her, even though it was. Her mother told me to tell Lola to call her." I removed orange juice from the refrigerator, and poured myself a glass. The juice chilled my throat going down, and my trachea struggled to return to room temperature. "She's with Madd Dogg," I said with finality, drying the breakfast dishes, placing them inside the upper pantry.

"You think?" Cleo said, standing beside me.

"As sure as I'm standing here. I'm going down to the studio. I need to see her with my own eyes. You don't just up and leave, without a thank-you or a goodbye, at least to you, Cleo." I dropped the dish towel, and slipped on my Atlanta Hawks leather bomber jacket with matching baseball cap.

"You need me to go?" Cleo asked as the telephone on her kitchen wall rang. "Cleo," she answered in a tone so low and sultry I just had to laugh, lacing my sneakers. Cleo smiled, too. Instead of engaging in a conversation, she extended the telephone receiver to me, smiling coyly, with eyebrows raised.

"Yes, hello?" I was curious as to who would be calling me on Cleo's telephone.

"I hope I didn't interrupt?" the familiar baritone voice asked. "It's Vernon. Vernon Blackwell."

"Oh hi," I said, looking at the winking Cleo as she tiptoed upstairs, wearing her white floor-length negligee and fur high-heel slippers.

"Cleo said that you were leaving in the morning. I wanted to see you. See if you were available for brunch."

"Well, um.... " I remembered how handsome Vernon looked at the fundraiser at the Sugar Bar, and I smiled at his boldness.

"I know it's last minute."

"No, that's not it. I mean, usually that is it, but I have to make a run to midtown. See about somebody." A little edge entered my voice as I thought about Lola.

"Are you taking the subway?" Vernon asked, determined to continue the conversation.

"In this cold, I'll grab a cab."

"Why don't I swing by and get you? I'll take you to wherever you have to be. And we'll just see how the day goes."

The interior of the canary yellow Corvette had the aroma of spice and citrus, and the supple, mud brown, leather bucket seats were soft enough to bring on a sudden slumber. Vernon and I looked like benefactors from a sports apparel sale, which was a relief as I'd been concerned as to what to wear, when he parked in front of Cleo's brownstone, having given no thought as to my appearance, only focusing on Lola's whereabouts.

Entering the West Side Highway at 125th Street, Vernon and I debated the merits of the Atlanta Hawks over the New York Knicks, his favorite team.

"Ewing always thought he was a point guard. That was his problem," I said, as if I was an ESPN commentator.

"Say what? Pat Ewing gave his sweat and blood for that franchise for over ten years. They could have showed the brother more respect than he got." Vernon signaled, veering into the middle lane of the three-lane highway.

"Tell me something," I said.

"What's that?"

"How does a man born and raised in Atlanta become a New York Knicks fan? Isn't that sort of like being a traitor?"

Vernon's chuckle sounded like an approaching thunderstorm. "Like everybody else in Georgia, I was a Hawks fan. In fact, I followed all the teams, even hockey. But I guess when I moved away, working in different cities, finally getting a syndicated radio show and spending a lot of time in New York, most of my friends were Knick players, so of course my loyalty went toward them, especially Patrick."

"Oh, so when I hear you on the radio in Atlanta, you're actually here in New York?"

"Sometimes. I have the flexibility to broadcast from wherever I want. So I'm pretty much back and forth, between New York and Atlanta." Another Corvette driver honked at Vernon, giving him the thumbs-up sign, as we drove west across Fifty-Fourth Street, parking in front of StarTyme Recording, across the street from Elite's adult entertainment emporium. "You want me to go up with you?"

"That's okay. Don't want you to get your car towed." Vernon galloped around to open my car door. "You smell great," he said, when I brushed against him as he helped me out of the car. I blushed, batting my eyelashes like a silent screen movie star. The glass wall mirrored Vernon leaning against his Corvette, watching my booty shimmy as I walked toward the office building; he then began robotically scrolling through his iPhone.

The two Rottweilers, Buddha and King, and the receptionist were replaced by a Dominican janitor who was glued to a beat-up miniature black-white television, watching a Yankee baseball game on Telemundo, not even looking up as I approached him until I pounded on the counter.

"Excuse me, is there anyone upstairs at StarTyme?"

The television announcer disappointed the janitor: "*MVP Jeter están de parte de batea. El tono se tira. El columpia. Se parece a un cuadrangular. Va, va y cogido en la pared por Rodriguez.* (MVP Jeter is up to bat. The pitch is thrown. He swings. It looks like a home run. It is going, going and caught at the wall by Rodriguez.)" The janitor pounded his temples with the side of his fist as I repeated, "Excuse me?" My appeal went unanswered and ignored, as he cried, "*Ah mí! Ah mi! Ah mi!*"

"I don't give a flyin' fuck what you think. Who gave you permission to think? You think you got skillz? Beyotch, please! I taught you everything! I fuckin' made you! Lemme put this in simple terms that you can understand; you know, the level you do ya rhymes at. That last line you kicked: 'I put more niggas to sleep than 1-800-Mattress.' That metaphor is like some shit I woulda said in junior high! You betta keep it real!"

Madd Dogg was on fire. Lola cowered in the corner, staring down at her dirty white sneakers like a zombie. The optimistic young girl who had emerged at Cleo's had again disappeared under Madd Dogg's verbal assault. The two were alone in the studio; the cherry-colored lights on the engineering board were still flashing. Madd Dogg was wearing the requisite hip-hop uniform: Levi jeans and beige sweatshirt, made in Korea. Lola was wearing the same clothes she had escaped in to Cleo's. Her confidence and vulnerability had again been stolen.

"Lola," I said, stepping through the door.

"Whatchu doin' here?" Madd Dogg responded, turning toward me, partially blocking Lola.

"Lola," I said again, ignoring Madd Dogg. "Why did you up and leave?"

"Who da fuck are you, *Auntie*?" he leered. "Comin' up here, uninvited, askin' questions, like you five-oh or some shit."

"Lola?!"

"She don't belong wit chu. She belongs here. Wit me."

"Excuse me, I'd like to hear it from Lola," I said tersely, snapping my arms across my chest.

Lola slowly stood, slipping around Madd Dogg. "You shouldn't be here," she said in a tiny voice, biting her lower lip.

"Lola, you said you wanted to get away, to have a better life."

Madd Dogg shook his head slowly, lighting a marijuana joint with swagger, purposely blowing a gust of smoke toward me, exhaling in my face.

"And was she saying how bitches always be pullin' on her? How that was what she always wanted? The better life. Fans screaming her name. Any life she gonna have and anybody in it, gotta come by this nigga first," Madd Dogg boasted, thumping his chest.

"Is that some kind of a threat?" I said, beginning to write checks I could not cash.

"Get this bitch outta here," Madd Dogg barked to Lola, hovering over her, flailing his arms like he was about to take flight.

"Lola, you don't have to live like this. There are other producers, other men who won't abuse you. You don't have to be anybody but yourself." The studio door behind me pushed open; it was Buddha and King, followed by the thug-looking receptionist and another skinny, sleepy-eyed kid, who slowly bopped into the room. The two Rottweilers sniffed curiously around my feet. The two men followed suit, sensing the tension in the room. "Whassup, Dogg?" they said.

"This old sell-out bitch thinks Lola is going somewhere wit her." Madd Dogg laughed. *Old* was what he'd called me. My breasts sank two feet, as I fantasized about biting his head off and spitting it back into his face.

"Lola, I'm leaving. And you're welcome to come." Lola maintained her stare into the floor.

The two males blurted laughter. "Who's dis, man?"

Standing with the studio door open, I pivoted toward Madd Dogg, steam plowing through my ears, my tiny nostrils flaring. The two men jumped to their feet as if I was a physical threat, pushing Lola behind them. Buddha and King growled, gnashing their teeth. "You talk about keepin' it real. Keepin' it real means lifting your culture, not debasing it and demeaning women because you happen to be bigger than them. If you want to be about keepin' it real, why don't you call the devil and see if you can get your soul back? Modern-day Sambo!"

Madd Dogg stepped toward me. Lola screamed. A strong arm reached around me, dragging me to the studio door, then this figure stepped in front of Madd Dogg. It was Vernon.

"You don't want to go there, my man. Trust me," Vernon warned, with hardened eyes.

Madd Dogg looked up into Vernon's serious face, evaluating his options. He had none. His homies were suddenly interested in reading *Source* magazine. Buddha and King whimpered.

"Hey, Vee," Madd Dogg said, "I didn't mean nothing." Vernon and Madd Dogg obviously knew each other. Still Vernon did not thaw his icy exterior.

"You okay?" Vernon turned and asked me. I nodded. "So what's left to do here?"

"Lola, you coming?" I asked. Lola sadly looked into my eyes, then shook her head, rushing out an opposite door.

❖ ❖ ❖

"It really hurts to see some of our talented starlets of color accomplish so much only to let some asshole drag them down. Millions of our young daughters idolize these famous women, wanting to be exactly like them, even if it means having a sorry-ass man like them. Just imagine what would happen if these divas would respect themselves enough to let those snakes go? Imagine if they showed the world that they love themselves too much to let a man, or anyone, destroy their lives? I'm not saying that there's something wrong with them for getting played, because it damn sure happened to me enough times. I'm saying that when the shit keeps happening over and over again it's time to show your dignity and show that asshole the door," I blabbed to Vernon, as he drove away from the studio, and up the Avenue of the Americas, turning right on Fifty-Ninth Street.

Vernon suggested a drive upstate, then dinner. "Let's just talk," he had said. Inside, I was numb, feeling anger and sadness for Lola.

"There's an Italian restaurant with great seafood, just above Nyack." Vernon steered his Corvette north onto the FDR Drive. Blue-gray clouds formed sharp streaks, and small boats idled in the waters of the East River. A tourist helicopter flew over the Harlem River Bridge.

Vernon knew of Lola, had heard the scuttlebutt about the frequent run-ins with Madd Dogg and far worse, the police. Colby Woods often courted him, pleading for Vernon to break out a single from one of his new artists. "He knew who he was dealing with when I refused to accept cash under the table. He figured everybody else in town was taking payoffs to play what they called music, why not me?"

Shifting in my seat, I turned slightly toward Vernon. "What did it? What made you so different?" Vernon made a clucking noise inside of his mouth, mulling an answer as we crossed the George Washington Bridge into New Jersey; early evening had rapidly fallen.

"Once you put yourself out there, letting people know you have a price, your integrity is compromised, and no one in any industry, particularly in radio, will ever respect you."

As we sat skimming the suede-bound menu, the aromas of roasted garlic and herbs gently floated throughout the candlelit dining area. My focus shifted to this homo sapien before me who had schmoozed the maitre d' into seating us, circumventing their dress policy; had held my hand, scooting my chair close to the table just so; his gaze soft, about a cup short of lustful. Half a day had passed before I noticed how good it felt being with him, my babbling affecting him as though I mattered. Vernon's replies were full of wisdom, and he stressed the importance of digging deeper to know myself, instead of focusing so much on the world. "Because when it comes down to it, you're all you've got," Vernon said, refilling my goblet from the bottle of Chianti, raising his in a toast. "To new beginnings."

A moist sensation formed between my legs that had not occurred since the morning I had had a dawn session of Bikram yoga; and before that, whenever I anticipated being with Achilles, whom I had not thought of until the Westminster Dog Show had advertised that it was accepting experienced participants.

Vernon and I were starving, our bodies tense; then relaxing as our tongues swirled around the mozzarella cucina and the hot antipasto, our breathing quickening as we devoured the clams oreganato, stuffed mushrooms, eggplant rollantini, and artichoke hearts. We exuded moans while devouring the shrimp and mussels.

We clutched one another as the eggplant exploded a blend of herbal flavors into our mouths, rendering us vulnerable, giggling, perspiration dotting our foreheads.

By the time the main course appeared, Vernon and I were pleading for mercy, but the shrimp and broccoli rabe with sautéed garlic over linguine offered no compassion, capturing us in our weakest moment, leaving us to lick our fingers in surrender. With extended stomachs, we offered no resistance when the pumpkin praline pie and the tartufo, consisting of vanilla and chocolate ice cream with hazelnuts, arrived. Then we allowed ourselves to be hauled in individual wheelbarrows to Vernon's Corvette. With new silver flatware from the restaurant secreted inside my purse, Vernon and I had had a completely satisfying evening.

My career as a budding kleptomaniac began by watching Lee Artist slip china in her purse during dinner in the restaurant at the Ritz-Carlton Hotel on Miami Beach, an innocent action, really. No one but me had noticed my mother slipping Orchard In Bloom flatware and a Floral Waltz plate in her Coach purse, thereafter dabbing the sides of her mouth with an elegant scroll damask napkin. The bewildered waiter, dedicated to delivering first-class service, kept bringing flatware and plates to replace the ones that had magically disappeared. "Excellent service in this hotel," Lee Artist beamed. "And most Negroes think that the hotels in Miami Beach don't like to serve us. Well, I beg to differ."

Judgmental people would have classified Lee Artist as a common thief, but they would have been wrong. My mother was merely helping the beleaguered waiter from carting dirty dishes used by us Negroes back to the kitchen, which they would burn in effigy, anyway. Everyone knew that, at that time, restaurants would have rather gone out of business than to reuse plates and flatware used by Negroes.

"This is 107.5 WBLS New York, the 'Quiet Storm.' Where the legends of soul live forever." Vernon leaned toward the microphone and melded his soothing voice with the show's theme music. His prerecorded voice announced the call letters of radio stations in other cities, followed by a series of upbeat commercials and urgent promotions. His voice calmed the hearts of romantics, offering hope to the lovelorn while he played the background music for creating love's fantasies, throughout the sixty markets in which he broadcast. It was the "Quiet Storm." Ten o'clock p.m. The on-air light was turned off. Vernon rested his headset on the console, casually rubbing the back of his hand against my cheek. An energetic male intern, busting rhymes under his breath, served us mugs of hot apple cider.

"You're beautiful, Iris. You know that?"

His eyes were weary from the long day, but when the engineer gave him his cue out of the commercial break and the on-air light came on, he was ready with his Southern baritone. "We're living in fifty-five minutes of pure soul at 107.5 WBLS, New York. In the last set, you heard the new single by Eric Roberson, Dave Hollister, and Rachelle Ferrell. Call me for dedications to the one you hold dear." He gave the station's phone number. "Hmm-mmmm... let me kick that notion off with my own personal dedication to Iris. Kenny Lattimore's 'If You Could See You Through My Eyes.'"

When I reached Cleo, who told me she was spread eagle under Delroy, she said she knew that Vernon would make me scarce, and reveled in the giggle in my voice. "Child, when you didn't get back here in time for '60 Minutes,' I knew you weren't coming. 'Cause you know you love you some '60 Minutes.'"

"I hope you TIVO'd it for me, Cleo," I whispered, as Vernon communicated last-minute changes in the playlist to the Midwest affiliates.

"Child, the only thang I'm TIVO'd is a sign to my boudoir saying, 'Do Not Enter.' Make-up sex is worth the argument." Cleo laughed.

"Well, I'll see you when Vernon gets off the air."

"At two o'clock in the morning? I think not. Just tell love man to play some Teddy Pendergrass for me."

"Teddy Pendergrass. You showing your age."

"You got that right. And my ass. Toodles. See you in the morning. And have fun, you deserve it. ...Ooooooh, Delroy, you better stop, ooh..."

ATLANTA

[15]

"Hi, Ms. Chickie," I said, calling home on impulse, after spending the humid morning running laps in a rain-drenched Piedmont Park. "How ya doing?"

"Child, you sound like some white lady calling to try to sell me something. Sounding so proper."

This was the standard reaction from a family member, particularly when I had been away from Opa Locka for a while, absorbing "Yankee ways," as Ms. Chickie often described my speech pattern. While I was away in college and Victor was still living at home, he could never identify my voice. A common scenario: "Hello, Victor." Without returning my greeting, he would slam down the telephone receiver. "Momma! Momma! Dere's a white lady on the phone."

Applying face moisturizer, I asked, "So what's goin' on down there?"

"Lawd, your crazy momma stay in the streets and your daddy must have a woman under the hood of the car, as much as he stays under there. I haven't seen nothing like that in my life. And your brother done left that gal. I never liked her no way. And he's back here, until he can find another dummy to move in with. And my arthritis is cutting up; feel like a pain is shooting up through my spine. Bertha died. Shot herself in the foot. But other than that, I'm blessed and highly favored. You having sex wit' anybody?"

"I still can't believe that Victor is still sleepin' in the same room, he used to wet the bed!" I exclaimed, now applying deodorant and ignoring her question.

"Child, he needed some place to stay. Plus, I saw it in a dream. Saw how nothing good could come out of a marriage with all of those nasty chickens walking around and those damn candles burning all of the time. And you know what else?"

"What, Ms. Chickie?" I responded, even though she was going to tell me anyway.

"Dat gal had a gap, right square in front of her mouth. And you know what that means, don't you?"

"What, Ms. Chickie?" I exhaled and rolled my eyes at the same time.

"Her lies were so big, her teeth needed the room for the lies to come out."

"Okay, so has Victor taken on some new religion or changed his name again?" I asked laughingly.

"Oh, you know that boy is fine as long as he got his momma to come running to. But you know it's never good for a grown man to be living at home. I tell you, your momma done ruint that boy. Ruint him! Umph, umph, I don't know where your momma gets her ways."

"I bet he's there now. Back there in his room asleep."

"Sho is. I just got done boiling his grits. Come on, Victor, before your food gets cold," she yelled, before continuing with me. "Your high-and-mighty sister is on the telephone."

I had lost my appetite for family bonding. The purpose in calling was to receive a warm, maternal hug from my belligerent grandmother, or my aloof mother, or at the very least, my nefarious brother or ever-absent father.

What was I thinking?

By the time I arrived home from Hartsfield-Jackson airport,

Vernon had texted and phoned, checking to see if I had arrived safely, and confirming if I had received the jade plant and the Kenny Lattimore CD personally autographed by the singer himself. I hadn't. Mr. Whitaker had intercepted them, using it as an excuse to dip into my business.

"When you leave packages on your doorstep, thieves know nobody is home."

"Thanks, Mr. Whitaker, but everybody knows you're the eyes and the ears on the block."

Mr. Whitaker took my statement as a compliment. "Heh, heh, well, I do keep my eye on things around here. Which reminds me, I haven't seen your man friend lately," he said, perching his foot on the threshold as if I had invited him to stay awhile. Suddenly, a pungent aroma threatened to strangle my nostrils, causing my eyes to water.

Dabbing my eyes with the back of my wrists. "Mr. Whitaker, what on earth is that smell?"

"Huh? Oh, that's my new cologne. Like it?" he asked proudly, leaning close so I could get a stronger whiff.

"Reminds me of..."

"I got it from my brother-in-law. His new business. He mixed my sweat with wood root tonic. And the beauty is that I can go around smelling like myself."

"Oh. No wonder it makes me sick," I slammed the door on his foot. Mr. Whitaker screamed and hobbled next door to his own house, where he should have been in the first place.

Vernon had attached a card to the luscious jade plant: "Let the life of the jade represent a new beginning." Recalling our last tenuous hours together, I thought, a new beginning is what I deserved. In spite of the rain, a raven landed on the windowsill, chirping, just as I was on the verge of believing it.

After Vernon's radio show, we had wandered around Rockefeller Center, holding hands, wrapped in a comfortable silence. My hormones had been on fire, frankly, but my heart had been on a retreat, while my persona had camouflaged my roller-coaster emotions. Vernon had purchased hot chocolate and cinnamon rolls at an all-night bakery near the corner of his high-rise condominium. He had stacked logs in the fireplace and built a rapid fire, then finally had settled on the brown leather sofa next to me, as we had argued over everything from whether the idea of reparations was a pipe dream to how music sampling had shelved the careers of recording icons.

Gradually Vernon had steered the conversation to more personal matters, needing to know what mattered to me. "Is there a man in your life?" he had asked, stirring his hot chocolate.

My palm instinctively covered my heart, perhaps recalling recent trespasses. "What did the brother do?" Vernon had asked.

At first, I wanted to appear noble, assigning equal blame and admitting that I should have seen it coming, that I hadn't accepted Achilles for who he was, but as Vernon had commiserated with me, my true resentment came out. "It didn't matter if Achilles and I were having problems. That didn't give someone who I treated like a sister carte blanche to infiltrate the relationship."

"Do you still love him?"

"Since my trip to here, I've thought about that, but I think what bothers me is not the fact that we broke up, but that Tammy became involved with him. I thought she was better than that. The relationship was ending, but I think I stayed with Achilles because I thought I deserved him."

Vernon and I had nodded our heads at my revelation and at how many times in our lives we had allowed toxic people to languish, draining our energies, leaving us with nothing, including our self-esteem.

"Let me hold you," Vernon had said. When he had felt me resist, then shiver under his embrace, he had offered, "I just want to hold you, that's all."

And so, Vernon and I had slept fully clothed, draped in each other's arms, breathing softly, denting his leather sofa.

When I shared this development with Cleo, she laughed so hard I thought she was going to make herself sick. "Iris, you're my best friend, but you are also are a sex-o-holic."

"But—" As Delroy was sucking on her toes, Cleo had not heard the whole story. Vernon had stirred first, a few hours later, waking to a chilly, gray morning. The now-dying embers had simmered amongst the coals in the fireplace. The telephone had rung. Vernon had scooted from under me, which had spurred me to sit up, smoothing my soft, fuzzy hair, gradually recalling where I was and whom I was with.

Vernon had spoken in low, personal tones on the telephone in his small kitchen alcove. Men do not murmur with their homies; instead, they tend to bellow as if they were in a hollering contest. Instinctively, I knew he was speaking with a woman. What happened to you last night, I imagined she would say, followed by, we could pick up where we left off, you know.

I had hovered in the bathroom doorway, then had pretended to rinse my mouth and remove the sleep from my eyes. I had eavesdropped closely, hanging on as the seconds slowly ticked away. Vernon's tone had explained, listened, then again explained, confirmed, before he softly had replaced the telephone receiver.

Returning to the living room, Vernon and I had converged at the same time near his walnut dining room table.

"Good morning," he had said.

"'Mornin'," I had mumbled, avoiding his questioning stare. I felt I was intruding, that the carefree comfort I had felt the day before was merely an illusion, and that the sooner we returned our emotions to reality, the better. Rummaging through my wallet, I had retrieved money for a taxicab, dialing my BlackBerry. "I wanna let Cleo know I am on the way."

"I'll take you to—"

"No, that's okay. Plus I have to pack."

"I'll wait. And then take you to the airport," Vernon had insisted, placing his hand on my arm.

"No, that's—"

Suddenly, Vernon was kissing me. Hard. Then soft, easing his tongue into my mouth, wrapping his arms around me, as warm as a comforter. I offered no resistance, relaxing, as we slid down to the plush rug in front of the fireplace, entwining ourselves around one another. Vernon cradled me, staring into my eyes, waiting for my signal, for him, for us to proceed. I nodded. A solitary tear flowed from my right eye. Vernon's tongue caught it before the salty liquid reached my earlobe. Then taking his time, he removed my T-shirt, kissing my shoulder like he was sucking on a cherry candy, warming it in response to my trembling. He traced my limp body with the brush of his lips. "The plane," I had murmured like someone coming out of a coma.

"Let me fly you. Just hold on."

Vernon's lovemaking was a combination of wild horses and blooming flowers. And right now, that's what both bothered and frightened me. He was too perfect. He had zero flaws on which I could hang my insecurities, or use as a valid reason to kick him to the curb. Well, there was the issue of family and what they would think. Vernon was not tall, nor handsome, but average looking, sort of like Denzel, possessing that *thing* that made you think he was handsome. You accepted what he believed about himself.

The fact was, in twenty-four hours, I had fallen in love with Vernon, more fully than I have ever loved any man. But I still questioned whether it was too soon to be jumping into an emotional involvement on the heels of Achilles' trifling ass and Tammy's betrayal.

Later, after private giggles and a teary farewell from Cleo, who could not wait to get back upstairs with Delroy, who brought us all fresh sweet potato pies, Vernon had held my hand en route to the airport, until his car phone had rung. Again I knew it was a woman; probably the same woman who had called earlier that morning.

"Vernon Blackwell," he had answered, pressing the phone knob on his steering wheel.

Upon hearing "her" voice, through the speakers, Vernon had planted his hands-free headset to his ears farthest away from me, responding to *her* in monosyllabic caveman grunts, as we had sped across the Triborough Bridge.

"Uh-huh...hmph...uh, uh...okay...mmmm...okay."

As we had passed a sign that read: WELCOME TO QUEENS. POPULATION 700,000. CLAIRE SCHULMAN, BOROUGH PRESIDENT, Vernon had hung up and glanced my way. "Hey. You okay?"

Since I was positioned somewhat like the Leaning Tower of Pisa, almost hanging out of the car door as trucks and other cars zipped past, I was an unadulterated liar when I had responded in a falsetto voice, "I'm fine," shrugging my shoulders. Vernon had reached for my hand, but all of a sudden I needed it to discover dinosaurs in the bottom of my carry-on bag. He had clucked his tongue inside his mouth.

Stinging tears had crept into the rear of my corneas. I had needed to get out of these comfortable bucket seats then.

"I'll get out here," I had said, when Vernon was forced to stop behind a car rental courtesy van inside the terminal area of La Guardia airport.

"Short-term parking is in the next lot," Vernon had said.

I sucked my teeth.

"What's wrong?"

A gust of air had escaped me.

Only truly brave men have the courage to ask that question. Most men know that the answer to that question could result in a purgatory-bound monologue over the infraction that they may have incurred ten minutes ago or in 1997, on the way back from Essence Music Festival, neither of which they remembered. So for a man to open himself to this kind of stress test, which his brain was doomed to fail, was truly courageous.

"There's no need to park. Just drop me off at American Airlines." A stiff silence had followed. Vernon was befuddled and I knew it. But the darkness lurking inside me had achieved momentum.

"Okay," he had said glibly. The American Airlines terminal was approaching fast. By the time I had gathered my words, the yellow Corvette, which had, in the last twenty-four hours, been the carrier of my dreams, felt now like a suffocating tomb. And I was the mummy.

"Iris, wassup?"

"Nothing," I had said, staring straight ahead. Middle-aged black baggage attendants had unloaded suitcases from a charter bus filled with senior citizens wearing bright, flowery, cruise destination leisure wear.

"You sure?" Vernon had asked, leaning forward, half smiling, attempting to gaze into my eyes.

"Of course," I had said, hoping he would ask again. He did not.

"Okay," Vernon had said, turning off the ignition and triggering the locked trunk. Vernon then had the audacity to actually open his car door, as if he was going to get out. And he did.

"Okay, Vernon, since you insist on talking," I had begun, deciding to play his little game. "Let's be clear. What happened this morning was what it was. I just want you to know I have no expectations. None whatsoever. It is obvious that you are a *player*, and I respect that. Just know that I can get my play on, too. If I try real hard."

Vernon looked like a black man on *Jeopardy*, so I could not ascertain what he was thinking, or for that matter, feeling. I was too caught up in my own confusion, which was exacerbated when he had the nerve to smile and say, "Okay. If that's what you want."

What I wanted, needed, was more time to ramble and plead my case. I now wished he would have parked in the short-term lot, as previously planned, and walked with me to the damn security screening area. But instead, Vernon had succumbed to my irrational statements and was unloading my luggage on-wheels out of his trunk.

Like an imbecile, I had extended my hand as if he had agreed to become a new client. "Vernon, it was nice meeting you."

Vernon squeezed my hand, raising my palm to his mouth, kissing it. My knees quivered. "Ms. Chapman," Vernon had said, "Whatever that was in there, I'm going to chalk up to jitters, nerves, doubts. And I can dig it. Because however afraid you feel at this moment, I feel the same way, too, but to the tenth power. I was buck-naked this morning, too, remember? Now I'm goin' to have to return to my condo with memories of you there..."

A group of Hasidic Jews sadly had bid farewell to a young couple, as Vernon had continued, "Yes, there are women in my life. Hello, ninety percent of my listening audience are women.

And none of my relationships measure up to how I'm feeling about you right now. I already miss you and you haven't even left yet. Look, I don't know about the future, but I feel strongly about this connection, so much so that I have decided to put you, Ms. Chapman, on a ninety-day warranty."

My bottom lip was hanging open. I was sure of it. How dare he use my ninety-day warranty tactic. A low-flying American Airlines jet had flown overhead, the sound from its engines deafening.

A skinny Port Authority police officer had parked behind us and leaned out his window. "You're gonna have to get movin', buddy, or I'll have to ticket you," he had warned Vernon.

Exposing my eyeteeth, I had snarled at the officer, but Vernon had intervened. "If I have to choose between a ticket and kissing this beautiful woman, I think I'll take the ticket." Vernon had swept me into his arms, kissing me harder than before, almost knocking my front teeth out, leaning me into a tango dip, forcing a slight muscle pull in my left calf.

The cruise-bound senior citizens had turned and applauded, while the Port Authority police officer had wistfully smiled, while writing out a $75 ticket.

Until late morning, I collected clothes from the dry cleaners and ran various other errands, returning in time to hear Jamie Foster Brown of *The Tom Joyner Morning Show* begin her entertainment report on the radio: 'Y'all heard another NextLevel artist is in the hospital again? Yep, that lowlife, nose breather, NextLevel record mogul Colby Woods, told her if she did not lose a hundred pounds she could lose her contract. Now the sister is back in the hospital again." Tom Joyner's cast of characters gave a collective groan and asked everyone to send cards and flowers to Atlanta Memorial Hospital.

As I paid bills at my desk, I spied two beady eyeballs peeking through the back door window at me. Seeing it was Theotis, I realized there was no way I could avoid him by employing the Jehovah's Witness-duck-under-the-furniture method. Reluctantly, I rose from behind the desk, lowering the clamor on the radio. "Slip everything through the door slot, Theotis," I yelled.

"Miss Iris, you needs to sign dis here paper." This must be the morning for the return of the stars of black vaudeville. I made a mental note to see if there was an AUDITION sign hanging on my door.

Snatching open the back door, I grabbed a lavender envelope with familiar handwriting along with a pile of junk mail out of Theotis' hands, before he could launch into some meandering story about how he avoided his boss' hound dogs. "Thanks, Theotis." I slammed the door in his bewildered face, yanking down the window shades.

Flipping the envelope over, I saw there was an unfamiliar return address, but no name. It was written in a handwriting that perfectly matched Tammy's. Instinctively, my hands tried to tear the envelope in half, but instead I ran out the door and down the street after Theotis, who was waiting for a police car to pass by so he could pee in Mr. Whitaker's bushes.

"Theotis, return this to the sender." I ducked behind the bushes with him, standing an inch away from dog cah-cah.

"Whatever you say, Ms. Iris. Tammy wrote down, she say, she sorry."

"She sorry alright. Make sure she knows not to ever contact me again, Theotis."

"Please don't let Mr. Charlie know Iz back heah."

[16]

Over the next few months, Vernon broadcast his radio show from Atlanta, and probably would have from my bed, if I had asked him. We became each other's shadow, though I would often question the depth of our connection or his devotion toward me. However, brother Vernon would be right on time with the right gesture, the right words, or supply the space I needed, at times, to breathe.

The ninety-day warranty expired without a hitch, without a need to backtrack on our emotions or to pretend to be people we were not. Vernon went to church. I did not. I appreciated the merits of World Wrestling Entertainment. He did not. He was close to his family. And I was afraid. Vernon never suggested that my laugh was too loud. Or that my ribald jokes were best suited for a barbershop; or that my dresses were too skimpy. But with all of our differences, our similarities made us that much stronger, and neither of us attempted to make the other one over.

Vernon appreciated whatever I revealed to him, which made me want to swoon. Vernon, however, did have one annoyance. The worldly Vernon had a penchant for talking to the screen while watching television, and even, to my horror, in a crowded movie theater.

Once, as I was being mesmerized by the sadistic cutlery delights of Hannibal Lecter, imagine my embarrassment when, in a crowded theater, Vernon suddenly screamed to a soon-to-be beheaded character, "Look out; he's got a knife!"

"The only thing you can find wrong with the brother is that he talks at the movies? Gurl, puh-leeze. Don't you think you are nit-picking?" Cleo had advised during one of my frequent reports on Vernon.

"But what if it's Tourette's syndrome. Think of our children, they could be exposed—"

"Iris!" Cleo exclaimed, laughing.

"You're right, I guess. I'm so used to people doing it to me, I guess it's rubbing off."

Vernon's parents, Vincent and Venus, were a happy pair; so happy in their merriment, I am told, they often made other black folks suspicious. With all that black people have to struggle against, the malcontents would say, what do Vincent and Venus have to be so delirious, so utterly peaceful about? Only white folks and those trying to ascend to whiteness, the grumblers would say, should be so preoccupied with an emotion as inconsequential and time-wasting as happiness.

Venus smiled so much; strangers presumed she was making fun of them. At work, her mirth became a distraction, as Venus always wanted to share a cheery story with a rosebud ending. She would anger co-workers as she shared a warm and fuzzy excerpt from *Reader's Digest*. A funeral home is no place for merriment, her supervisor, the head embalmer, would scold.

Vincent, Vernon's father, was also jovial, but he had a tendency, upon introduction, to abruptly lift people and swing them around. And so, Vincent, as he has urged me to call him, is now recuperating from a hiatal hernia.

Now he knows, I weigh more than I look like I do.

Since our first meeting had been unceremoniously interrupted, I had assumed that this *gaiete de coeur* would somehow be dimmed when I later visited Vincent in the hospital. Instead, as Vincent gnawed on laminated Jell-O in his hospital bed, he and Venus mulled over just how happy they were. The scene made me demented enough to want to go on a shopping spree with Lee Artist.

Vernon's doe-shaped eyes were rimmed with emotion as his mother relayed to me a story she thought I would appreciate: "This woman was recovering from knee surgery and the extraction of impacted wisdom teeth. And she was lying on the couch with an ice bag on her leg and hot-water bottles against both cheeks. From the kitchen, she heard her mother cry out in pain. Through a mouth stuffed with gauze she asked her mother what had happened. 'You know,' her mother replied, 'there's nothing worse than a paper cut.' Isn't that hilarious?" Venus squealed, as Vincent joined her, grimacing in pain.

Now, I agreed that Vernon's mother should have been reprimanded, or at the very least, hanged.

Vernon's midwest affiliates were not thrilled with his decision to broadcast from the Atlanta station, WVEE-FM, through most of the spring. Vernon informed the program director that it was restitution for all of the time he had spent in New York. This was partially true. However, when I had a business trip in a distant city where there was a "Quiet Storm" affiliate, suddenly he was there, broadcasting the show.

"Wasn't that what you always dreamed about?" Cleo had asked.

"Yes, but sometimes we don't believe we can achieve our dreams."

"And when you do?" Cleo had pressed.

"I don't know what you do, but I do the only rational thing."

"And that is?"

"Sabotage the relationship."

My sabotage took the form of flexing my emotional muscles, seeing how long this brother would be in for the ride. If we were supposed to have dinner, I would sometimes stand him up; or perhaps not return his telephone calls or respond to his text messages. All of my dastardly deeds continued without incident and stoked my devilish nature. Vernon would accept my vague explanations time after time.

Until the tables were turned.

It was my birthday, February sixth, a date I shared with Ronald Reagan, Bob Marley and Lucifer. On this day each member of every civilization throws their Kangol hats in the air, jubilant, waving their arms like they just do not care. When I am walking down the street, strangers will stop me and say, "Hey! Happy Birthday. Can you come to our 'Iris celebration' at our house?"

"Thank you, but I'm booked at the McCarthys and the Thompsons. But get your request in early next year," I would respond gaily, swinging my arms like Mary Tyler Moore along the Minneapolis waterfront.

Well, not really. But this is how I envisioned it.

During the preceding month, I had provided enough hints for Vernon to sufficiently "surprise" me on the appointed day. That morning I woke early, bathing, flossing, douching, humming, vacuuming, and meditating until six a.m,; by which time Vernon had not phoned. I surmised it was because he got off of the air at two a.m. But that did not compute as he still had four whole hours to have joined mankind in jubilation. And if you want to get funky about it, which I always did, the revelry officially should have begun at midnight.

Six a.m. turned into nine a.m. Cleo phoned in between pitch business meetings at ten a.m. Ms. Chickie and Lee Artist called at two p.m., upset that I had not called them. I should know, they had said, that they hate making long-distance telephone calls. By the time they had finished ranting about the long-distance telephone call, they'd completely forgotten why they had phoned in the first place. "It's my birthday," I wearily reminded them.

"Well, it's just another day, Iris," Chickie advised. "Once you get my age, it's just another day."

Just in case Vernon had broken an extremity that prevented him from dialing, I called him, leaving a message on his rude telephone machine. "This is the place," a bored-sounding Vernon droned, "leave a message." I whined something about calling me if he did not want an ass-whooping.

By the time the closing credits on *The Real Housewives of Atlanta* were rolling, I was into my third container of Bon-Bons and had decided living my best life was not what it was cracked up to be. After all, for weeks I had practiced my best surprised facial expression, a look even an Oscar-winning actress would envy. But now it would be for naught as my melancholy blended into fury. Angry that I had given Vernon the best six months of my life, I decided that prudent action was imperative.

First, I checked with BellSouth to make sure my telephone line, my BlackBerry, my fax machine, his telephone line and beeper, and our alternate cell phones were working. Then I called a police detective and an old booty call, to verify that Vernon had not been in an accident. Once I completed doing what any compassionate lover would do, I then sobbed at my computer, while mapping out a plan to murder Vernon Blackwell. First, I had to decide what would kill him.

1) Tape his mouth shut in a movie theater; or

2) Steal his New York Knicks season tickets; or

3) Deny him oral sex.

This list remained intact until guilt flooded my conscience.

Having second thoughts, not wanting to inflict cruel and unusual punishment on the brother, I crossed off the harshest of the punishments and let him keep his Knicks tickets. Around 11:45 p.m. on February sixth, as the world was winding down their celebrations in my honor, the doorbell rang. Keith Olbermann was lambasting on television a silver-haired politician who was reluctant to give a straight answer. The doorbell rang again, this time repeatedly, sounding like a wayward ice cream truck.

Tossing the floral box filled with used tissue into the wicker wastebasket, I peeked through the sheer, white curtains. There were no recognizable automobiles outside.

"Who is it?"

"Vernon." My hands reflexively flew to my hips, as my lips assumed a perfect pout position.

"What do you want?"

"Iris, open the door." I waited a few moments to make it appear that I was not an eager beaver, then slowly unlatched the top lock.

Once the door was cracked an inch, Vernon pushed his way in saying, "Hurry up! *24* is coming on!" My mouth flapped open like a drawbridge. Vernon offered no kiss, no hug, no "Happy birthday," no "Go to hell, skank." Instead, he beelined to my refrigerator to retrieve an ice-cold Heineken and was now lounging on my sofa as if he was performing another take in a beer commercial.

My sentry stance remained as defiant as Hattie McDaniel's in *Gone with the Wind.*

"What?" Vernon finally rubbernecked and asked cluelessly.

"What?" I barked, as if to say "How could such a stupid question come from an otherwise intelligent man," while I simultaneously stomped over and turned on the radio to Vernon's fiercest competitor (at full volume).

"Whaaaaat?" He was now really irking the shit out of me.

"Whatever," I said disgustedly.

"Whatever?" he said, as if he had never heard the expression. "Look, I don't have time for this; I'm getting another beer."

Those were fighting words.

As Vernon strode toward my refrigerator, I hurled every insult I could think of that would pierce his little "the world is beautiful" existence. Instead of going to the refrigerator, however, he continued to the back door, flung it open, and stood on the porch with his arms folded across his chest, grinning. Not until my lips ceased to flap, like seagulls flying south, did I wrap my brain around the fact that he was indeed, grinning. My eyes lifted past his shoulders, and shifted to the spectacle before me.

There were people whom I recognized. Cleo, Delroy, Seth, Basil, Lola, Daddy Cooper, and others, yelling, "Surprise!" and singing a flat chorus of "Happy Birthday!"

Vernon wrapped his arms around me, whispering, "Now you know how I feel when I get stood up. Happy birthday, sweet pea!" I punched Vernon playfully in the ribs, and then I bawled and cried until my eyes turned into red-rimmed slits, appearing as though I had smoked a kilo of marijuana.

Vernon must have quietly decorated the backyard sometime during my evening self-pity and searing heartbreak. The stone pathway was illuminated with Japanese paper lanterns. The pine trees were draped with fabric streamers. Wheelbarrows were filled with chilled fruits and drinks. Pink candles floated in the sand-cast water fountain. Daddy Cooper and his two stork-faced nephews manned the overstocked beverage bar and played R&B/

hip-hop music loud enough to garner telephone complaints from a neighbor—Mr. Whitaker, whose real issue was that he had not been invited.

"You were right about my wife's silly nephew," Daddy Cooper confided.

"I'm sorry that didn't work out," I lied. "But there's one thing I learned about people like that."

"And what's that?"

"Talking out of the side of your head always means free media coverage. The media loves a spectacle."

After the traditional but tired dancing of the Cha Cha Slide, the congregates laughed and assembled in small clusters. While I was congratulating and scolding Cleo for keeping this monster secret from me, Vernon led a humble Lola over to our boisterous duo.

"Iris, can I speak with you?" a doe-eyed Lola asked.

"Sure." I tried to sound lofty, as if I had forgotten her antics in New York. Cleo grabbed Vernon's arm and be-bopped toward the dance floor.

"Let's go inside, Lola," I said.

Lola, dressed in a casual maroon jumpsuit, seemed to have lost the edge I had been exposed to in New York. A pompous feeling came over me as I watched Lola squirm, waiting for the apology that she was about to bestow. Lola needed to atone for her sins, and I enjoyed being in the position to cleanse her tarnished soul.

"You were wrong, you know," Lola began. As I was practicing my speech from on high, angling my eyebrows at just the right position, lining up my points and handing down my edict, I was momentarily distracted by her comment.

"Excuse me?"

"You were wrong," Lola repeated.

My ego took quite a bit of rearranging before I was able to

continue. “And how was I wrong?” I asked, my arm swooping across my chest like an infuriated Spanish matador. Lola whirled around from the door and sat across from me, her posture erect.

“You thought that I was stronger than I was. That I could walk away from Madd Dogg just like that. Well, I couldn’t then.”

“And what about now?” I leaned forward, weaving my fingers together.

“He’s out of my life.”

“Just like that?”

“Well, a restraining order made the point.”

“A restraining ord—”

“Madd Dogg may think it’s okay for me to do twenty-five-to-life for his ass but I’m not tryin’ to go out like that…”

“He wanted you to sell cocaine again?”

Lola nodded, then collapsed into a chair. “When we first got together, it used to be good with me and him.”

Over Lola’s shoulder, out in the backyard, Cleo pushed a bungling Seth off the Cha Cha Slide line. Seth laughed sheepishly, his cheeks exploding a crimson red as he adjusted his satin scarf. Basil playfully nudged him.

“In de beginning, as they say, everything is great.” I smiled, remembering the pact between Vernon and me.

“We were going to be the hip-hop Ashford and Simpson. Writing and producing songs heard for generations, but now I’m on my own.”

Swinging my legs on top of the desk, I asked, “So what’s the game plan, Lola?”

“What do you mean?”

The brass doorknob jiggled; at the same time knuckles tapped against the windowpane. It was Colby. Lola hissed, blowing a stream of air through her teeth, while I rolled my eyes. Colby stepped through the door, carrying yellow tulips, grinning as if he was Sir Walter Raleigh. "What're you doing here?" I asked, my eyebrows narrowing.

"My secretary needs to be fired for losing my invitation," Colby said, stuffing the tulips into an already filled flower vase.

"You were not invited, Colby," I said, my heart championing my directness.

"Whereever NextLevel's star is, that's where I should be."

The partygoers slow danced, Seth and Basil included. As the night air became windier, the candles dotting the backyard gradually lost their flames. Vernon and Delroy were engrossed in a conversation, intermittently eyeing the house.

"Um, I need a word with Lola," Colby said, attempting to evict me from my own house.

"And I need a word with you," I retorted.

"Iris, don't leave," Lola said. "I need a witness to what he's about to say, just in case he decides to sue me or some shit like that."

I settled back in my chair as Colby crossed his arms and leaned against the wall next to the portrait of Ms. Chickie and Lee Artist, as if he expected a verbal pummeling. Beads of perspiration formed on Colby's pimpled neck.

"After today, I ain't gonna be kicking it with you. I'm bouncing up out of NextLevel."

"Wait just a minute; you have a contract."

"That contract ain't worth smack if you don't have any of my lyrics or any of my beats. What're you going to do, force me?"

Colby searched my face to determine if I was responsible for the words, the confidence emanating out of Lola. In response, Lola gave Colby a gleeful smirk. "I have to decide if I want to even keep doing this anymore."

"Lola, I don't know where this is coming from, but you're one of the best rappers, male or female, out there. People hang on to everything that you do, everything that you say."

"But everything that I'm saying is negative. I mean, yeah, I grew up in the projects, raised by my moms, but that didn't mean I grew up without love. And that's all y'all want me to act like, to rap like, like someone who never knew love. And it's killing me."

"Rap about whatever you want to rap about. I don't care," Colby said, throwing up his arms. Lola wagged her finger, shaking her head.

"Iris, tell Lola, tell her, that what I'm offering her only comes around once in a lifetime," Colby said, flinging his arms frantically.

"Thank God," I said, rolling my eyes.

"Say what?" Colby said.

"You heard me," I said, my head wiggling like a cobra.

Colby pushed slightly off the wall, his eyes darkening. "If it wasn't for me—" he began.

"If it wasn't for you, you wouldn't have an artist in intensive care, right now. If it wasn't for you, maybe the women in your camp might believe in their own beauty, instead of the European, Barbie-doll fantasies that you are determined to perpetrate."

"Nobody wants to see a fat, black woman rap!" Colby said, with a speckle of saliva flying out of his mouth. His moronic, retarded tendencies were now fully exposed.

"Your momma was fat," I shouted, not meaning to resort to the age-old tradition of playing the dozens. But Colby's mother was, in fact, a corpulent woman. And in the descriptions of her in jazz periodicals, it was often mentioned that she was also beautiful. A jazz singer before giving birth to big-head Colby, she had toured on the fledgling chitlin' circuit.

Staring through the window, seeing me dice the air with my hands, Vernon and Delroy froze, questioning whether they should charge through the kitchen door like the cavalry. Catching his eye, I signaled Vernon to remain in the backyard. This situation needed to be resolved without any extra testosterone being brought in trying to save my—our—honor. Our honor was our own to save.

"I quit," Lola said, rejoining the conversation.

Colby paced, with his hands on his hips, not knowing which way to turn. "I tell you what. Finish this album and then we will renegotiate everything," Colby said firmly.

"Didn't you hear anything I said? I quit. I'm out. And if I ever decide to perform again, it'll be on my terms and not with your label."

An oblivious Seth entered the door; then seeing everyone foaming at the mouth, did a U-turn, returning outside. Colby lurched to the door, seizing the doorknob, pausing, holding it, as if he was giving Lola her last chance to sell her soul. "So it's like that, huh?"

Lola nodded.

"You down with her, Iris?" Colby asked.

"Colby, I'd walk away. You already have a lot of bad press, in the street and in the media. If this gets out, that you're tryin' to force Lola to work with you, this will get very ugly. So since it's been all about you, you should just walk."

Colby looked as though he had been hit by a bag of quarters, then exited, slamming the door, rattling my windowpanes. Vernon and Delroy eyeballed him until he slammed the metal gate, disappearing into the night.

Lola hid her face in her hands for a while. Not knowing whether she was crying or not, I asked, "You okay?"

Lola nodded, then walked over and hugged me.

OPA LOCKA

[17]

"You wanna go in first, then bring me?" Vernon asked, as the impatient Cuban taxi driver thumped the steering wheel. We sat idling with the motor running, in front of 321 Napier Street.

"There's no way I'm going in there alone," I answered, tightening the strap on my orange-red sandals. "It's better to launch a surprise offensive. Maybe we should come back after midnight, when they're drowsy and goin' to take a leak. Otherwise—"

"Baby, we're visiting your family, not Afghanistan."

"They'll interrogate you like you're an investment banker in front of a Senate subcommittee in an election year. Don't say I didn't warn you."

Vernon touched my lips and quieted my jumpy nerves, then kissed me gently. "It'll be okay, sweet pea. They aren't going to run me away."

The time had long since arrived. Vernon and I were a couple, and had shared our joy with respective friends. To Vernon's listeners, I was his "sweet pea." Though I spent the holidays and some weekends with his parents, I had discouraged Vernon from meeting my capricious family.

At first I had lied, saying that my family was escaped convicts, or that they were a singing group on tour in the Congo, and had decided to remain there to fight the war. Other times, I had said they were at a vow of silence in a Thai monastery. The lie that I thought might be effective was the one about my family in the witness protection program because of their sixties radical activities. Still other times, I said that my family had been raised by wolves, and they shied away from human beings by living in the Alaska wilderness. Somehow, no matter how hard I tried to convince him, Vernon did not believe any of these fables.

One morning, Vernon plopped airline tickets in my lap, announcing, "We're going to Antigua. A beautiful split-level villa, with a sunken Jacuzzi, private staff, ocean view and king-size bed awaits us. We're flying out this afternoon on my station owner's private Learjet, with one stop—"

"…one stop where?!" I squealed, not able to guess what destination stop would surpass a Caribbean private villa.

"Opa Locka," Vernon said firmly, knowing just how to pop my balloon.

"But—"

"Today."

"Oh."

Now Vernon and I sat like detention hall-bound schoolchildren in Arriba, Arriba taxicab, waiting for the perfect moment to enter my family home. Although Vernon had generously compensated Hector, the driver, for his time, he repeatedly checked his watch, rubbing his forehead and shaking his head. "*Yo no me siento cómodo en un vencindario americano de Africano,*" Hector said under his breath. ("I don't feel comfortable in an African-American neighborhood.")

"*Ahora sabe cómo yo me siento en La Habana Pequeñ.* (Now you know how I feel in Little Havana.")

Startled that I understood Spanish, Hector's eyes nearly popped out of his head. "*Yo no supe que usted entendió el español.* (I did not know you spoke Spanish.")

"Well, now you know," I said in English, because I did not know how to say that in Spanish. Vernon muffled a laugh behind his right fist.

Like undercover cops, Vernon and I scooted down in the sky-blue vinyl backseat as Lee Artist and Ms. Chickie arrived from church. Even though his army green, oil-stained pants protruded from under the hood of his prized Oldsmobile, my mother and grandmother entered the house without acknowledging my father. A stray hound dog with matted hair stirred underneath a palm tree near the corner, yawning, then frantically scratched behind his ear.

"Okay, here's the plan." I patted Vernon's arm. "Whatever you do, don't allow Ms. Chickie to corner you by yourself."

"I won't leave your side. Promise." Vernon saluted.

"And we won't stay more than forty-five minutes. We'll say that you have to get back to Atlanta to perform an emergency lung transplant. And whatever *you* do, don't leave *me* alone."

"Sweet pea, I just said I won't leave your side. Come on now; it won't be that bad."

"You don't know my family."

"*No será eso malo,*" (It won't be that bad,") Hector volunteered, turning to face us.

"And neither do you!" I barked laughingly, as the meter clicked to $32.

"Anybody related to you can't be all bad," Vernon said soothingly, rubbing my sweaty back.

For good measure, I ordered Hector to circle the block once again; although having traversed the area twelve times, we appeared suspicious, as if we were casing the neighborhood.

When we returned to in front of 321 Napier, the dashboard clock read two p.m., the broadcast time of three of Ms. Chickie's favorite gospel programs. Entering the house now was my brother, a clean-shaven Victor, wearing a long yellow robe, followed by a group of white-robed, barefoot Hare Krishnas, beating on hand drums in rhythm with their chanting. Two dancing, sari-wearing women with tufts of red hair, swayed, playing their finger cymbals. One young man blew on a seashell; another beat on a tambourine. Vernon and I watched the spectacle, slack jawed, until they had disappeared behind the screen door, into my family home.

Despite my protestations to escape, Vernon firmly dragged me out of the taxicab, tossing the relieved Hector a fifty-dollar tip.

"I thought you loved me," I protested, attempting to squirm from Vernon's grip.

"I do. I do." He laughed; dragging me, across the street, my heels creating sparks against the cobblestone pavement. "Come on, baby, an hour and we're out."

"You promised forty-five minutes, Vernon!"

Hearing all of our commotion, Willie peeked from under the hood of the Oldsmobile. "Iris? Well, I'll be," He smiled brightly.

"Hi, Daddy," I replied, standing up, smoothing my ruffled clothes, then hugging him tightly. "Daddy, um, meet Vernon."

Willie's smile disappeared as quickly as Hector had rounded the corner, screeching away in his taxicab.

"Don't worry, I won't leave your side," Vernon whispered. "Mr. Chapman, it's an honor to meet you, sir."

Instead of returning Vernon's greeting, Willie wiped his oily hands on the paper towel and folded his body behind the wheel in the car, tapping the accelerator and turned the ignition. The Oldsmobile heaved, rattled and then became silent.

"Iris, go on in the house. Your momma and Ms. Chickie are around there somewhere."

❖ ❖ ❖

"You want some more sweet potato pie, Son?" Ms. Chickie offered Vernon, as he sat beside her in her Robitussin-smelling bedroom.

"Oh no, ma'am," Vernon answered, chomping on Ms. Chickie's infamous crunchy sweet potato pie, which no one enjoyed except local dentists who welcomed the influx of emergency patients after it was served. But the fault lie with Vernon. We had made a pact to remain together, but he committed a foolish act and had gone to the bathroom—alone. Feigning a search for her snuff, Ms. Chickie charged into the bathroom just as Vernon had zipped his pants, and from there she herded him into her bedroom across the hall. It was his fault.

As a slow bong, death march resonated from Victor's bedroom, Willie sat dejectedly on the sofa. "What's the matter, Daddy?" I asked.

"Iris, in all my years, have I ever asked anything of you?"

"No, Daddy, you haven't," I responded, confused as to why he was so upset.

"I have thought of you as my baby girl, my partner in crime, my compatriot—."

"Yes, Daddy, I have, too. Thought of you as my partner in crime, that is. But—"

"Then explain to me, if you would, why, after I specifically asked you not to, you have brought a short man into this house!"

"Daddy, Vernon is not short! He's, he's…average height!"

"He's shorter than you!"

"That's because I am wearing four-inch stilettos."

"Iris, I never told you this, but as far as I am concerned, the Chapman line is dead."

"What about Victor?" Seeing the incredulous look on my

father's face as the slow bong continued, I retracted that question. "Never mind."

"And so I was looking to you to bring somebody in here with some sense, and somebody with some height on him. These sawed-off boys today ain't good for nothing! Most of them steal, 'cause they can't get anything on their own. They can't even reach the top shelf and hand me a wrench if I need one! You might as well put 'em all on reality TV."

"Vernon is intelligent. And he can reach everything *I* need. You just have to get to know him, that's all."

"Is that a fact? Hmph, he doesn't wear those platform shoes, does he, trying to make himself look taller than he is?"

"No, Daddy. No." Feeling nauseous, I excused myself, seeking peace in the bathroom. I could have sworn that Woodrow, the statue of Ms. Chickie's husband, winked.

The Hare Krishna drums and tambourines continued their trance-like rhythm.

"You want some more sweet potato pie, boy? Eat all of it now."

Vernon thumbed his teeth to make sure they were still secure inside his mouth. His first molar felt loose. Feigning that he was stuffed, Vernon rubbed his belly. "Oooooh, ma'am, that's all I can deal with now. See, we ate before we got here."

"Iris knows I serve sweet potato pie after church every Sunday. I tell you that girl don't have a lick of sense. See how she shaved off all her hair? Used to have long, pretty hair, right down to her shoulder, like mine. And she wrote and told me that she gave away all of the clothes that I got from my white lady. When I growed up, I was happy wearing a paper sack," Ms. Chickie said.

Eavesdropping, I stood in the hallway outside Ms. Chickie's bedroom door and two closed doors away from Victor, where he, his cronies, and Lee Artist were now singing, chanting a song about being an anointed son.

"Iris is beautiful," Vernon offered.

"What grade of hair does your momma have?"

"Grade, ma'am?"

"Does she have good hair?"

"As long as it is attached to her head, I think she would consider that it is good."

"You not trying to get smarty pants with me, is you, boy?"

Conflicted, and wanting to rescue Vernon, I also relished hearing him do battle with Ms. Chickie's, um, idiosyncrasies. Willie suddenly appeared behind me, tapping me on the shoulder. I placed an index finger over my mouth, signaling him to do the same, while he joined me in listening.

"Oh no, ma'am. With all due respect, my parents taught me that everything we are, our very breath, is precious and good. So I've never divided people up according to their physical features to determine what is good, and what is not so good."

Ms. Chickie rocked her rocking chair, listening.

"So you want a woman to run around with nappy hair?"

"I want a woman with a good heart. That, you have to admit, Iris has."

Willie and I waited for what seemed like forever for her response.

"Iris is a good girl. But the world don't look at her heart when they see her. They look at that nappy hair. We tried to straighten it out, but she leaves here, runs up to Atlanta, and comes back looking every which-o-way. Lawd knows I've done everything I can for her. Introduced her to porn and what not. Her momma, Lee Artist, the one in the other room sangin' out of her head with her deadbeat son and those hippies, saw on *Oprah* all of these white people goes to see a shrink—, say it help 'em feel better and that we should go. I thought and prayed on it. Asked Jesus to speak to me in that voice that always leads me the right way. So I told Lee Artist today, on our way back from church, I told her, 'If anybody go runnin' around telling our business, I'll kill 'em dead—, warning her, being a lovin' mother and all—"

Pushing open Ms. Chickie's door, I clasped Willie's hand, pulling him in with me into Ms. Chickie's bedroom. Sitting next to Vernon, I gave him a soft peck on his cheek. He smiled, a thank-you for being rescued.

"Me and your grandmother are getting acquainted."

"I see. Daddy, do you have any questions for Vernon?"

"Only one."

All eyes turned to Willie. "What took so long for us to meet the boy?" And then Willie stomped out the bedroom, rattling a glass perfume table, and down the hallway, barging through Victor's door, the sound of the beating drums and tambourines flooding the house.

"Victor, stop that goddamn racket, and get those motherfuckin' people out my damn house."

Victor abruptly stopped shaving the head of a new convert. The Hare Krishnas gathered their cymbals, tambourines and drums and scurried down the hallway and out of the house, slamming the screen door behind them. Though the, um, music had been silenced Lee Artist continued twirling like a spinning top, doing her ecstasy dance.

"Lee Artist! Come meet this boy." Willie yelled down the hallway, "What's your name again, son?"

Lee Artist wobbled her spin, slowing with a delirious smile in front of Willie, tugging on her green sari. "Husband, shall I prepare your favorites for dinner tonight?"

Willie's chest caved, as he clutched the doorknob to prevent himself from fainting.

Vernon and I stole glances, and beamed like neon signs.

Witnessing this, the vultures, being repulsed by happy endings, scattered.

ABOUT THE AUTHOR

When Sabrina Lamb, a New York City-based media personality, hosted a tribute to the Poet Laureate of New Jersey, The National Conference of Artists exclaimed, "Sabrina Lamb is a master of satirical humor with an emphasis on political current events. Her bites at the current U.S. administration left no one untouched."

Sabrina is the best-selling author of *Have You Met Miss Jones? The Life and Loves of Radio's Most Controversial Diva* (Random House). Sabrina was named 16th on the list of 50 Top Black Women in Entertainment in *Black Noir* magazine. She has written cover stories for *Essence*, *Heart and Soul* and *Black Elegance* on subjects from Gladys Knight, The Evolving Black Church, Why Women Love Bad Boys to Surviving The Holidays with Your Family. Sabrina was featured twice in *Essence* magazine and was the columnist to *Black Elegance* magazine's "He Say/She Say" column. She is the recipient of the Rainbow Push/Wall Street Project Honors. Sabrina was designated as New York 1 Television's "New Yorker of the Week" and a member of Who's Who in Black New York. Sabrina has also been nominated for the following awards: Pine Sol's "Women Making A Powerful Difference" Award, Jumpstart Coalition's "William E. Odom Visionary Leadership Award" and Tom Joyner's Hardest Working Community Leader.

Sabrina co-hosted "The Morning Show" on 1600 WWRL in New York City, interviewing cultural figures to government officials. She co-hosted and contributed to the highly-rated "Open

Line," "Week In Review" and "Wake-Up Club" on WRKS-FM, respectively. Sabrina has been featured on CNN's *Nancy Grace*, Fox Business Network, WNBC-TV, WCBS-TV, BET's *Meet The Faith*, *Tonight with Ed Gordon*, HOT 97's Street Soldiers, *Sharp Talk with Rev. Al Sharpton*, WABC-TV, FOX-TV, Fox Business Network, UPN-CH9, Playboy Radio, WHAT 1340AM, WBLS-FM, WLIB-AM, WBAI-FM, *Philadelphia Tribune*, *Kansas City Star*, *Jet* magazine, Urban Buzz, *Rolling Out*, Daily Challenge, *Afro Times*, New York Newsday, MJI Programming, BRE Show Prep, *Time Out* Magazine. She also hosted and produced "Laughing, Lying and Signifying," the history of Black Comedy on WBAI-FM.

One may remember Sabrina, a Miami native, from Lifetime Television's *Girl's Night Out*, where she wove her comedic skills around issues such as homelessness, foreign policy and spousal abuse. Sabrina got laughs and delivered the message. She was also a political satirist on the America's Talking Network. Sabrina has become very popular in the New York City area. Other credits include NBC's *Saturday Night Live*, The Original Improv, Comedy Cellar, Stand Up New York, HBO/Toyota Comedy Festival and Black Entertainment Television's *Comicview*, which nominated her Best Female Comic and Best Impersonator.

Sabrina was a finalist at the National Association of Television Programming Executives Convention where she impressed a standing room audience with her pitch of the romantic comedy, *Callaloo and Cornbread*. She also produced the hairlarious docu-comedy *UnBeweavable: Woman, What Did You Do To Your Hair?* The film garnered The Audience Choice Award at the Jamerican Film and Music Festival in Montego Bay, Jamaica. Sabrina is very proud to be the Founder of the WorldofMoney.org, dedicated to the financial literacy of underserved youth.

Sabrina is active in the New York Road Runner's Club and has completed the 1995, 1996 and 2000 New York City Marathons.

Printed in the United States
By Bookmasters